JOHN F. DEANE was born on Achill Island, County Mayo, and now lives in Dublin. He is the founder of Poetry Ireland, the national poetry society, and of The Dedalus Press. His novels and short stories *In the Name of the Wolf*, *The Coffin Master and Other Stories* and *Undertow* are published by Blackstaff Press. His poetry has been shortlisted for the T.S. Eliot Prize and the *Irish Times* Poetry Now award. His latest collection, *The Instruments of Art*, was published by Carcanet in 2005.

GW00492716

The Heather Fields

and other stories

JOHN F. DEANE

BLACKSTAFF
PRESS

BELFAST

First published in 2007 by
Blackstaff Press
4c Heron Wharf, Sydenham Business Park
Belfast BT3 9LE
with the assistance of
The Arts Council of Northern Ireland

ARTS
COUNCIL
of Northern Ireland

John F. Deane has asserted his right under the Copyright, Designs
and Patents Act 1988 to be identified as the author of this work.

Typeset by CJWT Solutions, St Helens, Merseyside

Printed in Ireland by ColourBooks Limited

A CIP catalogue record for this book is available
from the British Library

ISBN 978-0-85640-800-7

www.blackstaffpress.com
www.johnfdeane.com

for Tim and Róisín Sheehan

CONTENTS

The Heather Fields

ONE

The trip out to Mason's boat was exhilarating. Reynolds had been on the sea before but never travelling at such a rate, the prow of the speedboat high and leaping waves like you'd leap clumps of heather on the heath, the water splashing on either hand, the spray only occasionally catching their faces with a sudden spit of the wind. The dog perfectly balanced. Mason and Reynolds told to sit down, out of the way. The master himself standing in the stern, his hand on the tiller, as balanced as his dog.

At first they moved cautiously, making their way like a servant with a piled-high tray weaving through guests at some grand reception, through and between the moored yachts in the harbour, and it was joyous to hear the rigging wires beat like little bells off the masts, a constant hymn of tinkling sounds that must be something like the sheep in high pastures of the Swiss mountains. Then they had left the harbour mouth and hit the open sea. The master speeded up the craft and the dog barked louder and they banked to the right, around the harbour wall and began to race towards the boats moored further out.

Reynolds was aware, or course, of the differences. Mason's little boat was anchored with other lesser ones, small fishing craft, clinker-built lighter boats belonging to enthusiasts, those who loved boating for its own sake and not for the show of the great hulls and gear and gleaming appurtenances of the rich craft in the inner harbour: their rigging and their displays; their flags and features and fistulas – these the glitter-days of the new and confident Ireland, and you could imagine the beautiful bodies laid out nude, or nigh to nude, on their gleaming decks, gloating under the sun. Except, of course, not here, not in this climate, not in these weathers.

Mason's craft was an old rowing boat that had belonged to the monastery of Heatherfield in the heady days of faith and sufficiency. Some of the monks had enjoyed coming out along the coast, rowing merely, and fishing. They chose the peaceful days and always came back with fish: pollack, mackerel, enough to fill the tables for a day or so, thus doing homage to their bellies as well as to holy poverty. There was an outboard engine as well as oars but the boat, clinker-built, varnished within and without, was no more than eighteen feet long, seaworthy, stalwart, pure. It reminded Reynolds of the old ass that was kept in the back field to graze into easeful old age, without labour, occasionally urged into a gallop for its own health's sake.

'That yoke,' the master ferryman offered. 'That yoke? Not worth a balloon. Not worth a buggered balloon in soft weather.' He shook his head and even the barking dog seemed to be of one opinion with the old man.

A little crestfallen, a little embarrassed, the two men transferred to Mason's boat, waved goodbye to the master mariner and his dog, and settled into their places.

Reynolds dragged up the little anchor, the rope rising with small knots of dark green weed hanging on it here and there, and he laid it down in the prow, winding the rope carefully, drying his hands on his thick woollen jumper. They pushed off, the engine sputtering a little, spitting water. But soon they were moving out onto the sea and heading for Gannet Island. The waves were big out here, the wind was cold, but Reynolds felt exhilarated, out on the sea with Mason. They hoped to get to the island, row slowly around below the cliffs to watch the fulmar, the gannets, the puffins, to listen to them squabbling and screeching like a high glass building filled with hastening businessmen. The rowing would be lovely and gentle, the boat sluppering along in peace.

The sea is predictable in its ways, responding as it always does to the conditions of its existence. Of course the weather changes, sometimes suddenly; and squalls come beating in out of nowhere. But all of that, too, follows a course set down and ordered from the beginning. There is an obedience about the sea, even in its moments of shift and shudder, that gives hope to the heart, an uplift to the soul that yet founders in its magnificent presence, and that keeps one happily aware of what obedience to the original commands of creation must have been. Unlike the way man himself behaves, erratic, uncertain and cruel. But the sea – beautiful. Like the sparkle, the inshifting outshifting gleam and silver-sheen of a shoal of fish rising and falling, turning as if all tied together in a net, then off, down into darkness, and away.

By the time they were half a mile from the island Mason and Reynolds were in trouble. The storm seemed to come on them like a headmaster pouncing from behind on an errant student. Out of the south it came and they could almost see the wall of it approaching from the horizon, the clouds heavy and blackening all the time, the surface of the sea rising and breaking into foam, and then, without warning, the outboard engine died. There was a silence in the little craft, they could hear the rising winds, they could hear the sea water hacking against the hull, they could hear the ringing determination of that afternoon to make them note its passing and remember it for ever.

The boat began to drift with awful speed, away from the coast and the island, and out towards the wild ocean. Reynolds grabbed for the oars as Mason stood in the stern and tried to get the engine going again.

'Is there … ph … ph … fuel?' Reynolds shouted.

Mason did not answer. He never answered again. There was no sput from the engine and as Reynolds shoved the oars at random into the sea and began to heave, a wave came huge and overwhelming from the starboard side and tossed the boat over. Just one heave. Reynolds rose in his seat with the boat and the fall was as slow and as silent as those you see done in slow-motion in the films. Mason simply flipped into the sea and disappeared.

There was Reynolds, tossed into the sky out of the little boat, poor stuttering Reynolds. Somewhere in the depths of his soul, though he had suffered long and grievously, there remained a sense of a radiant presence that, all alone, allows the suffering heart to hold purchase on its sanity and its hope, that allows the bleakest mind to see that all is not lost when all is lost. Reynolds seemed to hang in the air for a long time, like a rotten apple about to fall off a branch. And then everything came together against him in a great flash of ocean and terror and flailing. He sank into a silence so complete it hummed in his ears. He floated down through a darkness that was alert with cold, a dark green thickness with shooting flashes of white across his eyes like a shoal of a million flickering elvers. His hands and feet waved and grabbed and kicked, he could feel the sea water enter his mouth and catch against his throat, swirling against his life, choking him. His eyes closed. His body jerked and spasmed and then he felt as if strong arms were hefting him bodily up through the water and he opened his eyes to a salt and clouded greenness where everything went utterly still and quiet until suddenly he was on the surface again, shouting for breath and reaching for it out of the grey air. The boat was upturned just beside him and he grabbed for it, all the time sputtering out the water that was clogging up his chest. He cherished the feel of the hard timber of the boat and he clung on desperately for his miserable existence.

The slippery underside of the boat was slimed with a green-brown ugliness from its time at sea but the craft floated gently in the wilderness into which Reynolds had risen. He held to it with both hands, his ungainly body dangling in the water. The ocean heaved high and dropped sickeningly low all about him and he tried to climb onto the boat but could not find the strength. Reynolds was not young. And then he yelled and screamed hopelessly into the growing winds. Only now, when he heard no response except that of the withering storm, did he look around for Mason. Over the heaving and wallowing stretches of ocean about him there was absolutely no sign of the man, no bobbing head, no flailing arms, nothing. Reynolds had never felt the world so empty, so bereft of any hope or human presence though his recent sense of immanence had lifted him from darkness and he felt a desolation that must be like the desolation of the damned. He closed his eyes and leaned onto the ridged breast of the boat.

For a long and wearying time he held there. Minutes may have passed, or hours, and the boat lifted and fell, sea water stinging his eyes and freezing his body through. At times the far-off cliffs were visible through a driving rain and at others they quickly disappeared into the gathering darkness. Reynolds tried to pray, but the words would not form themselves in his soul. His head was down against the soiled timbers and the sense of Mason's loss was overwhelming; oh yes Reynolds believed, in that abstract intellectual way, in the existence of a kind God but there are so many times in life that this intellectual conviction is far from enough; now the whole weight of the surging of the world was down on him and all sense of beauty in that surging had disappeared. Order had fallen away, and with it had fallen hope, and with that, energy. His fingers were chilled through, his whole body seemed to be stiffening into an impossible numbness and he knew that all this had happened so quickly, out of the blue of an ordinary day into the very testing-places of the forecourts of eternity so that he wished fervently and uselessly that he and Mason had never left the house that afternoon.

But the ferryman who had brought them out had not abandoned them, had felt some misgivings as to their wisdom or competence and had kept a loose eye on their progress, through his binoculars. Reynolds was grabbed and prised away from the boat. Later he remembered a confusion of shouting voices, a crashing of waves, he remembered the great agony he suffered under his arms as powerful hands hoisted him out of the waves, he remembered the never-to-be-eased shivering of his whole body and how he was heaved over the gunwale of another craft and onto a wooden deck. He woke in hospital, tucked up and warm and completely broken-spirited.

Mason had disappeared into that world of turbulence and darkness, of chaos and chill, leaving no trace behind him. He was gone, as if he had never been.

The ward in which Reynolds came back to himself was tranquil, bright, clean, smelling of health and medicines, gleaming with competence; there were flowers in vases by bedsides, flowers in vases on window ledges, and a great clock working silently high on the wall. Around him he could see several people, about his own age, all shrivelled and leering, holding on uselessly to the pathetic little bit of life still left to them. Slobbering and muttering and pathetic, like himself. Unlovely. But holding on. Reynolds lay for a while, absorbed by grief, and knowing at once what he had to do.

Orderlies came, wheeling trolleys, trying to inveigle the men to eat. Dinner. A smell of mushed potatoes. Some vaguely brown, vaguely warm, gravy. A mess of sloshed-down turnips. Meat. Horse-flesh? Goat-flesh? Thin and fatty and noticeably stringy. What a banquet it was and on what a shore! And had they hacked the chines apart from the ribs, to expose the guts? Had they sliced the shivering flesh and fed the fires and set the cooking vats down along the beach? Oh yes, a reckoning! There must come a day of reckoning.

How they urged the weak old men, with their dribbling, drivelling, cave-awful mouths, to come, partake, revive their strength! Reynolds grew nauseous and motioned them away. Long, slow afternoon, while they lay back and mused in silence on the many that had been lost along the way, the dead companions, the special disappeared. What wrong had he done, Reynolds wondered, what wrong that the Almighty God had torn Mason, the last and most loving, from his life? The same ill-fortune had always dogged his disaster-ridden days. When, great God, will you let it be enough? Reynolds had founded no city; he had left no progeny; he had built no house. And now, he knew, the one remaining door had been slammed shut. He had come gradually to believe that mankind is dark. He was convinced of it now. He had suffered enough. He had lost, slowly, the ever uncertain grip he had had on life. He had lost motive, and with motive, energy. The energy to continue.

When they sent him home from hospital, Reynolds felt so lethargic it seemed as if he had just now been drawn from the harsh embrace of the sea. Perhaps they should have left him to drown, to be with Mason, wherever that might be.

Once inside he drew across the front door of his house, here in Heatherfield Gardens, a large and heavy fridge. He placed it so that it leant against that door, a door that was rarely knocked upon anyway by anybody other than whingeing politicians, insistent policemen or begging clergy. But it would deter any officious or merely quizzical persons from barging through. He drew over the curtains in every room. He retired upstairs. By day he opened the curtains in his bedroom, where he lived now, for the time being. It was time, high time, that he took the decision to ferry himself away from this world and find that better one he had suffered for and laboured towards. May the kind God have mercy on his soul.

TWO

There was Tom Molloy, bane of the early days. Tom with his big fists, his body lithe and cruel as a whip. Even then Reynolds had been reading books and used to repeat to himself, over and over, the little phrase: *Here! creep, Wretch, under a comfort serves in a whirlwind* ... Hopkins, taking his cue from Mad Tom in *King Lear*. Oh yes, how he crept away to read, often and often, the boy Reynolds, finding all his consolation in the pages of books. The comfort he used to creep into was strange comfort, though, the comforting of a thorn bush, its spines and blossoms, its contorted limbs. Out beyond the monastery school the heathland stretched, vanishing into almost desert places with only wild clumps of scutch grass, heather fields, colonies of thorn bushes. Reynolds loved to be there alone, among the gold-bloom and bird-feathers on the whins, the blood-flakes and the sun-stains.

Big Tom Molloy would come after him with his fists, for Reynolds was easy prey, even though he was bigger and heavier than Tom, bigger and heavier than anyone in the school indeed, though slower and more aggrieved than them all. Slower in body and slower, it appeared, in mind; Reynolds knew it well, and he knew it then, for Big Tom made sure he knew it, and so did almost everybody else in that fine house of learning. Tom drew for him the boundaries of peace and happiness for he followed him, oft and oft, out onto the heath when Reynolds would only be heading away for the comfort of his books and the company of skylarks and pipits and the occasional marauding kestrel.

'So!' Tom offered, as if only taking up where he had left off

a short while before. 'So! Reynolds, the fool, mad Reynolds the
fool, thinks he can leave us all and go off by his self with his
books, as if he could read, the mad eejit, an' him only the arse-
end of a jackass. What's the feckin' book anyway, Reynolds?
Give us it here!'

That day it was the poetry of Joseph Campbell and Reynolds
had been trying to figure out what the 'gilley of Christ' meant
and he didn't have a notion at all. But it was a lovely book, its
hard red cover had a lovely strong feel to it and Reynolds held
that book so close to his chest that it was warm when he took
it out and showed it to Big Tom and all his hordes of admirers.
'Ti … ti … ti … ti … ti …' was all Reynolds could get out of
his mouth before Tom snatched the book out of his hands and
glanced at it. 'Ba … ba … ba … ba … book,' Reynolds went
on. What he thought he was saying, of course, was that it was a
book out of the lovely treasure-chest of books the travelling
library brought once a month to the monastery door. Reynolds
believed that he was the only one, he and Brother Leo Mason,
too, but of all the rest it was only he, Reynolds, who had the
freedom of that treasure-chest. And he availed of it, with an
overwhelming hunger gnawing him inside.

Big Tom couldn't quite make it out for a while. He opened
the book, keeping Reynolds pushed away with his big body
nudging against him, forcing Reynolds to back before him. He
squinted at the page.

> As a white candle
> In a holy place,
> So is the beauty
> Of an aged face.

He read the words out with spittle showing at the corner of his
mouth. Then he snapped the book shut, flipped his wrist and
sent it spinning like a flying saucer off into the heathers.

Reynolds loved the world when the heath was covered in
the blossoming furze bushes. The earth burned with a lemon-
coloured fire then, but there was another fire in the bushes and
it was that fire that took him now. Big Tom caught him roughly

by the left arm and Joseph Michael O'Dea caught his right and they dragged him to the furze bush and pushed him hard, so that he fell back into the thorns. It hurt because the thorns were strong and long and sharp and they got into his hands and stung him even through his clothes. Reynolds knew he'd be picking thorns out of his hair for hours after.

There he lay, not for the first time indeed, on his back in the thorns, not daring to get up or move because they'd only fling him back in again. And if they did that, then they would jump in after him, Big Tom and Joseph Michael, and straddle him where he lay, the thorns spiking him, Big Tom sitting heavily high up on his chest with his big boots on either side of Reynolds's head, and Joseph Michael hopping up and down heavily on his stomach, squashing the life out of him, forcing him down further into the thorns. Reynolds was silent, he suffered, and waited.

Sometimes, too, you could creep inside the thorn bushes, being careful of the thorns that were everywhere; there was a kind of tent you could imagine, an igloo, maybe, because you were still young, and you could shelter with the gnarled old branches making roof and walls and the blossoms outside for comfort. It was cool and dim in there and the scent was delicate. The floor was carpeted with dead thorns; they didn't prick you because they were all brown and dry and had blended together into something comforting. Reynolds picked himself up off the earth; he was spotted with bits of grass and clay, he was sore all over but he went and got his book and came back in there and sat, he just sat and listened to the breeze and the silence outside and there was nobody in the world who knew where he was. Or cared.

THREE

Reynolds felt well in body even though the sea had taken all his spirit away. Poor Mason. Poor old man. Gone into that wonderful heaving mystery that is ocean. What was there left to Reynolds in the world? Nothing. Not in the world that he knew now, with all its speed and greed and selfishness. Mason was gone. Reynolds was bereft.

He took a little drop of water because he needed to keep himself alert, at least for the time being. The first few days were quite easy. There was the excitement of the moment of decision; after all these years, at last, at last! That was the feeling. He grew light in spirit. He had shucked off the burdens he had been hauling about with him for so long. He was elated. He moved about the house as if all happiness had broken loose. He was a bird released. He was an angel, one of the fallen ones, who had been freed at last from its prison in middle-earth and was beginning its fall back up into grace. And then, of course, he was tired, so tired. He was weary after all the effort. He was exhausted after years of holding back. And suddenly, too, he felt as if the responsibility he had known for the loss of poor old Mason had fallen away from him. What did that matter now? He would be joining him soon. And so he slept, those first few days, and dozed, and woke and half-woke, and slept again. Long, relieving, dreamless sleep. Delightful oblivion.

FOUR

And then, one night, his mother came back to Reynolds. He had been eating nothing and had only taken a few sips of water but he did not expect this kind of thing to have begun so soon. He came awake suddenly. For a moment he kept his eyes shut, recalling where he was and who he was and what it was he was about. Then he heard a rustling sound near him and he opened his eyes wide. The room was dark, except where the light from the back street, Heatherfield Walk, cast its usual sickly glow in through the ragged curtains. At first he did not dare turn his head; he swivelled his eyes to the left as far as he could. Raiders? Reynolds had always had a horror of violence; in any case he would not resist them, should they wish him harm, for they might merely help him achieve his objective the faster. But he could see nothing. Then he heard it, that sniffle. Unmistakable, even after so many years. That ugly, indrawn, noxiously wet sniffling that only his mother could make to announce her presence and her displeasure. He sat in the bed, shocked upright.

The bedroom door was still closed but there she was, that slight frame, that same black apron with a billion tiny white stars, the apron that insisted on how hard she was working for them all and how little thanks she was getting in return. Her hair in that fine, chocolate-brown hairnet, dragging it back from her forehead, emphasising her anger and distraction. Mother. Sniffling. Drawing the back of her hand across her nose and mouth, brushing the hand down along the side of her apron. It was she, without a doubt.

She just stood there, watching him. He sat petrified, watching her.

'What else could you expect?' she began, in that high, whingeing voice, that complaining, discordant melody in the words. 'Expect a fart from a runt, that's what you expect,' she said, 'that's what you get.' And she sniffled once again. 'Last time we met, remember, you oul' eejit? I told you I'd be keepin' my eyes on you. Gave you a task, too. And how well are you doin'? Like a cabbage tryin' to walk, that's how. That's feckin' how!'

But at least she was speaking to him. That was something. His mother's way of coping with distress or anger had been the cold-war method; she would simply freeze into a silence that was like the freezing fog you get on a January morning. She would not speak for hours, making a show of ignoring you, turning away, the space between you and her cold and thick. That could last for days, for weeks; there was absolutely nothing you could do about it. If you did not do exactly as Mother wished at all times, then you were in the freezer and you did not come out until something happened that made her soft and reasonable again. Reasonable! And what was reason to her might well be mystery to everybody else. There were times, of course, when that frost was more than welcome, and you could go about your daily stupidities and know for sure she was going to pretend not to notice. That had been useful, betimes.

Right now there was no cold war. She half-sneered, half-jeered at Reynolds sitting up there in the bed. But that task? What task it was Reynolds could not remember.

'So!' she went on. 'This is your decision, then, is it? Oh dear, what a wise boy you are, so wise. Where is this goin' to lead you, I wonder? But sure I know, I don't wonder; we both know where it's goin' to lead you. But don't expect me to be hangin' about waitin' for you, or indeed waitin' on you, when you do show up. I'm past all that. Long ago. A runt, that's what you were, that's what you are. And a fart is all we're goin' to get! God help us.'

She began to shift towards the window. Reynolds was still sitting there in the bed, the blankets up to his chin, and he knew that his face must have looked blank as a turnip. Except for fear. And sheer wonder. Except, of course, behind that turnip face he didn't think, not any more, not for many, many years now, that he was the greatest fool the world ever drew forth; oh no, not the worst eejit. In spite of what his mother thought and had always been quick to relate and to repeat. He knew well that this was a mirage, that Mother was not real, and that nothing she could or would do might harm him. Not any more. He was free of her, and she of him. But still, he wondered ... There is always that soft spot where reason simply comes to a dead halt and mystery begins; that curtain, of green baize, hanging dusty and heavy down before the great blank door that never opens, the mystery.

She sniffled again, loudly. Then she drew back one side of the tattered curtain and gazed out. Reynolds was astonished to see that the sun was shining outside, though in the room it was as dark as the hours beyond midnight. Not a beam of that light came into the room. There was a sort of dull glow, an otherworldly emanation, that surrounded his mother, a sickly lemon aura that was there and not there, but that at least made her visible in the darkness. She sniffled again.

'I see that herself next door is at it again,' his mother said, peering out. 'Lyin' out half-naked in the garden, arse to the sun, and himself away in Turkey, spreadin' his own wonders about among the dark beauties no doubt. It's your chance, you feckin' eejit you. You failed before, but now she's waitin' for you, ready for you. And you lie there in the bed as if you had no pecker on you at all, and no spunk in you either, and the whole of the Reynolds line will fall into the muck when you pass on.' She let the curtain fall back again. 'Jesus!' she hissed, the name a long, slow slither out of her mouth. She rushed her hand to her face then and apologised to the ceiling. 'I'm sorry,' she said. 'I'm truly sorry. Just slipped out, so it did. Bein' here with this go-boy is what done it. I'm sorry. Mortal sin does be every-where, ev-ery-where! there's no doubt to that. No doubt at all. Sorry.'

She was moving now back towards the door and glad he was to see her move.

'You're like the feckin' bird that thought the only beak he had was the one on the top of his head. Get the feck up out of that, you little bollocks, and don't make a show of your poor mother!'

And that was that. She wasn't there any more and the room was as dark as it had been before she came in. But Reynolds was wide awake, shaking himself like a dog with fleas, wondering at his own mind and the terrible labyrinths men have in there. His parents, God rest them both, and he wished, oh how he wished, that they would take their eternal rest and leave him in peace, his parents had given him the pip when he was a youngster, there was no question of that; as well as the boys who bullied him, and the girls, too, it was mostly his parents whose cussedness and irritability had caused him grief. Affliction, yes, that was the word; they had poured affliction on the young child's head, and there is nothing like affliction to make a body know how miserable is the condition of the human beings who walk the earth. And yet, if that affliction is taken into the poor soul and the being stands tall and straight in spite of it, it may well be the cause of instilling a greater sensitivity towards others and their sufferings. And that may well be the cause of Reynolds's care of Genevieve next door. At least, that would be a spiritual way of looking at it, and not a carnal way, as Mother no doubt believed.

It had been Mother's belief that everyone had rotting corpses in their cupboards. When she came to see Reynolds the first time, no, actually the second time, here in Heatherfield, oh several years after her death, and when she saw his next-door neighbour, Genevieve, she had instantly suspected foul play somewhere. Genevieve was beautiful, full-bodied, hair as black as a sloe with the sheen of winter sun across it, and she smiled and was open to the world. Genevieve, lovely, lovely Genevieve. Reynolds had known joy in her presence, and joy is a revelation of the wonderful beauty of the world; now pain and suffering had brought that same beauty, but oh how differently! into his miserable body.

Reynolds had brought Genevieve a dozen of his free-range eggs when she first moved into the estate, and she had welcomed him wholeheartedly, though Randy, her big, tall muscleman of a husband, had watched askance while Reynolds was there. Those were the days before Genevieve began to complain about the hens and the pigs, before she caught the smells their healthy lifestyles emitted from Reynolds's cramped back yard. Genevieve's husband had something to do with wine, importer or distributor or something, and Reynolds often watched him carry crates of wine into the house next door; a fine man like that, and where was the beer, Reynolds wondered, how could a hefty man go only for wine? Or perhaps the wine was for Genevieve and the women friends who used to come around for mornings; coffee mornings? tea mornings? wine mornings?

'We must get rid of the fat!' Mother used to say, meaning the surplus from our own lives, not the bits of the corpses we have stashed away. 'We must make ourselves lean and supple in the service of the Lord, reduce ourselves the way John the Baptist reduced himself, or Saint Anthony in the Desert, or Saint Eucalyptus Magnus of Tory Island. Sin abounds,' she would say; 'is everywhere, common as midges before the fall of rain. But grace abounds, too. We must punish ourselves so we are pure as a flake of snow fallin' through the ether and then, like the snow, we must let ourselves be made nothin' before the love of God, as if we were little more than skeletons dancin' in His courtyards.'

Oh dear, she did get carried away, Reynolds's mother, poor, poor Mother. That kind of thing came out of her on her good days and sure they were rare enough, God help us, rare as the sun that might split stones across the rocky island heather fields. And now, there he was, in the dark, still shaken after her visit. He tried to settle himself down again. He pulled the blankets up around him, closed his eyes, but all he could think of was what Mother had said. Oh no, not all that stuff about reduction and annihilation, but about Genevieve lying arse to the sun in her back garden. He knew for a fact that it was the dark hours of the night, but the mind is such a thing! it kept at him, playing and replaying that image until he had to leap out of bed to satisfy his all too vivid imaginings. Leap, no, not the right word; Reynolds was already reduced in his being so that what he did, in fact, was labour his way out of bed and over to the window. He flipped back the curtain and there he was, staring out into the darkness of a suburban night, only the sickly lemon glow from the streetlamps covering the drab back gardens and sheds of that unholy territory! He laughed at himself, and got taken with a sudden coughing spasm that left him weak and sitting back on the side of the bed.

For a long time he sat there, wracked and wrenched by the coughing that tore through him, his head down between his knees, awful dribbles coming from his mouth. And once again he had proved to himself what a total idiot he was and had always been.

FIVE

Brother Leo Mason brought Reynolds out to the Scots-Pine Wood one afternoon. It must have been afternoon and school was finished for that day. Reynolds thought he was going to cut a branch off a tree to beat him with but he was wrong, very wrong. There was a poem the boys were learning that had difficult names in it, names that felt like you had a big stone in your mouth and when you tried to say the names the stones went rushing about against your teeth and the insides of your gums so that you expected your teeth to come out in dust. *Chimboroso, Cotopaxi*, something like that, from some strange poem. Reynolds could write the poem down without a problem in those days; he knew it by heart too, apart from those awful words, and he liked the poem, especially when Brother Leo himself recited it. 'Butterflies, I think they are, those strange names,' Brother Leo had said. 'Or if they're not butterflies, they're volcanoes. Same difference,' and he had laughed quietly to himself, floating as he so often did a mile above his students' heads. Anyway, he had got some of the boys to stand up and recite the poem and they all did, pretty well. Then he asked Reynolds.

At that time Brother Leo was new to the monastery and to the school. Reynolds felt the new monk had been looking at him all that first week, trying to sum him up, trying to see what this silent boy was like, who he was, and what he could do with him. So when Brother Leo asked him to say the poem, Reynolds supposed it must have been some kind of a test, for himself as well as for the Brother. Maybe he wanted to be kind, to see if Reynolds could be like the rest of the lads, just normal, like them. Anyway, up he stood and tried the poem but the stones started in their dozens to rush about in his mouth. Reynolds didn't mind that so much, it was the spittle that came dribbling and bubbling out of his mouth that always made him upset. He kept trying, he really did. He looked Brother Leo in the eyes, he gripped the top edge of his desk, he pushed and pushed against the words that were there, lined up and waiting to come out. And the boys and girls were all laughing and banging the desks they were so merry at him and he got more and more frustrated. Because he loved that old poem and he would have given his whole week's lunches to be able to say it. It must be wonderful to be able to stand up and recite a poem, he used to think, like sucking a delicious sweet from the inside out or something. Like sending skylarks out of your mouth into the blue sky on a summer morning. But he couldn't, and the tears came, and then he knew the mucous would follow, flowing out of his nose, and he gave up and just stood there. A gom. Silent, apart from a gurgling noise in his throat, like the sounds that dishwater thickened with lamb-fat made when it was let down the sink-hole.

Then what happened? Well, it happened as if somebody else had complete control over his body. In shame and frustration and embarrassment Reynolds lumped it out of his desk and because he was so awkward his books and pencils and slate, his bread-and-sugar sandwich and new wooden ruler all went scattering onto the floor of the classroom. Poor Reynolds! He stumped out of that room and all he could hear was the shuddering laughter of the classes because the whole school, from second class to seventh, was in that one room. Out he spluttered and banged the door closed after him.

Reynolds had nowhere he could go. And Brother Leo had such kindly eyes that Reynolds particularly wanted to get the poem somewhere near right. For him. He mooched away to the end of the play yard and banged in through the small bushes and whitethorn hedgerow and found a hollow place and sat down on the hard ground. And that day was another day coloured grey and black in his mind, coloured for ever with the colour of pain. There were times when he was very good at being a rock. He could half-close his eyes, close down his little peanut brain, slow his breathing, and almost cease to be. Just sit. Sit. Thoughtless, almost, but all his senses alive to the birds, the insects, the rustling of the breezes through the whitethorn bushes, the distant sounds from the classroom, the occasional passing of a cart on the road, the calling of a cock from a far back yard somewhere in the villages across the heather fields. And time did not matter to him at those moments.

He came out of that pleasing stupor when the other children had gone to their homes. Brother Leo was out around the yard and Reynolds knew he was searching for him. He truly believed he was in for an atrocious hammering but he was prepared to come out, slowly, and show himself, willing to get it over with as soon as possible. Reynolds was brave enough to face the consequences of his own failings, he was willing to take his punishment. He couldn't avoid Brother Leo – wasn't he staying in the monastery itself and would be bumping into him at all hours? In any case, it wasn't Brother Leo that worried Reynolds, this new young Brother was untried as yet; no, it was Brother Sebastian Hardiman that was the threat, the man ever ready with the strap and ever keen to use it.

'Ah, there you are, Reynolds!' Brother Leo said kindly enough.

Reynolds picked himself, greatly embarrassed, out of the hedgerow. He shook himself off, picking thorns out of his clothes, rubbing his nose and eyes into some semblance of normality. They walked together then, in almost silence, Leo remarking on the flight of a goldfinch, Reynolds grunting in response. Leo remarking on the glassy sheen the underside of the leaves seemed to take on in certain positions of the sun, Reynolds silent but awe-stricken in response; that was something he had never noticed before. When they came to the wood beyond the monastery grounds Leo took him in to a clearing not far within the pine trees. There Leo found a small sally bush growing against a ditch.

'Choose one, now, Reynolds, a good one, that'll make the hands red and hot with its stinging.'

Reynolds knew all about that. He had become an expert.

Brother Sebastian used to clout the hands off him in the early days and Reynolds knew what a good sally rod was like. He found one, broke it off, stripped off the little branches and handed it to Leo. The young Brother swung it a few times, up and down, thudding it against his soutane. Reynolds was furtively rubbing his hands together, trying to warm them up against the coming storm.

'Good,' Leo said then. 'Good. That should do the trick. Now Reynolds ...'

He paused. Reynolds held out his right hand and closed his eyes, bracing himself. In Reynolds's mind the Brothers were the Lord's, they ruled the universe, God's messengers and activists, God's angels whom He had sent on earth to administer His laws and systems, rewards and punishments. And being beaten by the Brothers was being beaten by the Lord. And nothing but good could come of it. He waited. Nothing happened.

When he opened his eyes after a few moments Brother Leo had already begun to walk away, back out of the clearing, through the pines, towards the monastery grounds. He called back to Reynolds: 'The next child, boy or girl, that mocks you in my classroom will know what a fine chap you are at finding sally rods!' And he laughed heartily.

Reynolds felt he had found a friend.

SIX

Reynolds knew it wasn't an easy time for people, moving into a new neighbourhood, especially in the crowded estates where gardens and walls and rush-hurry-business-only and finances seem to keep people apart from each other. You can live in a crowded estate without ever speaking to a soul for days, weeks, even months. Reynolds knew that for a fact.

He turned up at Genevieve and Randy's house at noon that day. They had been in the place about a week but the front garden was already a wonder, with perfect irises in bloom, rose-bushes in bud, a lawn as smooth as a mirror, and all the mosses and lichens raked away from the driveway. There seemed some magic involved in that perfection, as if it had been dropped down intact from the skies to Reynolds's next-door neighbour's delight. There was a large and heavy knocker on the front door, a brass affair with a horny old man's head on it, curly hair down his back, curly beard, big eyes staring. Ulysses, perhaps, or Hector. Mouth wide open and darkness within, but the lower lip served as a handle to lift and bang against his chin. Reynolds heard the echo of his knocking within. He knocked several times. There was no reply. Then he saw the little bell at the side of the door, and beside it a sort of speakaphone apparatus. So he pressed that little bell and waited.

Just at that moment a great car drew into the driveway. You must understand the driveway was not a driveway; there was just enough room for a big car, with a little space left before the door and a little before the gate. This was a big, plum-coloured car, a Jaguar, all a-gleam and most impressive. It came to a halt, breathing softly for a while, purring gently. Then the engine cut out and this most wonderful woman got out on the passenger side. Oh God, Reynolds nearly fell over on top of his eggs. He had seen beautiful women before, and he had imagined them often enough, but this one was the T-bone steak ideal lady. Tall, six feet maybe, utterly beautiful with her sheer black hair, her bright blue eyes, her skin tanned and healthy-looking, her body simply perfect. She smiled at Reynolds and he nearly fainted. All he could do was hold out the eggs in their brown paper package and do his usual stammering routine.

'Di ... di ... di ...' he began wonderfully. 'And do ... do ... do ...'

He stopped. He realised she probably thought he was calling her Diana, or Dido or something like that when all he really wanted to say was, 'This is a gift' and 'I have been knocking at your door'. But she seemed to understand anyway. She did not back away from him, nor recoil in any way. She was coming towards him, smiling softly, and he felt as if an angel out of the blue sky were coming to sweep him up in clouds of glory. Until he heard a shout.

'Get out of here, now. Get away. We don't want your kind here. Go!'

It was himself. Randy, the husband, as Reynolds learned later. He had got out of his glory-car and had banged the door shut and was coming at Reynolds, threateningly, as if poor Reynolds was a burglar or a salesman or a politician. And was he big! over six feet and constructed to match. Scaffolding of steel. Fists, no doubt, like bricks. He could have taken Reynolds and broken him into little wedges. Now, Reynolds forgave him at once. If Reynolds had been in his position, guardian of such a goddess, and there was this lump of a horrible-looking man standing in her way, his hairy hand reaching towards her with a lumpy brown packet in it, well, he might have got suspicious too. Reynolds did not hesitate. He left the gift down on the perfect lawn, watching himself lest Randy leap upon him, then backed away, two hands raised in defence. Reynolds tried to smile at the woman but the smile was little more than a leer, the tongue shooting out and a great wobble of spittle following it, because the man shouted at him again, louder than before.

'Get the hell out of here and never come back, you hear me?'

Reynolds rushed, then, out their gate and in at his own. He glanced back just before he opened his own door and he saw how they stood, slightly abashed now, aware at once that this was their neighbour, this was the man they would be living beside before they moved from this estate to a larger, more exclusive one well away from Heatherfield. Reynolds was used to that; but he was pleased to have at least seen the woman. Dido. Queen of Carthage. She was looking towards him then, and he could see, he thought, apology in her blue, blue eyes, her features warm and gentle, her stance forgiving.

SEVEN

One of the greatest sorrows of Reynolds's life had been generated in him by womankind. His lumpy body, like a hessian sack of mangold-wurzels, as big and as ugly, had always driven every woman from him, except, of course, those who had enjoyed making fun of him and using him as their fool. Yet in his mind and heart and soul he had always longed for a woman, for the delight of their delicate and lovely company as well as for the physical pleasure of their incredible bodies. For their gentilesse, their poise. *Whereso'er I am, below, or else above you, Whereso'er you are, my heart shall truly love you.* Reynolds would repeat Sylvester's lines to himself, his heart longing to love truly and for ever. But how could a woman love a sack of mangolds?

When he was much younger, when the world was still daffodil-yellow and the roads were paved with sand and pebbles, when the ditches and hedgerows contained only wonders and scented blossoms, Reynolds had fallen in love and he had been in love since then. He was given his first bicycle a few days before. It was not new, Mother always felt that would have been a waste on Reynolds because he was sure to smash it or lose it or forget where he had left it. It was an old bicycle, a Rudge, big as a turf-cart, black and rusty, with the chain forever coming off. But for Reynolds it was a gilded chariot and he was Paris riding out to war, four black chargers prancing ahead of him, and the dust he raised sent terror into the hearts of his enemies. Within two days he had learned how to climb on it and pedal and move and not fall off. Within three days he had lost some of his terror of the open roads. Within four days he had scarred both knees for life.

That special morning he half-cycled, half-walked the bike down towards the sandy banks where he could practise without fear of breaking his body. It was a graceful morning; rabbits hopped and pirouetted in fearless freedom where a high bank ended in tall and secretive marram grasses; gulls were drawn up in ranks, all facing in the same direction, just above the tide-line, as if listening to a sermon on the goodness of God and the mysteries of the Trinity. The sea itself was softly whispering, humming perhaps, in a warm idleness. For a long moment Reynolds breathed in the beauty around him, sighing deeply, his two hands on the bicycle, his body planted on the earth.

Reynolds mounted on the sand-rutted pebble lane that led from the main road to the green banks. And he fell, heavily, almost at once. Oh dear, not only was his right knee badly bleeding but he could feel a big gash there and he knew that a small pebble had got right inside. His left knee, too, was gashed and bleeding. But God was with him and Doctor Weir came out from his surgery just at the end of the road, all packed up and prepared for home and elevenses. He saw Reynolds at once, the young boy sniffling and bent towards his damaged knees. Doctor Weir sighed, but Doctor Weir was a good and generous man. He took Reynolds in, jeering kindly at him. Reynolds was put sitting on a hard wooden chair and Doctor Weir tut-tut-tutted before reaching for his equipment: swabs, strong-smelling stuff in a small brown bottle, and a long, curving, lean mean scissors. Reynolds closed his eyes and prayed: *O Angel of God my Guardian dear ...*

Doctor Weir washed the blood away, cleaned the wound, took the long scissors and got the pebble out. He kept telling Reynolds to be brave, and he was. Poor Reynolds was used to pain and he just clenched his face shut and bore it without making a sound. The doctor showed him the little pebble. Reynolds took it from him and smiled, put it in his pocket and tried to say thank you. Then the doctor bandaged up the knee and sent him off.

Bandaged and healed and a little abashed, Reynolds came out onto the sandy lane. Doctor Weir's big house stood up to the right of the surgery, away at the end of a long fuchsia-lined laneway. Reynolds would always remember the forget-me-not blue of the surgery, how it gleamed with a kind of special light that day. The bike was strewn where it had fallen and Reynolds bent to pick it up. But a shot of pain went through his knee and he let out a little cry. He put a hand to his eyes to wipe away a tear and there were tiny rowan-berries of dried blood on his wrist, and on his palm, where he had fallen, a stippling of gravel-dust. He licked away the blood and then stood for a while. Absence fell across his eyes, like a warm shadow, and absence came over his addled brain, like a soft blanket.

It was just then that Doctor Weir's young daughter, Deirdre, came around the driveway curve. She was small and very pretty. There was something gossamer about the way she came along the lane, something blue-steel, too, in the way her loveliness suggested perfectibility. She was smiling at Reynolds. She knew. Perhaps she had seen the fall from a window in the house above. She laughed out loud at the big boy where he stood, mouth fallen open at the sight of her lemon-yellow dress with the tiny green leaves patterned on it. Oh she laughed at him, that red and blotched face, the short trousers hanging shapeless over the bandaged knee – but there was no malice or hurt in the laugh, it was a tiny, gurgling laugh of conspiracy. She said his name, that's all, 'Reynolds,' she said, and it sounded like music in her mouth. He would remember noticing how perfect were her teeth, how white. She said the name once more, 'Reynolds', then she turned and disappeared quickly back around the driveway curve. She left him more abashed than he had ever been in his life, more healed, too, sensing the possibilities of trust, the interventions in his life of what was beautiful.

EIGHT

Reynolds believed that his whole vocation in life had been one of self-annihilation. Now that he had begun the final process, inside his barricaded house, with complete awareness of what he was doing, he began to know that his life's work had consisted in just such an activity, if activity is the right word. Activity. Passivity. Words. Because Reynolds was born a clod and grew more cloddish as he took on flesh, and he knew the only skill he would ever have to get him along would be a skill with words. Written words, of course, not spoken. He had never, almost never, enunciated one word correctly in his life, without stumbling over it like a cow on rocks. His joy had always been in words. Now he would become bone and flesh, without impurity. He would become gold, spring water, he would become like unto God, without filament or filigree, without anything left on his ego-skeleton whereby he might sin. He would become love, pure love. Word, pure word.

Reynolds wanted to be original chaos, to be like the water pouring from the hill, willing to take the shape of the streams on the hillside, the ditches between the fields, the pipes among the houses. He would be putty in God's hands so that nothing more could be taken from his being by this difficult world. Because Reynolds saw God as an old man, he saw Him in His snuff-dusted waistcoat with its faceless fob watch, sitting late on His veranda in unaltering perfection: no note of birdsong or buzz of flies anywhere about, no breeze or rain, the light of dusk won't shift towards night; no one there to soothe His angers or ease away the strain along His back. Non-being is a glaur that waits malleable around Him; should He shift out of His stiffness, His every shift creates a universe, the glaur unsettling, viscid ripples widening out from Him where His being caught on the thorns of movement, and His blood dripples; the wild meadow of our universe marvellously wrought. Such was his view of God.

Dear grandfather God, here I am, Reynolds spoke without stuttering deep inside his own being where only that God could hear; *here I am at Your garden gate, waiting on You, waiting to be so pure that I may dare approach Your everlasting presence.*

Yet he knew, in his innocent foolishness, exactly where he was, there in his old house in Heatherfield Gardens, there in his bedroom, in the semi-darkness, alone as usual, cold and hungry and very thirsty. It was a thirst like this, though not nearly so violent as he was suffering now, that made him make a great oath to the world about him. Away back, years before, a day of great heat when the whole school was outside, doing tables or spellings or some such, and Reynolds was deeply dry within himself. Big Tom Molloy, the bully, was beside him, sitting cross-legged, as they all were, Brother Leo up on the grassy bank teaching them something. But there were distractions, a wren flitting busily about in the fuchsia hedge behind the brown soutane of the Brother, butterflies, mostly white cabbage butterflies but sometimes the unequalled beauty of a tortoiseshell, floating wonderfully by; sometimes too they'd hear the screech of a black-backed gull as it swooped low over the heather fields beyond. And everywhere the low humbuzz buzzhum of flies and midges and the soft low clarinet-music of the turning of the world. There came from the boys and girls, too, the low buzz of learning.

Reynolds was sick with thirst. Breakfast in the monastery was often nothing more than salty porridge and Reynolds, being slow and cumbersome, having to hurry to be up in the school on time, had missed his mug of tea. Big Tom produced a bottle of Lucozade from the folds of his schoolbag and Reynolds couldn't resist, he would have given his life for one mouthful of that red-gold, fizzing nectar. Reynolds leaned towards Big Tom, making sure Brother Leo was not looking or listening, and he tried to ask him, to beg of him, a great favour.

'Too ... too ... too ...' Reynolds began, and Tom knew he was saying his name. He turned to look at Reynolds and from the leer on his face and the disdain that he always maintained towards him Reynolds knew that he would not give him even the smallest drop of the stuff. 'Pa ... pa ... pa ...' he went on, and moved his hand gently towards the bottle.

Tom glanced up quickly towards Brother Leo, then turned back to Reynolds and muttered, 'Feck off you stammering stuttering eejit!' Then he raised the bottle on his mouth and Reynolds could see small drops of the precious liquid that he deliberately let fall down along his chin.

Oh God how he suffered for those terrible moments and how, when Brother Leo came rushing down from the grass bank towards Tom, he longed to be able to say even one sentence without making a fool of himself.

Brother Leo had seen Tom lift the bottle and now he cuffed him about the ears and took the bottle from him.

Like the total fool Reynolds was, he stood up awkwardly from where he sat and pointed to the bottle in Brother Leo's hands. 'Mi ... mi ... mi ...' he tried, pointing to himself. Poor Brother Leo thought Reynolds wanted a drink and he offered him the bottle, perhaps to punish Big Tom the more. But Reynolds shook his head and continued pointing to himself, 'I ... I ... I ...' But it was hopeless. How could he ever tell Brother Leo that it was all his fault. Brother Leo shrugged his shoulders and headed back up towards his grassy perch.

Big Tom snarled at Reynolds. 'Right, you eejit!' he said. 'In the lane after school. Me and you. A fight.' He leaned towards Reynolds, stuck the index finger of his right hand in his mouth and rubbed the finger down along Reynolds's arm. 'I'm layin' the wet finger on you, you bloody eejit!' he said. 'For this afternoon. After school.'

Nobody in their right mind would dare refuse the wet finger challenge or they'd be branded for ever as a coward. Reynolds decided that if he could not speak his soul and mind then he would learn how to write down his soul and mind as well as he possibly could, so that he would not pass through life totally unable to communicate with his fellow man. Reynolds sat down again, cross-legged on the ground, and immediately took up the old dirty schoolbook and looked at it with new attention. There was a funny little poem, a lovely one, wise and yet simple beyond belief.

> Four ducks on a pond.
> A grass-bank beyond.
> A blue sky of spring,
> white clouds on the wing.
> What a little thing
> to remember for years.
> To remember with tears.

Reynolds looked up from the page and he could feel his eyes water over with the truth of that. He felt the great power of words and knew that you didn't have to be able only to stand up in front of the world and speak them out. You could write them down, too, and they'd say even more than if they were simply whipped away in the wind. Reynolds had developed, suddenly, an even greater thirst and his ordinary one just faded away into the sunlight. Big Tom thought he was laughing at him, but Reynolds was only happy for that short time, that's all, and when he was happy he'd laugh, laugh out loud and the juice of his laughter came out in small white bubbles from the side of his mouth. He would write, that very evening, the great miracle that Murt, his friend, had shown him up at the quarry, and he would hand it over to Brother Leo, as well as an explanation of Big Tom's innocence with the Lucozade.

The quarry had been gouged out of the side of The Whinny Hill, a little over a year ago. The hillside had been a dull one of famine grass and low-growing heathers and ling, with small tussocks of moss and fraughans. But nearby the sand-and-stone cart-track that led over the hill and down the other side towards Doonanaine had suddenly become important in the advance of the world towards wealth, and they had come seeking stones for the new road. There had been exciting dynamite-explosions; there had been men dressed in thick trousers, wearing only braces over dirty off-white vests, swinging picks and shovels; there had been an enormous tractor that came with a great bucket in front of it and had lifted out the rocks onto the roadside.

Reynolds had become totally absorbed in the way the tar bubbled and flowed before ultimately lying still on the ground, steam rising gently into the air, then disappearing. And he would go, later on, and put his index finger on the tar, astonished, meditating on it without being aware of himself at all. But it was the hole in the hillside that they left behind that became the source of the greatest mystery to Reynolds, explicated only much later by the wisdom of Murt Quigley.

Murt was well disposed towards Reynolds and often took him in hand to give him explanations of the workings of the universe. Reynolds was fascinated by the quarry and often went there when his chores at the monastery allowed. The Quigleys lived not far away, the other side of a knot of small hills, and Murt would come and join Reynolds as he watched the evolution of this quarry. For weeks it was just a hole, the high sides riven by dynamite and pick, the bottom dry with stone-dust. But after a day of rain Reynolds noticed the hill-waters seeping down through and over the roots of the heathers and beginning to form a dark pool of water in the centre of the hole. Soon the pool had grown larger, much larger. It began to reach up the sides of the quarry; it covered the floor; it grew deeper.

He saw a scum growing on the surface of the quarry that began to spread into tiny, thin strands of green vegetation at one side of the pool. The water was very dark and it was now impossible to guess its depth and its dangers. There were tiny traces of old oil left on the surface, forming shifting rainbows of colour that gave the water a sickly look. This made it all the more fascinating, and when Reynolds and Murt discovered frogspawn shivering at the edge of the pool they were very excited indeed. They kept all of this a secret from Big Tom and his likes, just in case they would come and destroy the place.

By now, if you were still very young, you could call this pool a lake, and one day, when Reynolds was idly turning over one of the larger stones at the edge of the pool, he saw a tiny living shape glide out and slip away into the blackness of the darker water. An eel! finger-small, butter-lithe and butter-coloured. When Murt arrived later that afternoon they turned other stones together and saw more, several more, tiny, beautiful eels! Where had they come from? How had they got there?

For a while Murt thought hard. He was in the top class and was one of the brightest students, if not the very brightest. But he was modest with it and it was his modesty along with his brightness that set him free from bullying by the other, more dense, members of the class. Murt, if you pressed him, and Reynolds pressed him, had an answer, ultimately, for every-thing. 'Well,' he told Reynolds. 'If you were able to see them, there are tiny, tiny golden seeds contained in some of the raindrops that come down and fall into this pool, the tiniest imaginable golden seeds, falling from the very edge of the rain-bow, when the edge of the rainbow catches the edge of the pool. You can see them if you look very, very closely, some day when it's raining and the sun keeps on shining through the rain, and if you don't get too close to the rainbow's edge you can see the gold seeds in the drops, and it's these very seeds that, when they fall into the water, grow into these lovely golden eels. There for you. That's the very truth of it now.'

Reynolds was satisfied with this explanation and from then on watched the rain when it fell, especially on those days when there were sun showers, soft, slow rain that gleamed and glit-tered with wetness and with more than wetness. He treasured the thought and grew more fond of the miracles that he saw around him in the world. 'Praise God!' he would have said aloud, but he didn't, because he couldn't, and only his lips plopped, and a thin bubble of spittle formed and burst on his mouth.

NINE

Reynolds knew he was growing irritable. Perhaps the fasting was beginning to get to him. He was starving. There was a severe pain in his stomach, a pain so big he began to believe his stomach must be a much larger place than he had ever believed. Sometimes, too, great stabs of light hit him behind the eyes somewhere and seemed to travel down through his body, touching every bone and vein as they passed. This was not going to be as easy as he had thought.

He had another look out into the garden next door. There was a sort of disarray in that back garden, worse than Reynolds's own, for his had been trampled down till there was no weed nor plant nor stick left that could grow. His small back garden was a moon-scape. Apart from the two humps of earth down against the back wall. Now and again, when Randy was away somewhere, Reynolds would leave a few eggs at Genevieve's door, ring the bell, and walk away. He was happy imagining her delight at the gift, imagining her boiling the eggs and thinking of Reynolds.

Reynolds had kept three pigs out in the back garden, and about twelve hens. There were the neighbourhood cats, too, who wandered into his garden, scratched his already trampled soil and relaxed their bowels. Reynolds didn't mind; it was all natural, and the cats were fairly wild things, occasionally bringing in some delightfully small and marmalade-coloured kittens. The pigs lolled about under the old apple tree in the far corner where he used to let the apples just fall off the trees for them. Sometimes, in the special fruit-filled season, they smooched under the plum tree, the great softness of the fallen plums being specially good for them. The hens muttered contentedly here and there among the weeds and high grasses, pecking away at whatever insects they found, and enjoying the grains he flung out to them every day.

Mason used to come to see the pigs and hens and once he asked Reynolds if he had names on them. Reynolds pointed to one of the pigs; she was lying in by the wall, in the sunshine, and there was a hen standing on her big round body, pecking gently at something on the pig's flesh. 'Ve ... Ve ... Venus!' he managed to get out of his chest and Mason laughed heartily. He pointed to another pig that was snouting happily under the tree; 'Ka ... Ka ... Ka ...' he tried.

'Kavanagh?' Mason suggested.

Reynolds shook his head. 'Ku ... Ku ... Ku ...'

And Mason offered 'Cool Runner?'

Again Reynolds shook his head. He slapped the palm of his hand against his forehead and the name burst out of him: 'Cupid!'

And again Mason laughed aloud. He pointed towards the third and suggested 'Aphrodite?'

Reynolds shook his head and tried: 'Jay ... Jay ... Jay ...'

'Janus?'

He shook his head again.

'Surely not Jaysus?'

Reynolds tried again and eventually got out the word. 'Juno!'

Then he brought Mason out into the grass towards the old shed that had once housed the central heating engine but was now only a half-standing henhouse, tucked in behind an old wooden fence. In a warm nest amongst the grasses and up against the wall of the henhouse he found a delightful brown egg, still warm, one tiny white feather clinging to it. He picked it up and, grunting like one of his own satisfied pigs, he handed it to his old friend Mason. Oh was he enjoying himself! King of the castle, Hamlet the Dane, Peter at the Golden Gate. But Cupid, his oldest pig, suddenly made a sort of slow and lazy bolt towards Mason, who let out a small shriek of fear and gripped

Reynolds by the shoulder. It was easy for him, because his pigs loved him, and he just blew loudly at Cupid and he stood still, watching towards the invader. Oh yes, Reynolds had felt at home and at ease among his pigs and hens.

TEN

Big Tom and Reynolds had their fight one afternoon just at the start of summer. Reynolds had always looked on such events with a great feeling of dread that seemed to linger somewhere in the lower bowels but affected his whole body with a strong trembling. He dreaded what was about to happen. Reynolds's thought was: set a stone rolling on a cliffside and it will keep going to the sea. Set the world turning and it will turn for ever. Set the lion on earth and the gazelle for its food and the lion will tear the gazelle into little pieces. It has begun, and it will continue so. That's what Reynolds figured out. And he figured out, too, that it's a man's task to draw out of the banal a pattern of love. Not an easy business, either.

Reynolds was determined to draw something fanciful out of the misery of that fight. He knew he was not going to beat Big Tom, because he didn't want to beat him. Reynolds knew Big Tom would pulp him, and he would try only to harvest something presentable out of the afternoon. Tom was big; Reynolds was big. Tom was wiry; Reynolds was plumpy, like a hippo. Reynolds could storm over Tom and tread him into the ground, but that is not the way of love.

It seemed the whole school had gathered at the gates that afternoon. Reynolds heard the skylarks out over the bog somewhere, and their song was a distant waterfall of delight. He longed to be in his thorn shelter to listen to it. Somewhere else, in the village, he heard a cock crow. Big Tom was grinning hugely. Most of the boys gathered behind him, on the green patch between the road and the bog. Most of the girls too.

Reynolds saw Nora McGreil and Doreen Murphy there with him, Nora holding his bag, Doreen his jacket. Reynolds threw his bag onto the gravel at the school gate. There was really nobody, you might say, that could be counted on his side, even though he was that big and heavy. A few of the innocent young boys and the simpler young girls just happened to hang back behind him, maybe because there wasn't enough room on the grass at the other side.

Big Tom taunted him. The crowd jeered, echoing Big Tom. He rolled up the sleeves of his white shirt and bunched his big, iron fists. Reynolds did the same. Reynolds stood, taking up a pose he thought might be considered pugilistic, artistic even. Could he draw a work of art out of his movements in this dull, painful and banal situation? Tom came at him like a windmill, arms flailing. It was easy to step aside and as he passed him by, Reynolds's right fist came so close to his right ear he must have heard the whistle of it. He turned to Reynolds again. And again he rushed, and again Reynolds stepped aside. The gang were calling 'Coward!' at Reynolds, but what did he care? So far they were both unscathed. And then Reynolds made the usual mistake, he distracted himself, for he felt a dribble of saliva going down the right side of his mouth and he reached for a hanky to dry it away. Tom rushed, head down, taking him in the stomach as he had one hand in his pocket. His head hit Reynolds hard in his flabby belly and it was already all over. Reynolds was breathless. He fell back and Big Tom fell on top of him. He straddled Reynolds and began showering his big fists down on his head, left, right, left, right. There was no beauty in it. Reynolds had both hands up trying hard to parry the blows, to deflect them, but he was hit again and again.

One thing above all others Reynolds had always hated and that was a blow to the nose. And Big Tom hit him hard, right on the nose, and that awful pain shot into his head and made a greater fool of him than ever. Dulling him with the pain that seemed to fill his whole head as if the nostril were the spout and through it his head had filled up with sluggish water. Reynolds howled like a pained ass. It was pathetic. He suffered. And he could salvage not the slightest morsel of dignity. He just plastered his hands over his face and accepted the pounding. Big Tom shifted his fists from face to chest and then raised himself a bit and thudded him again in the stomach. He stood up, goading Reynolds to get up and take it like a man. Reynolds tried to stand up. He could sense the blood streaming from his nose, mixed with mucous and saliva, and the tears were blinding him. It appeared that a purple-red light was flashing on and off right through his brain. When he was almost upright Big Tom rushed him again, his arms flailing, and Reynolds fell once more before his blows. He was so winded this time Reynolds knew he couldn't stand up again. Not for some little time.

It was then he heard, amidst the jeering and howling of the mob, a small, shrill voice call out.

'Stop!' she shouted. 'That's enough. That's enough!'

A kind of silence fell about them and Reynolds began to gather himself up again, deeply grateful that a halt was called. He felt a soft, small hand take his right hand, and as he wiped the wet away from his face with his other hand he could see it was Deirdre Weir, the doctor's daughter. Where Reynolds and Big Tom and Nora and the others lived, the doctor, the teacher, the priest and the chemist held all the power of position and advantage. Deirdre's authority derived from some ancient honouring of position and status in the community. It wasn't that she would tell, Reynolds believed, nobody told tales in that world, but that somehow the doctor just mightn't cure or fix anybody that went against his little Deirdre. Reynolds stood there, a slob attended to by a gentle maiden.

The silence became a murmuring again and Big Tom shouted: 'Anyway, it's over. I knocked the lard outa him. It proves he's an eejit, and a yellow eejit, and a thick gom!'

Reynolds heard Nora and Doreen laugh aloud and he half-watched Tom go to them and take his jacket and bag. The rest of the boys and girls began to drift away.

'Are you OK?' Deirdre asked him in that little fuchsia-honey voice of hers.

He looked at her and nodded. He tried to smile thanks to her, but nobody could tell what expression was on his bloodied and tear-stained face. She only smiled. Then she picked up his jacket and handed it to him. As he was climbing into it, she picked up the schoolbag and handed that to him too. And then, do you know what she did? and everything came clear to him at once. She recited a bit of a poem to the air, quietly, but with a voice so wonderful it added still more stature to what she recited.

> How sleep the Brave, who sink to rest
> By all their Country's wishes blest!

Then she got stuck; she had forgotten the rest of it. Reynolds was of no use to her; he could have written it out on the ground, but he couldn't say it. He managed to get the name out, though: 'Co ... Co ... Co ...' he tried, sounding like an old crow. 'Co ... Collins!' He smiled at her.

When she left, Reynolds stood there for a long, long time, more happy than he had ever yet been. Small drops of blood continued to plop plop plop out of his nose, but what did he care? he had made a friend, a true friend, and that was something very, very special.

ELEVEN

Reynolds loved his father. He had a special name for him, though nobody knew it, because Reynolds was never able to say it out loud; Hugey, he called him, from the word *huge*, Hugey. He was big, bigger than Reynolds, and tough. And oh boy, was he tough! Hugey worked on the roads when there was something to be done. And there always did seem to be something to be done. Other times he collected the dole. He brought Reynolds, occasionally, to sit on the ditch and watch the workings, perhaps when he was feeling more guilty about things than usual. Reynolds would sit among the daisies and grasses, the sorrel leaves, the buttercups, and inhale the wonderful purity of hot tar. He'd have a book with him, poems usually, Byron, or the sonnets of Shakespeare, some such, *When to the sessions of sweet silent thought* ... but he wouldn't have to spend much time reading in it because the road-building or mending was so exciting to watch.

There was the big green wooden caravan that came first, towed along by the magnificent dinosaur of the steamroller. They parked it somewhere off the road, where it stood, always a little tilted, that small wooden ladder leading up into its mysterious interior. And there was the pile of stones delivered by a great lorry and making a wonderful heap on the road, a heap that Reynolds could wander through when the day's work was done, a heap he made into an impregnable castle, locking out Big Tom and his cohorts. The stone-crusher was a crude-looking machine, great leather straps linking it to the wheel on the side of the steamroller. He watched them fork the big stones in at one end, he heard the grinding of the great metal molars, the crunching and tossing and spewing, and out on the road came the perfect little pieces they took away in barrowfuls and spread on the road. But most of all, dear God, most of all, the black and blackened box that was the tar-sprayer; the heat that came from it, the smoke, and the smell that spoke of heady excitement and difference and magic summers and oh! to see how it came spreading out from under two blackened flaps, pouring out like treacle onto the little stones, gripping them all into one perfect mass. And Packie on the steamroller, up and down all day, that wheel with which he guided the great machine spinning under his big hairy arm, how he stood like a captain on the bridge of a mighty ship, eyeing the roads ahead, the roads behind, and up and down and down and up, levelling the world, that vast stone wheel with the water dripping off it, oh yes and oh my God, it was a world of wonder and excitement and Reynolds drooled and dribbled away many a blessed hour watching it.

Father. Hugey. He just had his shovel and he had the task of shovelling stones into the crusher and shovelling them away into the barrows at the other end. Nothing magical in that, except that it was a part of the great thundering wonder of the whole. The way a small human sound uttered in the back of nowhere would take its place in the great symphony that was the turning of the spheres. He would stand, ages on end, leaning on that shovel, his red face dreaming, or he'd talk and talk as if every stone in the road was a chapter of words and he needed to get them out. And at midday he'd beckon Reynolds to him, and they'd have sandwiches, ham, or eggs, or mutton, and they'd drink milk from a paper-stoppered bottle and Reynolds would sit, among the men of myth, inhaling the scent of tar, listening to the incomprehensible talk, feeling part of something wonderful and without end.

He had a problem, Hugey had. The common one, the drink. Perhaps his life was dull, dulled and dulling, perhaps his brain was dulled and dulling too, and perhaps the body of his living was already impregnated with the alcohol problem down the dark generations that had gone before. He drank in secret and

with an overpowering guilt. He drank in public, loud and ag-
gressive and challenging anyone to tell him that he was drink-
ing. And he disappeared for days at a stretch, drinking to forget
that he was drinking, swallowing his guilt, swallowing the roads
he had been working on, swallowing the happiness of his wife,
Reynolds's mother. Hugey would set himself up, at those times,
as if nobody else existed in the whole world, and nothing
mattered but himself, Reynolds's father, centre of the universe.
While on a binge he would not allow anybody to come near
him, and his conversations quickly died away into morbid
self-anguish, where he cut himself off from everyone and
everything.

Hugey's retreat was Alice's Harbour Bar, a sprawling, dark
and enticing pub at the edge of the sea. Standing with his fierce
arms resting on the counter, at least three pints already inside
him, Hugey would become an island Plato, an Aristotle, a
Heidegger. 'We moor,' he would say, 'on the shores of a mighty
ocean and the currents shift, north, south, north south, through
the sound.' Then he'd pause, considering. The window of
Alice's Harbour Bar watched out over the sound and the glass
was grimed with the spittle of the wind and sea. In the gloom
of the pub Hugey's big fist gripped the pint of stout as if he
would crush it into bits of glass and black fluid. He stood on the
dark sawdust-sprinkled floor, like a sailor on the deck of his
trawler, finding purchase. Here he was confident, out of the
swing of the world. 'We are all,' he would state, and drink,
pausing, and go on, 'water. We are water and returning to the
state of water.' And all his companions, his fellow-sailors, nod-
ded their heads in agreement, knowing the coarse heave of
seaweeds, and the grail warmth of the liquor that warmed their
bodies through. Oh the thirst of these men, the colander of their
big and dry bodies.

Mother knew these times where her good man had hidden
himself away and sometimes sent Reynolds in with messages.
Written messages. Reynolds knew the dust of the place, the
souring smell, men big as shadows who leaned at him, their
teeth a seaweed brown, their hands dry and callused where they
touched. They were intent, all of them, as if embroiled in the

most serious of businesses. Hugey would hoist him off the boards, showing him off, onto the counter where Reynolds felt the spillings cold on his bare hocks, where he pulled to get away but Father's grip was fierce, not to be broken by the pudgy boy he'd fathered. And when, those times Hugey was locked away for days in Alice's Harbour Bar and he and Mother prayed together, *Eternal rest grant unto them, and let perpetual light ...* Reynolds, forehead pressed against the back of the chair, knew what it meant, this phrase, he knew those souls in purgatory and the noisy, noisome dimness in which they strained.

Sometimes, though rarely, Hugey came home in the middle of a binge, bottles in his coat pockets, the half-hearted attempt at a cry for help drowned in the noise of his own screamings of guilt and the wheedling calls of the bottles. And it was on one of those occasions that it happened.

Reynolds was small at that time. He was very young. He never knew whether he was an idiot before the event or whether it was the event that made an idiot out of him. How could he know? As a young child, maybe he was four or five, his mother told him later, he did mutter and mumble a good deal already, stuttering and stammering and drooling, but she did not put it down to anything other than his being a small child, not that bright, perhaps, but not abnormal either. An only child, then, and who was to know that he was to be the only child? So who's to know or tell? But Father, down in that dark well where his guilt and angers swirled, added the crime he believed he had committed to the crimes of which he was already guilty, and that added guilt became even more of a reason for him to drown out his agony in drink. Poor man. Poor, helpless man.

Reynolds was sitting on the flags of the kitchen floor, his mother was pottering away at the table, making a soda-bread cake, an apple tart or boxty cakes, who knows? Just an ordinary, special day, in an ordinary, special time in an ordinary boy's life. But Mother stopped her humming and pottering all at once and stood in a strangely tense way that made the child, too, pause and look up. Then they heard the iron gate of the back yard squealing in complaint and banging shut and they knew that

Father was home again, and he was drunk and that meant sadness and trouble. Reynolds was only a poor young fool but he already suffered for his mother, and for his father too. They waited. There was silence, except for the clunking of boots along the pebbled track to the yard.

They waited to hear the back door into the scullery open and shut. But there was nothing. The footsteps fell away into silence. They listened. Reynolds could hear a bluebottle struggling away against the windowpane. Then Mother began pottering again, at the range, and Reynolds felt as if everything had fallen back into place. Now, Reynolds had never done this before and he never knew why he did it then. It was as if he was wiser far than his silly years permitted, but he came out from under the table and went, quietly and slowly, towards the back door. Mother scarcely glanced about at him; she had her own troubled thoughts to deal with. He went into the scullery, opened the back door and went out into the back yard. Father was moving through the meadow gate and Reynolds knew he was heading for the outside toilet just inside the shed wall of the meadow. Normal, everyday things; and the sun shining modestly on their modest yard. Reynolds went into the yard. He mooched about a while, waiting. Then, as nothing was happening, he went towards the meadow gate. He waited again. The toilet door was shut; Reynolds knew that Father was within. But he was taking a long time. Reynolds waited.

Then, very slowly, the toilet door swung out on its hinges. Slowly. Silently. Reynolds expected Father to come out, mumbling, doing up his braces, turning to close the door after him. But there was no movement. Nothing. So he moved forward into the edge of the meadow and around under the shed wall. He could see into the open toilet. Father was sitting on the toilet, leaning forward, his forehead down on his elbows, his elbows down on his knees. Reynolds grew anxious. He moved forward quickly then, and came up to the open door and he could hear Father sobbing to himself, lost to everything but his own misery. So, it wasn't only children that sobbed and cried wet tears, not only children who were bold and scolded and slapped that cried and felt sorry for themselves; it was grown-ups too, poor, poor grown-ups. Poor Father.

Reynolds should have called out to him then, and stayed where he was. But he didn't. He was young, so young, and perhaps a little foolish. But he always would remember the surge of love and even compassion he suddenly felt for that big, hurting man and he moved forward and tugged at his sleeve. He said something, something like, 'Daddy, come on in; you'll be all right.' Reynolds tugged at his sleeve and then, as if out of a mighty storm, the man rose up before him and his great fist came crashing against the side of his head and he went stagger-ing backwards, out into the meadow. Reynolds often relived that dreamlike, backwards fall; he would relive the blow, like a silent awful thud that went deep into his head and thundered there, and the terrible voice shouting at him, 'Get the fuck out of my life! you stupid fuckin' cretin!' Those were his words, exactly those. How could words like those, from Father, from your very own, very special father, ever leave your memory?

They say you see stars when something hits you on the head; Reynolds saw no stars, nothing like that; there was only blackness, a deep and somehow scarlet blackness. None of it made sense, really, none of it, neither then, nor ever, except that later in his life Reynolds would know too well how all of us are nothing, how our lives are a negative quantity, minus ten, minus thirty, and that our only hope is to approach some kind of zero where we may pass through into a positive dying. And he knew that poor Father then was at his most negative point of all, minus a million, minus, minus, minus. God help him. God help Reynolds. God help us all.

TWELVE

Another morning, if it was morning in Heatherfield Gardens, for Reynolds had lost all trace or sense of real time, he woke up, or came more fully awake – he wasn't sure about this either, for he had lost any true sense of whether he was awake or dozing – with the most atrocious headache. Here. Right across his forehead. A kind of migraine, he believed, that same pain like a rusty knife-blade cutting roughly against your nerves within. His whole head screaming with it. He buried his head in his hands where he lay in the bed, and waited. He suffered from such headaches all his life, coming at impossible moments, giving little warning, then bursting in through the door of his life, an unwelcome, an intolerable and intolerant guest. But this, somehow, this was different.

There is a darkness within the darkness that you impose on yourself, when you close your eyes and bury your head in your hands. That darkness inside is the most dangerous of all. In there, where there was a roaring racket alternating with a high-pitched prolonged screeching noise, lights flashing and strobe lights whirling, Reynolds could find no comfort. In there he found himself weakening. He saw himself getting out of the bed, taking a drink of wonderful, hot tea sweetened with sugar and following that with many, many slices of hot toast, the butter dribbling off the sides, and marmalade flowing over the butter. The vision was too much to bear. And he began to get up. He swung his legs out of the bed, his eyes still closed, and he sat there a while, a great flood of relief taking him, that now he had changed his mind; he would eat again, he would live again. He would …

And as suddenly as it had happened so often before, that final emptiness hit him once more; he would ... what? What was the point of it? What could the point of it possibly be? There was no point. He was a waste. He was useless. The only thing he could do would be to become zero. Just empty, a nothingness, ready then to be filled with meaning.

Reynolds made his way to the bathroom, took the toothpaste glass and filled it with water from the cold tap. He kept his eyes closed. He drank the water and he could feel it, wet and cool, coursing through his body, mapping out and announcing the name of every physical part of him within. It was enough for the moment. He felt revived. He returned to the bed, his eyes still closed, and he settled back among the covers. The suffering eased a little. He stilled himself fully. He rested.

That cool sensation from the water brought him back almost at once to the day they spent in the meadow, Father, Mother and Reynolds. For a second he opened his eyes; was this just a memory that came to him unbidden now that his body was fraying into air, or was there someone there, someone whispering to him, someone suggesting? Or was this, in fact, the happening he had so often heard about before, that a man in his dying will see his whole life, or at least the scarlet parts, flash before his mind? He did not know. He did not want to fight it. He allowed the memories their freedom.

Reynolds was very much alive, one day, very much part of something bigger than himself, working in the meadow with his parents. It was a day in late July, hay-day! The sun rose and shone out of a perfect sky. There seemed to be birds singing every-where, larks high above the meadow, a corncrake in a nearby field, a blackbird, a thrush, a robin, a wren, oh he didn't know nor care how many others or their names. There was a wondrous low bubbling and buzzing sound from the life that stirred in the high meadow grasses, a pleasing sound, so soothing. And just over the tips of the grasses were the butterflies, a whole variety of them, white and brown and purple and red, all fluttering slowly, as if they, too, knew what leisure was and were set on enjoying it.

Father had begun with his scythe down the left-hand side of the meadow, swinging rhythmically and powerfully, pausing regularly to hone the blade, when that great, soft, rasping melody came from his work and filled the world with confidence. Then he set to again and the lovely grass fell in swathes as he went. And there was Reynolds, close by Mother, his big head bound in a white handkerchief that he had knotted at the four corners, his trousers tucked into his socks, all his senses alert to the scent of fallen grass and clover and all things wonderful. He moved behind Hugey, raking the swathes into a thin, neat row, the long wooden rake behaving itself as he flung it out and drew it back. He was a king then, with his father, with his mother, and the world was at peace, and all was well.

That was one of the times when Reynolds thought that perhaps life could be something, that all of them together in some sort of peace and harmony, working together, could make life all right. They sat down against a haystack late in the afternoon, Father and son, and he ribbed Reynolds and he laughed, he told Reynolds he was his God-awful foolish son and he laughed again and Reynolds laughed. Mother brought out a flask of boiling hot tea with sandwiches thick as bricks, buttered and oozing red jam and she, too, sat with her back against the haystack and they all laughed at the wonder of the world. And for a short, wonderful while, Reynolds thought he could be happy in this world.

That was a long time ago. Another lifetime. Another person. Now, in these later years, there was Genevieve next door. And there was Randy, big Randy and his Jaguar car. Randy had a small penchant for growing sunflowers, the Giant Russian variety; he grew them against the sun-warmed side wall of his back garden, staked them, fed them as if they were his children, and took pride in their height and the great plates of flowers they produced. Reynolds admired him for that, enjoying the way the great flowerheads peered in over Randy's wall at the pigs and hens and cats in Reynolds's back yard. Idly Reynolds wondered if the flowers were growing now, and what happened the sunflowers when the sun disappeared at night? Did they feel the darkness? Did they know where to turn? And then he remembered: there were no flowers now, no sunflowers in the back garden, not any more.

THIRTEEN

The most terrible loss of all occurred the day the girls, Nora and Doreen, with Imelda Foley and Joan Macken came upon him in his little hide-out among the furze bushes. It was after school. He had been laughed out of it again because Brother Sebastian had asked him to try and say even one line of the poem they had been learning. And what a poem it was! 'Elegy', written by somebody called Gray. It was so lovely that Reynolds knew almost the whole of the long poem by heart; indeed, he knew it still, and could sound it to himself, inside his head, whenever he wished.

> The curfew tolls the knell of parting day,
> The lowing herd winds slowly o'er the lea,
> The ploughman homeward plods his weary way,
> And leaves the world to darkness and to me.

When you look at the first line of that poem there's only one *s* in it, in *tolls*, and you can skip that, sounding it like a quiet *t*. So Reynolds believed that Brother Sebastian must have thought he could manage that line without spitting out a bucketful of spray. He tried. Hard.

'The cu ... the cu ...' he began. Sebastian stood there, a grin on his red face. Behind and around Reynolds the giggling had begun. He tried again. He had a long pause on the *r* of *curfew* before he managed to get the *f* sound out, it came out like a small pistle of rain. It took a while to get *tolls* out, and Reynolds knew that it came out as *tollt*, but it came out.

Brother Sebastian took out his fob watch and regarded it, very ostentatiously; then he looked up at the big clock on the schoolroom wall. 'School ends at three o'clock, you know, Reynolds,' he said and the whole class burst out in a gale of laughing.

Reynolds, too, must have grinned. Not, you will understand, out of a sense of gladness for causing mirth, but as a kind of grimace of effort to get the little word *knell* begun in his mouth.

'So!' Sebastian said ominously. 'Reynolds thinks this is all one great joke. Eh? Eh? Eh?' and all the time he was drawing the sally stick out of the drawer where Leo always kept it.

Reynolds's whole body sagged. He knew it would probably be a less painful thing if he just accepted the stick and gave up trying to get the line out into open air. Sebastian gave him eight slaps, four on the right hand, four on the left. And goodness but he could lift that stick high and bring it down without a pause so that the whip of its elasticity was still in it and added extra force to the slaps. Then, slowly, the class fell silent as Reynolds's spittle came gasping out of him with the ferocity of each slap. They were scared, for themselves, not for Reynolds. When he sat down his hands were so sore he could scarcely keep from leaping up again in pain; they were so red and raw he could not stuff them in for comfort under his armpits. He let them hang down on either side of the desk and he let the tears and the mucous come from his eyes and nose as they would.

Brother Sebastian leaped down along one of the rows of the class. He grasped Nora McGreil by the shoulder, almost hauling her green woollen cardigan off her back, dragged her out of her desk and up to the front of the class. 'Now, Nora,' he shouted at her. 'You thought all of that was just great fun. Didn't you?'

'No, Brother, no, I did not.'

'But you were laughing your sides sick, now, weren't you, Nora. Weren't you?'

To lie to Brother Sebastian when it was quite clear he had seen her laughing would have been to add trouble to trouble. Nora squared her shoulders, drew her mouth tight and held out her right hand.

Sebastian shrugged with the pleasure of it, and Nora received six withering slaps, three on each hand. When it was over she turned slowly from him and walked back down to her desk. She was not crying, there were no tears in her eyes, her face was composed, her hands down quietly by her sides. But her face was red, very red. She sat down and folded her arms and looked at the wall in front of the class.

None of this prevented Reynolds from loving that wonderful poem. And that's why he was in his little furze-bush den; he did not want to go home after school because Father would know he had been beaten and he would probably beat him again, his philosophy being that if the monks had slapped him, then he must have done something that deserved punishment. And he would give Reynolds more for humiliating him in front of all the other fathers' sons and daughters. Reynolds wanted to recuperate. He sat in the tent of bushes, sunlight coming in warm and filtered through the spines and blossoms and whorled branches of the furze, a curlew somewhere in the distance crying for him, the hard floor of the world dry and welcoming. Until suddenly a sod of earth came crashing through the furze and landed against his left shoulder, startling him.

He remembered how Nora had been one of the loudest gigglers during his punishment; he had seen her look at him with such a face of contempt and loathing as she walked back down to her own desk. And later that same afternoon Brother Sebastian had actually turned on Nora's best friend, Joan Macken, another big girl with a stook of red-brown hair and freckles all over her face. Reynolds had often looked at Joan, maybe because of her green eyes, which appeared remarkable to him, beautiful, bright and clear. But he knew Joan's nature did not really go with her eyes, not then, not yet. Perhaps it was her hair that drew Sebastian's attention; it would have been good to drag her up out of her desk by her hair, that was what was going through Sebastian's mind, Reynolds sensed it, even through his suffering.

Brother Sebastian, smirking, had asked Joan to recite the same poem. But Joan got through the first stanza quite well, except for changing the third line, 'The ploughman,' Joan said, 'plods his eerie way homeward.' Reynolds knew, even though he was in pain, that he had looked up at Joan, thinking she was trying a wonderful joke on Sebastian, but the Brother did not notice, or he did not bother. He moved on from Joan to Michael O'Cleary for the second stanza; Michael knew it and Sebastian got bored and gave up on the rest of them. But Nora had noticed how Reynolds had glanced up at Joan's mistake and she had shaken her head towards him, as if he had been trying to draw punishment down on her best friend. Now, it seems, they were going to punish him too.

Another clod of turf and grass came thumping in through the furze and scattered thorns about him. He heard the girls laughing. He closed his book and bundled himself into a ball. One of them shouted, 'Come out, dunkey Reynolds, come out!' He didn't stir. More sods came flying in about him, but they were soft and the branches broke their strength and they did him little harm. But he could hear the voices of the girls as they came nearer. He could see them, out through the furze, their skirts, their shoes, their stockings down about their ankles. 'Dunkey, dunkey, dunkey Reynolds!' He stayed perfectly still.

He could hear them talking then, saying amongst themselves that they would not come in to drag him out as they'd probably get hurt by the thorns. Then they giggled again and he heard them moving away a little bit. There was silence, although he knew they were not gone far. He didn't move. Then he heard one of them call, 'One, two, three, go!' and a whole shower of stones came flying in on top of him and all about him, several of them hitting him on the head and shoulders. He put up his hands to cover his head and the book fell on the ground. That made him sad. There was a pause, then another shower of stones came in and he decided that was it, he'd better give in to them. His book was a little soiled as he picked it up and crawled out of his lair onto the bank of grass.

'There you are, at last! little dunkey!' It was Nora. She had some stones in her hand and she held them as if she was prepared to fling them at him. Imelda was there, too, with stones; and Doreen. And he could see Joan, watching him; she had a big stone, a rock almost, in her hand, ready to fling. 'Will

you be good now, dunkey?' Nora asked him. 'So we won't
have to throw any more stones. You owe me, you know. It was
all your fault.' And she held out her right hand; it was red and
swollen where Brother Sebastian's rod had glanced off the palm.

He nodded his head. He was rubbing the book against the
side of his jacket, trying to get the little bit of muck off it.

'So!' It was Doreen, and she was coming slowly towards him,
the stones still in her hand. 'You were hoping to make a fool of
poor Joan, too, were you? Not enough to get poor Nora
thwacked. Ready to have a good laugh at her, were you?' With
the hand that held the stones she thumped Reynolds on the
shoulder; she was a strong girl, as big as him, and the blow
shook him. He stepped backwards, shaking his head. Then the
others closed in on him, giggling, and they surrounded him. He
stayed still. Waiting. They were girls, what could he do?

'You must be punished, you were bold!' It was Imelda this
time. She was a smaller girl, pretty, with very black hair. She
came up right close to him, looked up into his eyes; she pointed
up then, skywards, and he, like the fool he was, looked up and
suddenly she thumped him, hard, in the belly. It winded him
and he bent forward, holding his stomach. The girls laughed.

'Isn't he the awful eejit?' Imelda said. 'And he couldn't even
say one line of the poem, the fool, the eejit.'

Imelda lived in the house next to Reynolds, just two hundred
yards down the main, tarred road; he had always thought she was
a nice girl. She was not too big, not too small, and he had
believed her gentle and quiet. She took his chin in her right hand
and lifted it up, to look at him, then with her left she thumped
him again in the stomach. He groaned and staggered forward.

'He's a dunkey! Dunkey Reynolds!' Nora laughed. 'He'll
give me rides on his stupid back.'

'He'll give us all rides,' Imelda said. 'He'll be a good dunkey.'

Joan had said nothing and he looked at her. Her green eyes
were clear and wide open and he saw the pattern of freckles on
her fine face. Her red hair was tied up tight at the back of her
head. She was wearing a pink cardigan and a plaid skirt. He
thought, as she had said nothing yet, that she might be kind, and
get them to stop. But she did not move.

He was gasping for breath now. Bent forward and holding his stomach. It was then that Nora jumped on him from behind, flinging her body up on his back and her hands about his neck, clinging on to him, half choking him. He stood up straight, bracing himself under her weight, but she was taking the breath out of him. He put up his two hands to loosen hers from his neck, when Joan came right in and thumped him with her clenched fist, very hard, in the stomach again. He couldn't take that. He fell forward onto his face in the grass, gasping. Nora held on to him and fell on top of him. He could hear the girls laughing.

Nora lifted herself upright then and straddled him, her full weight on the small of his back. 'Right, dunkey!' she said. 'Up, up, up on your four legs.'

He could hardly move for want of breath. She waited a moment, lifted herself off him and let herself plop down on his back again. Winding him once more.

'Up, I say, up!'

He managed to lift himself onto his hands and knees and she stayed heavily on his back, laughing. He began to get his breath back. He breathed deeply. She held him that way for a while, bouncing her body a little on him. Then she moved forward and Reynolds felt Imelda climbing onto his back behind Nora. They were laughing. They were heavy. And then it was Doreen, too, who got up behind Imelda and they all three straddled his back, giggling, bouncing. He was gasping, his head bent towards the earth. They were so heavy, and he could hardly sustain them. Suddenly Joan kicked him, hard, on the backside and he fell forward onto the grass, flat on his face. The girls stayed on him for another while, laughing, tumbling a little. Then all three of them stood up and he thought for a moment that it was over. But instead of walking away Nora stood on his back and he cried out with the pain of it. He could feel the hard soles of her shoes digging in against his spine. She lost her balance, stepped to the side a little, then stepped up onto him again and stepped down the other side of him.

'He's our mat, girls!' she cried out. 'Only useful to be stood on.'

They took turns then, running and jumping on his back and

running on again across the clearing. That was the hardest of all.
Reynolds knew he could have gathered his strength and got up
and clomped away; he was big, after all, and strong. But they
were girls, what could he do but wait until they were finished?
Each time they jumped on him it hurt, and each time it hurt
more and more and more. But it wouldn't last for long. They
would get tired of it very quickly, he hoped, and they did, there
was no fun in it as he just stayed lying there, doing nothing, not
crying out, nothing.

He lay for a while in the dirt, aching and exhausted. It was
Joan who came up and saw his book lying on the grass not far
from him. As they were going Joan kicked the book as hard as
she could. It flew into the air, its pages flying every which way,
and some of them came loose and fluttered slowly about.
Reynolds felt that this was the unkindest hurt of all and he lay
down on that grass patch and sobbed. He lay a long time,
miserable and alone. At last he gathered himself together and
tried to clean his clothes off; they were covered in grass and bits
of dirt and the more he rubbed the more he seemed to spread
the dirt about. He tried to pick up the English book and put it
together again, but it was a mess. He knew, if Brother Leo
wasn't back, that Brother Sebastian would make him suffer for
that too.

He went home slowly. Mother would scold him for his
clothes. Father might give him a hard slap across the cheek.
Reynolds would try to make his way in the back door, and
clamber upstairs without being seen.

When he got home he could see at once that Father wasn't
back yet. He peeped in the window. Mother was in the front
room, sitting idly at the window, just watching out. All of that
meant, Reynolds had seen it so often before, that Hugey was on
the tear again and mightn't come home till late, or mightn't
come home at all that night.

When he was home, Father would always leave the old bike
leaning up against the wall of the turf shed; it would idle there,
propped up, like an old man ruminating over past times,
smoking his pipe. There was no bike to be seen when Reynolds
got home. He tried to sneak in past Mother but there was no

chance; the back door gave a long, skreeking sound that would have hauled the dead up out of their rest. Mother came to meet him at once and he knew what that meant too. She took one long look at him and sighed. Reynolds knew there would be no beating from her; she was too weary. She looked pale, her small face pinched and empty. Even anger seemed to have washed away out of her, leaving only despair.

'Right!' she said. 'Fightin' again. No supper for you. Out you go at once and spend the night you know where; and don't you dare peep out of there until it's breakfast time. Shame on you, shame! A big boy like you fightin' an' grishterin'. Me with all me troubles and you only addin' to them. Out you go now, out!'

Even if he had been able to speak properly, it would have been pointless to try and explain. She shooed him out the back door and closed it after him. This had happened several times before and Reynolds understood perfectly what would go on. It was for his own safety's sake she was hustling him into the hayloft, for Father would most likely go for him when he got back, drunk, foolish, looking for something to do violence against. Reynolds had been slapped and beaten often enough before and he was grateful to Mother that at least he would not be found in the house when Hugey got back. If he got back that night. And Reynolds knew then that if Father had not come home before midnight, she would go to her own room, lock and barricade herself in because, if he did not find the boy, he would go after her to take out his deep frustrations and angers on her poor body. Oh yes, they knew him well, Our Father, the bastard! When he was as drunk as that he simply accepted what was presented to him; if Reynolds wasn't in bed he would forget about him; if he couldn't get into Mother's room easily, he'd go back down into the kitchen and fall asleep on one of the big chairs by the fire. The poor old gom, oh the poor, dirty old bastard.

That evening Reynolds had mooched around the sheds and hayloft for a while as the darkness drew in over the lake and across the bog and came slowly over the outhouses; he could hear the jackdaws coming to roost in the tops of the pine trees, settling noisily. Once he heard the soft and lovely hooting of an owl before it set off in pursuit of its prey. He loved the sound, but he knew that it meant death and destruction to some other creatures, helpless voles or fieldmice, that evening. How sad the world is, he thought, how deeply soaked in necessary and unnecessary blood!

He kept a watch for the arrival of his father, though indeed he'd announce his coming from a fair distance off with all sorts of noises and preliminary threats. Reynolds saw Mother lighting the oil-lamp in the kitchen; he could see her sad figure moving over and back against that orange-yellow light. Then he shaped for himself a bed in a corner of the hayloft, as far as possible from the trapdoor, just in case Father got a bright idea. There was a wooden bolt fixed at the back of the hayloft door and the heavy wooden clunk it made when he pushed it to gave Reynolds a modicum of comfort. When it was dark he laid himself down and hoped to sleep, but fairly quickly he knew that he was in for a long and difficult night.

The base of his spine was killing him. It was that spot the girls had taken turns jumping on and jumping over and it hadn't really caught his attention until he was stretched out on the hay bed. Now he could not lie still, there was an ache that was continuous and every so often it grew into a sharp pain and he had to shift himself about. As he shifted he began to get, for the first time in his life, a sense of what desire is all about, though, at the time, he was unable to put words or coherent thoughts on it. It was the eyes of Joan Macken that kept swimming before his inward vision, he knew that even if his back wasn't giving him prods and knives, it was that freckled face of hers that would have kept him awake. Of course he was profoundly sad that she was the one who had beaten him most; she had seemed to take a special delight in hurting him and then, when she kicked away his book, that was the cruellest thing of all. He kept wondering if he would ever get to speak with her, just stand in front of her, be able to look into those soft green eyes and listen to her speak to him, gently, gently. And of course he knew that would never happen, never, what with his mouth and the clods of muck and clay that rolled about between his tongue and throat and palate and would not let him speak.

Suddenly his senses were wholly alert once more; he had heard the clang of the gate out at the road; Father was wobbling home. Soon Reynolds heard muttering, and the turning of the wheels of the bicycle along the loose stones of the yard. He astonished himself with his alertness; he was all attention, he scarcely breathed. He heard Hugey fling the bike against the wall; he heard his footsteps, none too steady, the back door being flung open and slammed shut again. Reynolds listened. Later on he was sure he could hear movements inside the house, he could imagine how the big man wandered about in the kitchen, how he dragged his way up the stairs to Reynolds's room, found the door open, looked in, cursed and headed for Mother's room. Reynolds imagined him trying the door, cursing again, calling her name, then stumbling back down the stairs. This, for Reynolds, was the crucial moment; if Hugey decided he wanted to break his anger on somebody then he might search for his poor, foolish son. Reynolds was near the wall of the loft and could, if needs be, jump out the small hayloft window and down onto the soft grass below; it would be quite a fall, but he had done it before. Then he could escape in among the trees of the grove where Father wouldn't follow him.

Reynolds shifted and let out a moan. The pain in his back! His attention had been so wholly focused on Father's movements he had completely lost awareness of his own pain. He lifted himself onto an elbow and looked over at the kitchen window. The oil-lamp was still burning and the glow from the window should have been one of comfort but Reynolds could see the huge shadow shifting slowly along the far wall and there was no comfort in that. Then all was silent for a while. The boy waited, attention still firmly directed. Nothing happened. All seemed still. He sighed with a certain relief and lay back on the bed of hay; perhaps they would get through another night without major angers breaking out; perhaps the morning light would see them all creeping stealthily but safely about once again, still scared of the big man, what with his after-the-night sickness and his soul-guilt. Reynolds closed his eyes and let Joan Macken move in a slow and kindly dance before his mind. He let her be warm towards him; kindly, she took him by the hand

and led him gently across the floor of the grove, they stood together under the trees and she told him things, about herself, her hopes, her dreams, her desires, and Reynolds featured in them all, she said, he featured greatly.

He must have slept for some time. When he came to with a suddenness and alertness that surprised him, the world seemed to have changed. The hayloft was lit with a strange light. Reynolds sat up straight and the pain in his lower back made him grunt aloud. He thought Father must be in the loft, carrying the oil-lamp. But there was no sign of him; and the trapdoor was firmly shut. He could see that the light in the loft was shifting, shadows ripping and dancing all about the place. For a while he sat there foolishly, perhaps even more foolishly than usual, until all at once, with a terrible chill taking his entire body, he knew. He forgot his pain, he forgot everything. He got to his feet and looked out the window to discover what he had already guessed: the house was ablaze. It must have happened very quickly because the whole back yard between the hayloft and the house was bright as day, hot-looking as the scullery of Hell, and the flames came bursting out, just then, through the window, bringing with them a mighty explosion of glass. Reynolds stood there, gazing at the spectacle, for too long, mouth open. Then he moved.

In certain aspects of living Reynolds, the fool, was wise enough, and this was one of those moments. Outside the door of the hayshed was a big rain-butt that took the water from the chutes and drainpipes; Father kept it there, for the cow, for the ass. As he came out the door of the hayshed Reynolds could already feel the heat from the blaze. He was trying to say the names out loud, Mother, Father, he was blubbering. He climbed right up and dropped feet first into the rain-butt, ducked his head under, came up and out again, soaked and shivering with the suddenness of the cold. He took out his handkerchief, soaked that in the rain-butt too and tied it round his face, leaving only his eyes uncovered. Then he ran to the back door of the house.

The rest of it was always to remain a blur, a recollection of Hades, of dimness, of smoke swirling everywhere, of objects on fire, objects in his way, objects falling over. And flames, flames like great angry gobbets of curse-words swinging at him. He passed through the scullery and into the kitchen. He saw Father on the floor by the legs of the table and he could tell at once that he was unconscious. He was not moving. Reynolds did not know if he was alive or dead. He saw, too, the oil-lamp smashed to little pieces on the floor of the kitchen. So that was it. That must have been it.

He took his father under his armpits and tried to heave him into a sitting position. It was impossible. The body was heavier than anything Reynolds had ever tried to lift before and the great pain along his back kept him grunting and suffering. He tried to drag Father along the ground towards the door. He could not shift him. Just then the table itself took fire with an awful whooshing sound, the flames relishing the black-and-white oil-cloth, and the fire reached at Reynolds like great claws trying to grab him. He gave up on Father. He ran through the kitchen. Luckily the door between kitchen and hallway was closed so the flames hadn't engulfed all the lower part of the house. He burst through that door and made his way upstairs. He was trying to call out, but he couldn't. He made his way as fast as possible, smoke everywhere, flames now gushing through the kitchen door and reaching for the parlour, flames beginning to reach up along the banisters behind him. He banged hard into Mother's door; the other side of the upstairs landing was aflame, the fire having come through the floor of Father's bedroom over on that side. Mother's door was locked and he ran at it several times, crashing into it, trying to get through. The lock smashed, the door gave way. But she had piled things up behind that door, furniture of some kind, probably the wash-hand basin, a chair, perhaps even the edge of the wardrobe. He began to panic. Why didn't Mother come awake? The smoke was thick everywhere now and Reynolds could see the flames begin to tickle the carpet on the upstairs landing. He smashed the landing window and put his head out, taking in great gulps of fresh, cool air. Then he ran at Mother's door again. Each time he crashed into it the pain in his back made him call out in agony but he persisted, he had to. He managed, at length, to push the door in sufficiently for him to get through. The room was thick with smoke; even with the handkerchief about his mouth and nose, even after the air he had just taken in, he found it hard to breathe. Mother was lying on the bed, fully dressed. Her eyes were closed. Reynolds swept her up in his arms as if she were a child and turned for the door. He was out on the landing, at the top of the stairs, before you could know it and as he headed down those steps he could see the flames rising to meet him.

Reynolds howled. He howled like a stricken animal, and he was truly stricken. He charged down the stairs, Mother lying limp across his two arms, and he was scarcely conscious of her weight. He turned at the bottom of the steps and faced the hallway. It was a mass of flames. Reynolds paused, but just for a moment, and then he charged, howling like an utter madman, for the front door. He turned his shoulder towards that door as he came thundering through the flames so that when he hit the door, Mother was safe and the timbers collapsed before him. Reynolds was a big boy, big and heavy, and he was possessed. When he burst out into the open air in front of the house his back was one great mass of pain.

He laid Mother down on the grass of the front garden. His clothes were on fire now, in spite of the water from the rain-butt. He didn't care. He lay a moment on the wet grass and rolled himself over in it, dowsing the flames. Then he was up again and racing back round the angles of the house, back across that yard, and he leaped once more into the rain-butt. He ducked his head under, handkerchief and all, and then he was back in the scullery, back at the kitchen door. Now it was the noise about him that filled him with terror. He was flailing his arms against the flames and smoke, as if that would do any good, but he pressed forward. The heat, as well as the noise, terrified him but he got to where Father lay on the floor. He knelt down through all the confusion and tried again to lift him. He was heavy as a sack of wet sand. Reynolds tried to drag him along the floor, but there was no movement in that either. And the boy felt that he must allow his whole body, soon, very soon, to go stiff and permit the pain that took his back to ease a little. But

Reynolds got right down and heisted the big man's head and chest off the floor, got his back in under him and tried to straighten up with him across his back. He could not. He managed to get on his hands and knees with Father draped across his back, hands dragging one side of him, legs the other, and he began to crawl towards the kitchen door. He made it out that far, then he had to pause. He was exhausted.

There was no possibility of getting a breath and Reynolds knew he would suffocate very soon with all the smoke. Things were beginning to collapse in the kitchen, too, and he heard the roar of ceiling and beam as the upstairs bedroom burst into the room below. He had been just in time. He pressed on, slowly, out through the scullery until he was hit by a welcome blow of cool night air. He was out!

Reynolds carried Father a few feet out into the yard, then he had to give up. He lay down flat and let his father's body slip off his back onto the stones of the yard. Gratefully Reynolds lifted the handkerchief from his mouth and took great gulps of air into his racked body. After just a few moments he was able to stand up again. He took Father by the hands and dragged him, inch after painful inch, onto the grass under the wall of the grove. The fire flung enough hellish light on him for his son to see that he was dead. His face was puffed and red. His eyes were open, the hellish light was in them too. Reynolds grew terrified again and let him fall back onto the grass. He turned and ran round the corner of the house to the front garden and Mother.

She, too, lay where he had left her, on her back on the grass. He ran to her and knelt down on the ground beside her. Her eyes were closed. She seemed to be in a very deep and peaceful sleep. For a long time Reynolds knelt there, taking her head onto his lap. He soothed her hair, his hand brushing it ever so gently away from her face. It seemed to him that she smiled at him, a slow, gentle smile, but it may have been only the flames playing on her face. He felt that harsh and throbbing pain start up again at the base of his spine. But he stayed there, kneeling, Mother's head in his lap. He could hear shouts of neighbours somewhere nearby. They were coming, at last, someone was coming. He did not stir. He was very, very cold. He was crying.

FOURTEEN

Reynolds's hands were cold. In fact he was shaking with the cold. He had been in the bedroom for about four or five days. A week? Who knows? He had lost count. Day or night, what matter now? All he had taken was water. From the cold tap in the bathroom. That morning, or that afternoon, or whenever it was, he turned on the hot water in the cistern. He thought he might try and take a bath and see if that would warm him a little. He went downstairs a few times, just to keep himself moving about a bit. When he was down there he felt a great desire for salt. That's all. Ordinary kitchen salt. He lifted the container to his mouth and let some salt pour in. Then he went back upstairs and took great slugs of water. That was good. That had helped him keep some strength up. He needed to focus. He needed to give his whole attention to this, to the last pages of his life.

After that first whish of water and salt Reynolds had suddenly grown quite elated. He went about upstairs, just looking at things, his old and shabby things. It was clear that nobody had been to the door of the house. Not yet, anyway. No bills. No letters. No demands. Not even the publicity rubbish they shove in through your letterbox. Nothing. It was as if he were already dead.

God is love. So they say. So he had been led to believe. But there are times, long times, when that statement seems little more than a mockery of what life appears to be. It depends on a definition of love. Reynolds had tried hard to define love over the years. Take Genevieve, for example. Take Deirdre. Take

God. Well, God asks a lot. Now Reynolds was giving Him everything, his body, his life. His soul. That, surely, must be love. OK, that's God sorted out. Now take Genevieve. How often did his thoughts turn to her; there was that day, for instance ... but suddenly Mother spoke to him from the corner of the living room. He heard her loud sniffle and looked up, startled. There she was, leaning against the corner of the room, arms akimbo, watching him, a sneer on her face.

'Why didn't you make a move, you fine eejit?' she said to him.

'What?' he answered. 'How do you mean, move?'

'She needed you. You, you big oaf. She needed you. She wanted you. Not that big corpse of a husband hasn't given her son nor daughter nor chimpanzee. She wanted you.'

'But she always shied away from me, she moved back from me, she did not ...'

'Of course, of course she'd do that. Wouldn't she? But don't you know a woman does the opposite of what she means? The direct opposite. She wanted you to be a man. Go after her. Take her. To show her you could be a man. But you couldn't, could you? You whimperin', slack-jacked eejit you!'

That left Reynolds stunned. He sat down in the dusk of the living room. He had not lit a fire there for a long time and the hearth was black and lonesome-looking. A jackdaw must have been pecking at something up on the chimney because just then a pittering of soot came down and landed in the hearth with the strange, rustling sound that a skirt would make moving through a room. Reynolds felt so lonely, so black and dark and hopeless, right at that moment. He sat there all the evening, just watching how the darkness came, slowly, so slowly, to embrace him.

Then there was the question of Joan Macken, for instance. Take Joan. Joan was so pretty, so pert, and with all of that, Reynolds knew, she was wicked. Mean. Bold. That very first night after the fire, the Mackens, Mr Macken and Mrs Macken, had offered Reynolds a room in their house. What else could he do? What else could they do? Reynolds's home was no more than a black mess of walls and timbers and unrecognisable items. And the rain had fallen most of the next day, making black and grey pools and puddles of horror in the great bleakness. How could they let him sleep in the hayloft that night? At first they were kind; they fussed over him. Reynolds spent that day in a complete miasma, moving like an automaton when anybody suggested he should move. The medical people and the police had come. They had taken away his father and his mother. The police had begun to ask him a few questions. He had simply looked at them, the spittle forming slowly at each side of his mouth, and dribbling down his chin.

That evening Mrs Macken had made Reynolds sit down in the scullery, and had given him a boiled egg, with toasted bread and butter, and a big mug of hot tea. Then she left him. For a long time he stared at the egg. He had a spoon. He knew that soon he would knock the top of the egg with the spoon. The egg would be hot. It would comfort his hands. But he hesitated. Then Joan had come into the kitchen. He glanced at her. She was pretty. She was silent. But he remembered how she had been with him the day before and he drew back a little from her. His back still hurt and perhaps, somewhere along his spine, there might remain the trace of the sole of her shoe. She sat down at the top end of the rough scullery table, put her head onto her two hands and watched him. He gazed at his egg.

'Do you know how to break it?' she asked him quietly.

He nodded his head. Of course he knew how to break it. He had eaten eggs before in his life. When he had a life. If ever he had had a life. And suddenly his head drooped forward onto the table with a loud thud, his forehead resting on the rough boards. As if the stem of his neck had yielded and allowed the head to drop. He closed his eyes and stayed there. Joan did not move. He closed his eyes and let whatever it was the world was doing to him drift over his whole body. His heavy frame sank slowly, like a great sack from which sand had drifted away. He shuddered. He found an ease in it. He relaxed.

With a certain gentleness, Joan came round behind him. She took him, quietly, by the shoulders and helped him to sit up straight again on the chair. Then she patted his shoulder and bent down and took his spoon, cracked round the top of his egg and lifted it onto his plate. Then she took his right hand in hers and put the spoon into it. Her hand was strong, kindly and very warm and comforting. Reynolds slobbered quietly. 'Salt!' she said. 'You'll need salt. And do you know what? what's lovely in a boiled egg is some butter. Plopped in, and let melt. It's just lovely.'

She reached and took a little curl of butter on the spoon and folded it in, part on the top of the egg, the rest in the egg itself, all the time holding Reynolds's hand, as if he couldn't do it himself. 'Now all you have to do is lift the egg to your mouth and eat it!' she said, as if he were a complete idiot. Which, of course, he was. But the only true comfort Reynolds had known since yesterday morning when he had left school was the warmth and gentleness of her strong hand guiding his big one. He was grateful. He felt he was going to cry again. Would life ever show him kindness any more? Could moments such as these not last for ever? Salt would never be quite the same for him, ever again.

Reynolds sniffled loudly and drew his large body together. He would not cry. Not yet. Not before this pretty girl who made his whole body burn. He took his slice of toast and broke it into three fingers; he took one of the fingers and dipped it into the yellow of the egg; the lovely stuff rose like a tiny wave and little droplets flowed out onto the shell of the egg. Reynolds put the finger of eggy toast into his mouth. Delicious. He closed his eyes in pleasure.

'That's disgusting!' said pretty Joan Macken from where she was sitting. 'My God, but that's disgusting. I'm sorry for you and all, I really am, but I am very glad that you'll only be staying in this house for a very short time. You're a pig, that's what you are, a disgusting pig!' And she flounced away out of the scullery, leaving Reynolds in the darkness by the kitchen table, leaving him with his eyes wide open, the taste of lovely egg rich in his mouth.

FIFTEEN

Reynolds tried to face up to the funeral, but he could not. Somebody came and organised everything, who, he never knew. He spent two nights in the stiff and resentful house of the Mackens. They gave him a little room off the scullery and he just stayed there. Somebody came with food for him, now and again, Mrs Macken, he thought, or Mr Macken. Joan never came again. He must have eaten something. Later, he simply could not remember. One of the monks from the monastery – it was Brother Leo – came to bring him to the chapel. He went, that first evening. But it was all so unreal, so echoing, so distant from him. People came up to shake hands with him and he knew he was in clothes too big for him. People were kind. Well-meaning. They came up and spoke warmly, with sympathy. Men. Women. Even the girls. Even Nora came up to him where he stood, dulled and gawking, at the top of the chapel and she took his hand and shook it and muttered something, something kind. But she didn't look at him. Big Tom, too, he came and shook Reynolds's hand and even gave him a gentle clap on the back, said he'd be there for him, something like that. Reynolds thought he meant that he'd be waiting for him, to give him a right beating-up for letting all of this happen.

And little Deirdre came, with the doctor. Deirdre Weir, the sylph. Deirdre. She came and shook Reynolds's hand and looked up into his face. There were tears in her lovely clear eyes and that knocked Reynolds backwards. He could not stand. He had to sit down, hard, on the wooden bench.

Reynolds tried to pray at the Mass, too, the following morning. It was awful. So many priests, all vested in black or grey, and they chanted those terrible, moaning hymns, like two groups of people pulling a big rasp slowly, over and back, over and back, over and back across his suffering. It was dreadful. The air was filled with incense. People came again, everybody he had ever seen, it appeared, and shook his hand. The two coffins were there at the head of the centre aisle, just resting there, six high, brown candles like sentinels about each of them. Someone had put a hat on top of one of the coffins and people were dropping money and envelopes into it. It was all so very strange. At last everybody got up to go and people carried the coffins out into the day. One of the monks took Reynolds by the arm and shoulder and urged him out after them. But that was it. He couldn't do any more. He made a sign to Brother Leo that he needed the toilet and the Brother nodded kindly. Reynolds hurried away, around the back of the church.

It was quiet there. He heard a yellowhammer chinking out its song somewhere over the furze and heather. *A little bit of bread and more cheese!* The sun was warm and there were all the village sounds as usual, as if the world hadn't veered away from its path into some strange and sickening spin: a cock crowing, some sheep somewhere, and in the distance that Atlantic ocean swell, its soft, mourning sound, all of that eased him into some kind of peace. And then he ran, as fast as he could, he ran across the fields to his own special furze bushes in the low hills. He crept in and squatted in his usual place, on the shaped earth, on the decades of dead spines and petals, with the roof of branches and thorns and blossoms, the sun speckling its way through. Reynolds curled his arms about his knees, put his head down on his arms and waited. The sounds were wonderful; a skylark singing as if it were filling the whole sky with musical water; and now and then the lonesome, far-pitched, down-falling call of a curlew. Reynolds vanished into himself, away from the world, away from pain and suffering and incomprehension.

He heard the little podded flowers of the furze pop every now and then, scattering seeds into the world. It was wonderful to listen to. He watched a beetle, its black back with an emerald sheen when it shifted towards the specks of sunlight that came through, as it laboured at some enormous task that seemed to be taking it for ever. It moved and turned and redoubled its way just at his shoes. He was absorbed. It had something to do with an awareness that he was powerless to influence or change anything that happens in this enormous universe in which he moved and ate and slept. He knew only that the world goes on, and everybody suffers, things, people, animals, and the onrolling push of the universe is indifferent. That everything depends, every moment, on this world, and yet there is nothing to be done about it. Reynolds just sat there and let a sense of that enter his body and his whole soul. He remained still. He paid attention. He implored in silence.

After a period like that there grows something in the body and spirit that retains a certain sense of indifference to whatever happens. Not that you become a stone to it all, but that, even in tears, even in the deepest suffering, you remain somewhat removed, knowing that this is part of the great growth of the world, spiritual and physical, in which we live. So when the voices of his school comrades broke through his long reverie, there where he lurked within the furze bush, Reynolds came back into the world a different person.

The afternoon had drawn on. The sun was still warm. Through the branches of the furze he could just about see the legs and dresses of the girls, the shoes and floppy socks and knobbly knees of the boys. They knew where he was. Once again his heart began to fail him. Could they not leave him alone? Why must they always torment him. And then he heard an adult voice call out his name.

'Reynolds, come on out, man, come on out. I'm here to help you. We are all your friends here. Come on out and we can have a nice, good chat.'

Reynolds felt himself absolutely chilled to the core. This was the voice of Brother Angelo Maria Spenser, one of the biggest-built men Reynolds had ever seen, at least six feet six inches tall, built like a truck and as threatening as a truck come loose on a steep slope. Angelo was Brother Superior in the monastery and was rarely seen out and about in the world, only on occasions of serious import and on raids of awful magnitude. And on those tremendous days when he stood in the classroom and took the place of Brother Leo or Brother Sebastian. Reynolds believed himself, now, in desperate straits. But there was no choice; he gathered himself up and prepared to face whatever was prepared for him.

There was one other thing about Brother Angelo Maria that was a whispered story all over the civilised world: Angelo, they said, had a glass eye. He wore dark glasses at all times, and so there was nobody who could swear on the Bible that he had ever seen that false eye for a fact. But it was bruited abroad, and behind the rumour there must be some truth. Reynolds came out to face that terrible presence. Several of the boys and girls from school were there, shifting about, watching. Reynolds saw Big Tom, Joan Macken, Nora. He hadn't time to take in the others because as soon as he emerged from his hiding place Brother Angelo Maria pounced. Well, perhaps not pounced. He came forward quickly and laid his two great hands on Reynolds's shoulders. Reynolds looked up at him. Angelo had a shock of grey hair and over the rim of his glasses his eyebrows, too, were thick and grey. Reynolds could only vaguely make out his eyes; but he felt an intense power coming from what must be the one glass eye (left or right?) that threatened dire consequences should things go wrong. Reynolds lowered his eyes and found himself folded into the great brown soutane, with its white knotted cord that surrounded the monk's belly. There was a strong scent, Reynolds believed, of roast beef and turnips, and of something else, tobacco perhaps, or sour apples ...

He had no more time to think, as Brother Angelo Maria turned him forcefully and began to propel him away from the furze bushes, across the field with its clumps of scutch grass and wild heather, towards the road.

'Now, my dear Reynolds,' boomed the voice above him, and Reynolds found that this was not a threatening start. 'We are going to look after you. It has been decided. Brother Leo, Brother Aloysius and Brother Martin and I have had a long discussion about this, and we have spoken with your Uncle William who has been and has gone away again. He being your only traceable relative, we believe, he has given his assent. You are to stay with us. You are to stay in the monastery. With us. We will take care of you. You will be looked after, never fear.'

The voice was loud and strong, but there was a kindliness in it that brought Reynolds to the very edge of tears. He looked up again and the Brother's face was red with bonhomie and care, and his smile was warm and welcoming. Reynolds moved away from the rough fabric of the soutane and reached out his right hand to take hold of the great, powerful left hand of the Brother. So what if he had only one eye! there was goodness shining out of this man, and protection, and hope.

SIXTEEN

It was afternoon. Reynolds could see a faint glow of sunlight forcing its way into his bedroom. He felt very cold. Mid-morning he had got up and draped a dressing gown over the bedclothes. That had helped a little. This dying was not easy. He wished he had gone with Mason when he had disappeared into the great and quickly destroying ocean. Wishing. No use to anyone. Not worth a balloon. Reynolds laughed. The laugh came out like a dry cough and was followed by a serious and weakening effort to retch. But there was nothing in his stomach; a few tiny puddles of water perhaps, a small stain of salt.

He lay on his back, his hands holding the edge of the dressing gown up under his chin. He watched the off-white ceiling and looked for cracks and failings in the wholeness of the paint, but he could see none. His teeth chattered. Yes, that was the word; he could hear them, as if they were in a corner of a crowded shop and were blathering away, gossiping for all they were worth, at speed, about nothing at all.

There was a sudden bang from downstairs. Reynolds was startled. For a moment he ducked his weakened body down under sheet and blankets and eiderdown and dressing gown, as if he could hide somewhere down there. All he could hear was the sound of the clothes settling over him, and then his own heart pumping, and his brain thudding. But, he thought, what was there to fear? Especially now, what on earth could he have to fear?

Cautiously Reynolds pushed his head out into the stale air of his bedroom. He listened. There was silence in the house; just the usual dull noise of traffic outside the estate, an alarm bell on a house some distance from his own, and nothing more. Nothing. No feet pounding up the stairs after him. Nothing. Perhaps he was beginning to imagine things. He got up, with difficulty, and wrapped the dressing gown round his already emaciated body. The gown was old and frayed, a dark purple colour, and the loops for the chord had long since disappeared. He held it shut about him, stood into his old slippers, and opened the bedroom door.

He waited a while on the landing, listening. There was nothing. Or was there a sound from his kitchen? Was there someone in there rustling about? Reynolds drew in a big breath. If there was, he thought, so what? Wasn't he preparing himself to fade into the new world in any case, so what could an intruder do but help him on his way? Indeed, it would be the opposite; if an intruder clouted him hard over the head with a length of piping, with the heavy head of a lump hammer, with a hurley stick, wouldn't he just be shortening the suffering that Reynolds had taken on himself? He would say thank you, thank you so very much, before falling down dead at the intruder's feet. If he was able to get the words out.

Still. Very cautiously Reynolds began to move down the stairs. The door of his kitchen was wide open. But perhaps he had left it so. He couldn't remember. He could see that the fridge and the other stuff he had shifted were still piled up against the front door, so nobody had come in through there. Whoever, or whatever, it was must be in the kitchen. He reached the bottom of the stairs and moved slowly along the hallway. A board under his feet groaned loudly. Reynolds heard an answering sniff from the kitchen. Mother! He should have known. Mother, back again to irritate and annoy him. He stepped boldly into the kitchen. And there she was, sitting at the table, eating something that looked like an uncooked roll of white pudding. Laying into it, with gusto, as if she hadn't eaten for years. She barely glanced up at him, but Reynolds had a terrible pang of hunger that shot through his entire body; he himself would gladly lay into an uncooked roll of white pudding. He stood a moment, watching down at her; she ate greedily, saliva dripping from her lips, her two hands stuffing her mouth with the food.

'Where did you get that?' Reynolds asked her.

She shrugged her shoulders. 'Thought you mightn't want it,' she muttered. 'Seein' as how ... Shame to let good food go to waste, that's what I always say. Have you anythin' else that's bound to go bad around here? Where's your bloody fridge?'

Reynolds gestured towards the door where the heavy bloody fridge was leaning, doing its work of guarding the dying man from intruders. He looked to see if the door of the fridge was open; but it was facing the front door, it couldn't be opened. He grinned; there! he had thwarted her again. When he glanced back Mother had disappeared, leaving behind her that old musty smell he so well remembered from decades back, and a heavy sense of her disapproval. She also left a great hunger rumbling in Reynolds's stomach. He headed for the fridge. He knew, of course, that it had been left leaning against the door. It wasn't plugged in. Anything inside would be mouldering away gently. Still, he leaned his head in towards the door and saw a small slip of paper that someone had shoved in through the letterbox. He reached down and picked it up. A message from the world outside. Perhaps, perhaps there was still somebody out there who was concerned, who knew, who cared. He took the paper back into the kitchen, into the bright light of the afternoon. It was a menu, a takeaway menu from a new Chinese restaurant about three miles from Heatherfield. Free delivery. Quick service. Don't be hungry.

Reynolds sat down, deeply depressed, where his mother had been sitting. The menu dropped from his hands onto the floor. He drooped his head. He wanted to cry, but he couldn't. Only a few drops of snizzle dripped out of his nose onto the floor, onto the menu. He picked up the bit of paper again and looked at it.

Dinner for Two
Chicken Sweet Corn Soup
Satay Chicken or Honey Ribs
Beef with Green Pepper & Black Bean Sauce
Sweet & Sour Chicken (Cantonese style)
Young Chow Fried Rice, with Prawn Crackers free!

Reynolds's tongue came out from between his dry lips and hung there, as if dead. For some reason, the sauce of the sweet and sour food came to his mind, its golden-orange flow, its pineapple lumps, how it would moisten the mouth, how it would ease all pains and anxieties moving down the corridor of the throat, into the vacant rooms of the stomach. *Chicken Balls. Kung Po Sauce (Hot!). Roast Duckling with Plum sauce. Boiled Rice. Fried Rice.* He let the menu drop from his hands once more. There were tears now moving down his cheeks; how wonderful life had been, but how rarely so, and should he wait and hope there would be special moments still? Or should he carry on across the desert, without oasis, that led to the welcoming tents of his God?

Reynolds sat a long time, his head drooped, until he fell asleep, sliding gently down off the chair onto the floor. The world moving ever more rapidly outside; the world seeking ever more and more wealth and pleasure and success. There, beyond his door. Beyond him.

SEVENTEEN

Brother Angelo Maria called Reynolds in to the office. Reynolds had spent that first night in the monastery in a dream of comfort and peace. They gave him a small room above the dairy; he had a comfortable bed, plenty of covers; there was a small wooden chair and a desk under the window. Out from his window he could see the orchard with its several trees in creditable rows, and beyond the orchard the rhododendron wood, the laneway leading up to the main road, the school. A tallboy placed just inside the door gave him ample space for any clothes he might have. At the moment he had none at all, only those he was wearing when Angelo Maria had called him from the furze.

Now he was scared again. What if the Brother Superior removed the glasses and watched him with only one eye? The large monk was sitting behind a vast desk that was covered with papers and books and, where it was visible, a green baize cloth. The office was dim, although Angelo Maria had a small oil-lamp burning at his elbow. He was leaning out over the material on the table, a pen in his hand, hovering now over an inkwell, now over some papers he was working on. The light from the window was very faint; the room was dark with bookshelves crammed with books. Reynolds stood a moment just inside the door while Angelo Maria muttered something, more to himself than to the boy. Reynolds closed the door, ever so gently, then turned and faced the man. It was actually true! He was sitting there without his dark glasses on, though as yet Reynolds could not see his eyes.

At length the Brother looked up at Reynolds. He laid his pen down on the table before him and beckoned to Reynolds to approach. Reynolds stood stock still where he was; even through the dimness he could see that one of Angelo Maria's eyes was a pale blue colour while the other was definitely green! But which was the real eye? which the false? He could not tell. He was still certain that the man, even without those dark glasses on, appeared gentle and kind, if only for the moment, if only under the influence of Reynolds's unbearable loss.

The boy stood, his mouth open, small dribbles of spittle moving on his chin. Brother Angelo Maria was talking but Reynolds, fascinated, could not pay attention to the words.

'Right!' Angelo Maria said suddenly. He stood up abruptly and turned his back to Reynolds. There was a moment's silence that brought the boy to his senses. Angelo Maria raised his hands to his face then turned, quickly, and called out 'Catch!' He threw something towards Reynolds and, with simple and perfect reflexes, Reynolds caught it. Then he dropped it and cried out. It was the big man's eye! It fell to the floor at Reynolds's feet and the poor boy gasped with terror. The eye was glass, but it had been warm and ever so slightly moist. He gaped at the man. The right socket was empty, little more than a tiny, dark cavern. Reynolds shivered slightly. Angelo Maria stood before him, grinning.

'Thought we'd better get that over with for a start!' the Brother said. 'Now, you see, I'm no more a monster without the glass than I am with it. What do you think?'

Reynolds shook his head. He was abashed. He looked down at his feet; the glass ball with the light blue iris inside was lying, lazy as a marble, on the wooden floor. He stooped and picked it up. It was cool now, round and perfectly like an eye. Reynolds came forward and handed it to the Brother, who took it, rubbed it carefully against the material of his soutane and with one quick, deft movement, replaced it in the socket.

'I would appreciate it, dear boy,' he said, 'if you would not make a habit of talking about this to the silly boys in the school. OK?' He sat down again behind his great table. 'Now,' he went on. 'I had been telling you of our plans for you ...' Reynolds was still standing foolishly, his mouth agape. 'You know,

Reynolds, when I'm dead, they will bury me, and like every-body else and everything else in this world, my body will decay; the coffin I am buried in will decay. All gradually, all certainly. But do you know what? This little eye of mine, this little orb of radiant and perfect blue, will last for ever, there where I have been, and in a thousand years time, should they bother to dig, all they will find will be the eye. Not the *I*, mind you, not the ego. Just the glass. Tells you something about the value of a human life, does it not?'

Reynolds nodded, then he grinned and suddenly felt at home.

Brother Angelo Maria explained. Reynolds was to live in the monastery for as long as he needed to; should he ever wish to leave, to find a job somewhere, then he was wholly free to go. In return the Brothers would expect certain duties to be per-formed by Reynolds, small tasks about the monastery and about the little farm, tasks which, however, would not be allowed to obstruct his course of studies. Then the Brother stood up and came around the big desk. Reynolds stood awkwardly. The big Brother hugged him and Reynolds found the tears coming, falling quietly, soundlessly, on the rough wooden floor of this holiest of holy places.

EIGHTEEN

The road down to the school from the monastery gate was a
sand-track, trodden hard by generations of would-be
scholars, of monks, by generations, too, of the village people
who flocked there to early morning Mass on weekdays. There
began for Reynolds a long period of calm and certainty, under
the sometimes hard, sometimes gentle, guidance of the monks.
He attended school, as usual, until he was fourteen and they
thought he had learned all he could possibly squeeze into his big
but disordered brain. He worked in the afternoons and at week-
ends, any jobs they could find for him, and there were many.
The one he enjoyed most was the task of ringing the great bell
in the louvred belfry at noon and again at six o'clock every
evening. There was a thick rope hanging down from dusty
rafters and Reynolds had to reach high, in the first years, to hold
it, then swing himself off the ground in a rhythmic pattern until
the first peal of the bell rang out. Then drag the thing, with all
his body's weight, down to the earth, rise with it again, when it
would peal out once more. Three peals together, a pause, three
more peals, a pause, a further three, pause, and then the glory of
the last nine peals ringing out together.

For weeks the people and the Brothers were amused to listen
to Reynolds's efforts on the bell, the stuttering and stammering
of it as he tried to learn the independent will of the great heavy
thing. He could rarely start the ringing without some small
banging of the bell first of all, then he could scarcely stop it to
allow for the pauses. But time is a wonderful thing; it is a prison,
out of which one can only escape into death, but it is also a great

teacher, and at length Reynolds found the rhythms, he bowed and lifted his hulking body in as graceful a way as the bell demanded until, after weeks, the bell rang out across the townland with a wholesome certainty, three, three, three, and then the nine, while the people paused to remember God's coming down to earth, and they prayed, and struck their breasts in thoughtless habit or in thoughtful contemplation, and by the time their prayers were finished, Reynolds's bell had gently pealed into silence. *The angel of the Lord* ... oh how wonderful! and how he rose and dropped with a special rhythm, every time, relishing the wonder of it, the miracle. There were times, even after some months, even years, when Reynolds, held by the music of the rhythm of the world to which the bell responded, forgot how many threes he had pealed out, and either cut the ringing short, or went on for far too long. But he didn't care, nobody cared, in those days of innocence, the ringing was all, and the moments of recollection, and the hope.

Brother Juniper McGrath had charge of the monastery kitchen, and of the rearing and killing of the hens and pigs. For several reasons he reminded Reynolds of the rain-barrel that he had dived into at the back of his own house; or even of the bell, he was that shape, round and solid, and not easily moved. Yet you could come to him for comfort and reassurance and for exhibiting the kind of holy foolishness that must be part of the humour of the Lord God. He kept his kitchen spotless. He scoured it after every session, polishing the cutlery, sheening the dishes, hanging back the knives and instruments in their places. And he never allowed anyone in there, ever. Except Reynolds, for Reynolds could always come and poke about, among the chests and the drawers and the cupboards, even in the cold room where the sides of meat were hanging and the ling was set up to be cured and salted. Reynolds, according to Brother Juniper, was the closest to God he had ever met and therefore he was allowed to have his way about Juniper's kitchen. And Reynolds never abused that privilege, taking only what he truly needed to satisfy the hunger or the thirst of a big and growing boy, and he always mentioned to Juniper what he had taken.

One of Juniper's tasks was the killing of the hens for the monastery table. It was the task, of all tasks, he truly hated. But he had his own method that excused him from physically laying his murdering hands on the poor, selected hen. He would enter the coop like a ballet dancer entering on the quietest of music, on tiptoe, chuck-chuck-chucking softly. He would crouch on his hunkers and wait to see if one of them would volunteer. But the hens knew, in spite of all his care, they knew what was in store and they scattered squalling and feather-bursting all over the place. Juniper grew tired of this game and grabbed a hen, stuffing her head first into a hessian bag which he then tied about the neck. He walked slowly and sadly to the belfry of the monastery, the bag in his hand, the hen inside doing all kinds of hennish acrobatics. Juniper climbed the many steps to the little platform where the great bell hung, high above the world. He bowed his head, said a prayer, and dropped bag with hen onto the unsustaining air. Whatever efforts the poor hen had made during her lifetime to acquire the power of flight now proved utterly useless, this greatest and final flight taking her plunging down from an awful height onto the gravel of the pathway below. Breaking her neck, or thudding her into unconsciousness where she would yield her neck, without demur, to Juniper's sudden blade.

On the very first day when Reynolds wandered about the monastery, still dazed, he had heard a rumpus in the hencoop. He saw Brother Juniper emerge, a sack in his right hand jittering and jumping against the barrel-body. He saw the holy monk disappear in the small door at the foot of the belfry. Soon, while only half-aware of what he was watching, Reynolds saw him appear high up at the top of the belfry, up there where the bell hung in all its wonder and heaviness. He saw the monk lean out sadly over the wooden railing and then, suddenly and wholly unexpectedly, he saw the bag come falling down through the air. Of course Reynolds moved to catch it, and he did so, his arms outstretched, and the bag knocked him off his feet onto the ground. He lay there, astonished for a while, hearing a screech from the monk on high, feeling a curious trembling coming from the bag he held. But he was proud of his catch, he looked forward to being thanked by the big Brother.

Brother Juniper lifted Reynolds gently from the ground, took the hessian bag from him, dusted down both bag and boy and then explained what was going on. He laughed, so heartily that Reynolds joined in with him and suddenly, without warning, Juniper slapped Reynolds hard on the cheek, knocking the stunned boy backwards.

'That's for putting the poor hen through her agony twice!' the monk said. And he moved away, back through the door of the belfry.

Then there were the pigs. The butcher from the village came every fortnight to the monastery, bringing mutton with him, all prepared for the table. And every second fortnight he disappeared into the back yard and Reynolds heard the awful war-agonies of the pigs as he stalked one down, caught him, heaved him upside-down onto the muddy earth, tied his trotters together, and prepared the knives. For Reynolds, both Juniper's depredations in the hencoop and the butcher's savagery in the pigsty brought back a roaring and screeching sound into his brain, exactly similar to the scarlet agonies he had known when the Reynolds home had burned down. How he felt for hen and pig! how he suffered on their behalf, hiding in corners, his hands pressed tightly to his ears, lest he hear the screams of a stuck pig or the thud of a fallen hen, and how he shook his own big body and imagined himself falling, blinded and trussed inside a hessian bag, or watching that awful knife hovering over his own so delicate throat.

But then there was the orchard. After the monks had tried him out at several tasks around the monastery buildings, farm and outhouses, they eventually decided that he could manage a few small, but essential, tasks. The ringing of the Angelus bell. The peeling of potatoes and the plucking of hens for Brother Juniper. The gathering of windfall apples, again for the use of Brother Juniper in his feeding of the pigs. The polishing of the parquet floors of the monastery and chapel. And the tending of the monks' small and private graveyard.

The orchard had many old trees, fruitful yet, though wizened with age and sanctity. Most of the trees produced a bitter apple wonderful for the making of pies and tarts, for the preparation of sauces to go with various pork dishes, and for the use of Brother Sebastian in the chastisement of erring pupils in the school. Reynolds spent many long and passionately quiet hours in the orchard. It was hedged around with dense and high-growing rhododendron bushes that offered endless nooks and caves for hiding and lying low. Between and amongst the trees grew a soft undergrowth of grasses and wild-flowers, daisy and wort and pimpernel, and it was little short of dreamlike to go searching among such growth for Brother Juniper's fallen apples. But best of all, down at the sunniest side, where the orchard ended in a hedge of mixed rhododendron, fuchsia, olearia and furze bushes, and where a small, white-painted iron gate led from the quiet of fruitfulness to the quiet of rest, from the orchard into the monks' graveyard, Reynolds had found an abandoned cart hidden under creepers and bushes and branches and flowers, and in under the heeled-up boards a perfectly dry and hidden cave glorying in fragrances and silence beyond even his furze-bush hideaway. And here Reynolds often sat and squatted and gave his complete attention to the world and its ways, allowing it to enter his being in all its strange and difficult, its wearying and attractive properties. And in here, distraction being rare, Reynolds was able to give all his attention to God's creation, all desire for the unreachable falling from him, allowing himself to be Reynolds, fully Reynolds, as he came tumbling from the hands of God the day of his conception.

He had his own wheelbarrow, too, cobbled together from pieces of timber nailed into shape, and having for wheel a slightly buckled tyre, a beauty from an old pram. Reynolds wheeled his contraption from orchard to graveyard and back again, simply for the delight of the sounds he made, shifting from the whispering jealousies of the soft grass and wild-flowers, with the occasional hump over a fallen fruit, through the soft and swooshing sound as it passed through the sometimes muddy, always wet gap of the little gate, and then up and down the neat rows of gravelled walkways between the tidy graves. This, above all, was his great pleasure: the wheel muttering and whistling through the tiny white stones between the cement borders, the different sounds the barrow made when full, the almost cheeky and challenging song it sang when empty. He was a bus-driver; a truck-driver; a train-driver; he was a hearse-driver, and the Brothers, dead or alive, watched him with pleasure, remembering their own early days and their own dreams.

There were some twenty graves in the tiny graveyard. They were neat, each grave having a small, black-painted iron cross with the Brother's name and his dates, birth and death, nothing more. Brother Anselm Rafferty, 1834–1877, Brother Angelo Harte, 1888–1924, and some of them so young, Brother Anthony O'Hara, 1848–1867, Brother Jeremiah Goldsmith, 1902–1921. Amidst blackbird-call and thrush-song, under the swaying branches of pine and elm, under the occasional mocking laughter of rooks, or the cackling aggression of magpies, Reynolds would stay for a long time. Among the dead. And he would tidy, cleaning the white marble chips that formed a blanket over the graves, picking out the little weeds that insisted on showing their faces, washing down the cement borders and the iron crosses, and this, along with his hideaway under the hoisted cart, brought him peace and absence and forgetfulness.

It was easy to hide away human limitations in his dreams. It was good, then, to purge as far as possible all desires from Reynolds's heart. If there are no longings there are no expectations, if there are no expectations there are no disappointments, and hence no angers, no recriminations, no rebellions. Blessèd are they who do not expect. Without knowing it, Reynolds became pure as a spring flower on one of his beloved apple trees. As he stood there, rake in hands, or shovel, or kneeling on a piece of timber at the side of a grave, trowel at the ready, he often passed into a dreamlike state of being, the breeze blowing softly against him, all sounds else of human activity reduced to a faint murmuring, and he ceased to exist, as a suffering and desiring being, and became part of the furniture of the dead. And what a relief that was to his nature, to his ego, to his soul.

Brother Sebastian knew well the bitterness in human nature that comes from longings thwarted, and every autumn, when the apples were plentiful on the boughs, he had Reynolds gather several of the finest, most darkly green, most plumped of the bitterest fruit, and carry them to the schoolroom. He would pick a day at random, a Tuesday, a Thursday, and send Brother Leo away for the morning, or for the afternoon. And then he, Brother Sebastian, would ask the lessons! Those were the terrible days, and they were many in the fall season, and the poor students suffered greatly, on their flesh and in their stomachs.

Like that afternoon, years before, when he strode into the classroom and dismissed Brother Leo. 'Brother,' he said. 'You may leave them to me for the afternoon. I shall examine their sinful souls.'

Leo glanced about the classroom with some sorrow and a lot of sympathy, gathered up his few books, nodded and went out.

'Reynolds!' was the first command from Sebastian. 'The orchard, please! Gifts for the boys and girls. A dozen of the finest apples, the cookers, fine ones, mind! plump and health-giving.'

Reynolds knew the adventure. He moved awkwardly from desk to door, he walked to the orchard, he gathered the apples, stuffing them into his pockets, carrying some of them against his chest. Not hurrying; trying to delay the inevitable but meanwhile running down the time during which Sebastian could indulge in his nastiness. When he got back, Sebastian was asking Big Tom Molloy to recite a poem for him, one they had been reading for a week or so, one that left Reynolds himself simpering with joy and pleasure.

'Big Tom!' Sebastian was saying. 'It is not growing like a tree, you know, in *bulk*, doth make Man better be,' and he laughed cruelly.

Jonson, Reynolds muttered in his own mind. And finished the stanza silently to himself: *Or standing long an oak, three hundred year, To fall a log at last, dry, bald, and sere,* and he watched Sebastian, the oak, balding, and that awful fist, clenching. Tom was standing at his desk, bemused, scared.

'Right!' Sebastian continued. 'Let's be having you, Tom, like a good lad. The poem. *Happy those early days, when I shin'd in my Angel-infancy.* Your Angel-infancy, Tom, tell me about all of that, tell me about these happy early days of yours. Off you go, and don't let our poor old Henry Vaughan down.'

Tom began, rattling the words off, rushing them, as if they were a raspberry feast all squashed together. Reynolds piled all the apples up on the Brother's desk, where they rested, their sheen and shape, their deep green and occasional flush so rich and innocent. Tom got along fine for a while, Reynolds sounding the words with him. '*When on some gilded cloud or flower my grazing soul, em, my grazing soul ...*'

'Your grazing soul, Tom, well, well, well. Are you a cow, Tom, a bull?'

'No, Brother, em, *when on some gilded flower, I, a gilded flower ...*' and Tom trailed away into hopelessness. He stood. Silent. Defeated.

Brother Sebastian smirked. 'Not good enough, Tom, not good enough. Branch or fruit, Tom, branch or fruit?'

With a certain amount of relief now that the worst had arrived and the danger frontally approached, Tom chose branch. Four slaps from the sally wand on each hand. The slaps sounded through the afternoon sun-motes like small explosions. Another day bathing the world in pain. And Sebastian picked his victims. None of them got through the first twenty lines or so, their bodies tensed, their minds already scarlet with confusion. When he called out the name, Joan Macken, Reynolds's heart gave a jump of sorrow. Joan, so pretty, that lovely red hair, those green eyes, and she was so small, standing there in her desk, facing the great bulk of Brother Sebastian Hardiman.

'I think, Joan, we have heard enough rubbish from the first half of poor Vaughan's lovely poem. We have heard it destroyed often enough. Let's hear from you the second half of this lovely, simple piece. Where it begins *O how I long to travel back,* off you go, Joan, impress us.'

The girl was pale with fright. She began. '*O how I long to travel back, And tread again that ancient track! That I might once more reach that plain Where first I met,* em where first I met, I met, *Where first I felt my glorious train; From whence the lively spirit sees,* the lively spirit ...'

Reynolds gave a great sob of sorrow. Joan juddered to a halt. Her two white hands were gripping the sides of the desk. Reynolds could see the freckles and his heart was swollen in empathy. She looked down at the inkwell, she gave up.

'Well, well, well, Joan, such a disappointment. You too. A fool, an idiot, a layabout. Tell me then Joan, branch or fruit, branch or fruit?'

Without looking up, Joan muttered 'Fruit.'

Sebastian was annoyed. 'That's no way to address me, girl!' he shouted. 'Where are your manners? Are they lost too, along with the words of the poem?'

'Fruit, please, Brother,' the poor girl said, her head bowed even lower.

Sebastian picked out the largest, greenest apple on the table and gave it to her. She had to eat it then and there, in front of everybody, silence all around except for her crunching and gulping, Sebastian standing over her, his hands on his hips, his great bulk shadowing her. They all heard her as she sobbed and ate and slobbered her way through the fruit, her body cringing, her mouth skewed, her face contorting until there was only a small core left. And they all knew, because most of them had already experienced the punishment, that the rest of the day would be filled with stomach cramps, that for days after there would be itching, hives and all sorts of unpleasantness to be suffered. But Joan, and those white hands with their delicate freckles and the tiny red hairs just visible on the wrist, how could she face the cruelty of four scalding slaps from a sally stick on her lovely flesh?

Reynolds wept for Joan Macken. When school was over he tried to talk to her. Although he had to go back to the monastery and she was heading out towards the road to go up to her home in the village, he wanted to walk with her. She was hanging back, walking slowly, stopping occasionally, holding her stomach. Reynolds knew, for it had happened him before, several times, he knew that the apple was causing her stomach pains, and that she would suffer far more than if she had taken the slaps on her hands. He stayed close behind her for a while, then, when she dropped her schoolbag on the laneway leading up to the main road, he darted forward and picked it up for her; she was standing at the side of the lane, holding her stomach, a look of pain on her face.

'So ... so ... so ...' Reynolds tried. I feel so sorry for you.

She just looked at him as if he wasn't there, her face contorted with pain. Then she turned and stumbled away in among the rhododendron bushes. Reynolds watched her, that primrose-yellow cardigan she wore, the dark blue skirt, the grey woollen stockings, one down about her ankles, the other halfway up her leg. He noticed her hocks, perfectly beautiful to his eyes, and for a moment he turned his head away, ashamed at the thought that he was taking advantage of her distress. But there was something terribly sad, too, about the backs of her legs, something finite and utterly vulnerable, their whiteness, their uncertain flush of red, and he longed to tell her something, he was not sure what, something about the futility of all living, something about laying oneself down, empty, before the rough but kindly hand of God.

She was putting her fingers in her mouth. She was trying to vomit. And at last she did, Reynolds waiting, as he always seemed to be – waiting, attending, but ignored; and the girl retched loudly, getting rid of the trouble in her stomach, throwing it all away into the shrubbery, all the meanness and the suffering and the poetry, vomiting it out of her system into the darkness of the undergrowth. Reynolds looked away, feeling for her. When she stepped out again onto the laneway he offered her a handkerchief, a clean white one he had collected only that morning. It had the name of the monastery embroidered in red thread on the corner: St Francis. She looked at it for a moment, then took it from him and wiped her face with it, gratefully. She was sweating. She looked pale. But there was also a glaze of triumph over her eyes. She reached the handkerchief back to him and he took it, putting it carefully into the pocket of his jacket. Then he hoisted her schoolbag onto his shoulder, smiled at her and nodded towards the road. He was delighted when she nodded her head and began to walk along the laneway beside him.

The afternoon was peaceful; the green leaves of the rhodo-dendron bushes hung dusty and still on either side; now and then they could hear a shuffling sound, some tiny life busy amongst the fallen growth, an occasional wren would dart through the branches, its song so much louder than you could expect from such a tiny bird. Reynolds's heart was singing. Joan Macken was walking alongside him; he was helping her, she would be grateful. As they neared the main road Reynolds saw a wild dog rose bush growing amongst the rhododendron. He hesitated. Then, gathering courage, he put down Joan's bag, smiled at her, then dug his hand carelessly into the bush, breaking off two full dog roses, one red and perfect, the other pink and not fully opened yet. His hand caught against the thorns and he cried out, but then he smiled, saw a tiny bead of blood on his thumb and sucked it off. He came back onto the laneway and offered her the two roses. Awkwardly she took them from him, but took the red one by the stem and the thorns caught her, too. 'Yow!' she yelled and flung the two roses away into the hedge. She, too, put her finger to her mouth. Reynolds stood, waiting.

'You're an eejit!' she said, though there was a little hint of kindness in her voice. She stooped and gathered up her school-bag, flung it quickly over her shoulder and moved rapidly towards the main road.

Reynolds stood, emptied.

Just as she turned right on the road to head for home she glanced back momentarily at him, smiled and said, 'Thanks, Reynolds.' Then she turned away and was gone.

Everything that happens, Reynolds thought then, is wonder-ful. Everything that has happened had to happen and everything that will happen will have to happen too. Everything is in the hands of something greater than us. And all we can do is wait, and obey, and agree. Her word of thanks to him meant so much, it lifted his heart and he went back down the laneway towards the monastery with some joy in his step. In the quietness of his room that evening he wrote out a poem, as carefully and as neatly as he could. He would give it to Joan Macken some day, when he got the chance, and it would say everything, far more than he could ever utter himself, or even write, in a lifetime.

> Drink to me only with thine eyes,
>   And I will pledge with mine;
> Or leave a kiss but in the cup
>   And I'll not look for wine.
> The thirst that from the soul doth rise
>   Doth ask a drink divine;
> But might I of Jove's nectar sup,
>   I would not change for thine.

Reynolds, poor Reynolds.. He folded up the sheet of paper and put it between the pages of his poetry book. Then he took out the handkerchief, unfolded it, rubbed his face slowly in it, and put it in under his pillow. Outside dusk was falling over the old orchard; somewhere he thought he could hear an owl call. It would be a warm night, filled with wonder; he would sleep well.

NINETEEN

How many days and nights had it been now? Reynolds had lost track, between the dim and the dark and the half-dark, the light and the un-light and the near-light, spending all his time in the bed, or in the old horse-hair broken-down armchair on the landing, or sitting on the toilet, voiding nothing. It appeared to be around noon that day when he struggled out of bed. He had lost a good deal of weight, of course, and was beginning to look very different to the large and bulky Reynolds of not so long before. He was pale, except for the great red blobby flesh around his eyes. It was his aim to make himself nothing in the world so that he could become something else, to become transparent in the eyes of God.

He was trembling, shivering; his whole body shaking like a willow tree in a stiff breeze. He was cold, cold through. He took down his dressing gown from the nail behind the door and put it on. He was shivering still. He took off the old frayed blanket from the bed and wrapped himself in that. He moved towards the door, still shivering, hardly able to move. There was saliva around his lips, though he hadn't taken a drink for hours. Holding on to the banisters and taking a step at a time, resting with both feet on each step, he made it to the bottom of the stairs. He did not head for the kitchen and a glass of water, at least, or some salt, but turned into the chilly sitting room and fell-sat on the armchair at the side of the black, cold grate. He wrapped himself tightly in dressing gown and blanket, hunched forward towards the fireplace, and continued shivering.

The afternoon, if it was afternoon, was very still. Scarcely a sound from outside. Once the noise of an aeroplane lifting into the sky could be heard through the chimney and Reynolds's heart lurched a little at the sound. Remembering his own journey, his once-off, hope-filled journey. Then silence again. He imagined he heard someone whisper down the chimney to him, whisper about God's will, about how it is not a good thing to deliberately and consciously set out to destroy yourself, but years and years of effort in the keeping of his poor body and soul together had made him deaf to that plea.

There was a small thud from the hallway. Reynolds hardly looked up, he hardly noticed, he simply sat there, shivering. His thoughts were vague as fog moving over the marshes, he was dwelling on things of the past, most of the time, but now and then they took on a kind of swirling murkiness about them, just like dirty dishwater does when it is being released from the sink and away into the horrors of the system. It was so with him then, for a long time.

Eventually he sighed, and with a great effort he mustered strength enough to struggle to his feet, holding first to the arms of the chair, then to the mantelpiece, then to the edge of the table, stumbling, slowly, slowly back into the hallway. His eyes were watery but he noticed, peeping around from the corner of the fridge, a small packet of biscuits. He bent down, with difficulty, and picked it up. Another message from the great world beyond! He rubbed his eyes and looked at it and he was shaken. Free ginger biscuits. Amazing. Ginger was one of Reynolds's favourite tastes. He took a sudden decision, turned towards the kitchen with some speed, trying to tear open the little pack. He turned too quickly for his own good, he stumbled and fell heavily against the wall and toppled slowly to the floor. He released a little cry of anguish and lay there for a while, believing he was already being punished for this movement to undo his fast. But he clutched the little pack in his hand, as if it were a truly precious gift. Then he struggled to his knees, his hands and knees, and pushed himself upward. Holding to the wall, he moved with extreme slowness and caution to the kitchen.

His fingers were dried-out twigs and he struggled to get the packet open. The three biscuits fell to the floor and he sat down heavily beside them, picking them up, dusting them off against his blanket, putting one slowly into his mouth. He closed his eyes and chewed, licking off his lips the tiniest morsel that might escape. Slowly, relishing everything. When he had finished the three biscuits he sighed deeply and remained sitting on the floor.

Almost at once there were cold currents of guilt and a sense of failure rushing through his entire body. Had he abandoned, then, by not eating, by not looking after himself, had he abandoned the certainties and the physicalities of the world, or that which is, for that which, perhaps, does not exist? The answer was a resounding no! Reynolds had not abandoned that which is for that which is not, if that which is, that which the world knows exists, is not in fact what is good, and if that which perhaps does not exist, and in the eyes of the world certainly does not exist, is indeed the good. He tried to fit the thoughts and the words into some order that might console him. He could not.

But the Lord plays strange tricks! Reynolds, where he sat, began to grow pale and clutch his stomach. Quite suddenly and violently he began to retch and within minutes, perhaps seconds, the three ginger biscuits he had so greedily consumed were back, in a mess of vomit, on the floor and on his blanket. Of course his stomach was not able so quickly to absorb such a strong taste, such a difficult food as ginger biscuits. He was sweating with the great upset and heaving he had undergone. He was worn out. He lay over on the hard floor of the kitchen and faded away into unhealthy sleep. The remains of the last little trick the world had played on him lay stinking on the floor about him.

TWENTY

Reynolds, after the death of his parents and the destruction of his home, after the induction by the monks of this lost creature into their care, had taken on several levels of mystique in the eyes of the pupils in the school. They treated him now with some deference, owing to their sense of his tragic loss. They treated him with a little more caution, owing to his insertion among the great wonder that was the monastery, and his everymoment contact with all the Brothers, including their teachers Brother Leo and Brother Sebastian. So when Reynolds stopped Joan Macken on the laneway the day after her troubles, she gave him her full attention.

Reynolds took off his bag, took out his English book, took out of that the folded paper with the poem on it, and handed it to Joan. Then he stood, his head down, his hands irritating the book, his shoes scuffing the clay of the laneway.

Joan looked at him, then glanced at the paper. 'Is this a letter?'

'A po ... a po ...'

'A poem?'

Reynolds nodded.

'Did you write it?'

Reynolds shook his head. 'Beh ... Beh ... Ben ...'

'Somebody called Ben wrote it?'

Reynolds nodded.

Joan began to read. Her lips followed the words on the page, slowly, shaping them. She hadn't gone far when she looked up again at Reynolds. 'What's this about a kiss? In a cup?' She laughed. Reynolds moved forward, wishing to explain, but she pulled the page away, still laughing. Then she called out to Nora and Doreen who had passed them and were heading to the main road. The two big girls turned and came back.

Joan showed them the page. The three of them read, Nora and Doreen leaning in over Joan's shoulders. Reynolds wanted to say it was OK, they could give him back the paper now, if they liked. But he simply waited.

'I don't understand a word of it,' Nora said, becoming angry. 'It's weird. How can you drink with your eyes. *Drink to me only with thine eyes.* That's rubbish. Just rubbish. What's this, Reynolds? A love-letter. To Joan?'

The three girls looked at him. He knew he was the colour of beetroot. He kept scuffing the clay, then pointed at Joan, and nodded. Bravely.

Doreen read: '*Leave a kiss in the cup* … Did he, Joan? Did Reynolds give you a kiss?'

Doreen was laughing, too, and Joan began to blush. 'He did not, the eejit!' she insisted. 'I wouldn't accept a kiss from an eejit like that.' Then she took the paper, rolled it up tightly in her fist and flung it into Reynolds's face. 'Just you feck off and leave me alone,' she said. 'You hear me? I don't want anything to do with you.'

'Anyway,' Nora added. 'You're nearly a Brother now. Brother Reynolds. Sure you'll be living with the Brothers all your life. You can't be expected to be looking at beautiful women like me and Joan and Doreen. So you just feck off, Brother Reynolds. You just feck off.'

The three of them turned and ran up the short distance to the main road. They were laughing, turning back a few times and screaming at him, 'Brother Reynolds! Brother Reynolds!' He was glad when they turned the corner from the laneway gate onto the road up to the village.

Reynolds squatted to pick up the crumpled bit of paper. He rolled it round in his hand, thoughtlessly, then sat down on the little grass verge at the side of the lane. Everybody had gone home. He was alone. The afternoon warmth was pleasant but he was hardly aware of it. He slowly tore up the sheet of paper with Ben Jonson's poem on it and threw the bits into the rhododendron hedge. Then he put his head down in his hands. There was a long line of the tiniest black ants moving steadily near his feet; they seemed to cross the laneway in a straight line and had now veered to get past his feet. He watched them for a while, fascinated. Some of them were carrying bits of rhododendron leaves far bigger than their own bodies; others had insects, flies or small worms, and they were shoving them with enormous difficulty towards the verge where Reynolds was sitting. He got up, quickly, not to bother them, not to cause havoc amongst their labours.

The words came back to him, *Brother Reynolds. Brother Reynolds.* It didn't sound all that terribly bad. He knew now that he would find it increasingly difficult to speak to girls, to be with girls, and he was tired of them making fun of him, making him into a total fool. How nice it would be if he were to become one of the Brothers and live all his life in the monastery, taking care of the orchard, for instance, or the kitchen, or the graveyard, or better still and best of all! if they would make him sacristan and he could keep the chapel gleaming, fresh with flowers, glowing with candles, oil in the lamps, floors sheening, cushions neat and plumped. And that way he could serve his God without having to make a fool of himself before the world. What a wonderful idea that was!

But for a long moment, while his body sagged heavily again, Reynolds could see Joan Macken, how pretty she was, that red hair, those freckles, those big and wholly distracting green eyes! And he thought of his new hope, his dream, the Brother Reynolds dream, how he would have to hide himself away for all of his life, from that red hair, from those green eyes. What he was contemplating, he knew, was a kind of death, even a suicide. Even the busyness of two gulls that came swooping low from the direction of the sea, calling loudly, could not distract him for the moment. Nor the patient, ongoing labours of the tiny ants at his feet.

Later that evening, homework done, chores completed, Reynolds waited until all the Brothers had finished their evening prayers and had gone to their rooms, or to the common room where they might read, or perhaps play a game of cards together. Then he slipped quietly into the chapel through the little door with the frosted blue glass that led directly from the monastery cloister. The shutting of the door behind him echoed loudly through the empty chapel. There was only a small red flame from the sanctuary lamp, and the remains of daylight that came in from the world outside through the brightly coloured and frosted mullioned windows that opened, or closed, on the earth he was thinking of abandoning.

Reynolds moved quietly up to the altar rails and knelt on the long step. He felt the hardness of the marble under his knees, its coldness against his skin. He could hear his own breathing. He closed his eyes, entering into a greater blackness than ever, thought of all his days and months and years up to this moment, how they weighed heavily, sadly and uselessly on him. He sighed with grief, and the sigh seemed to echo all around the empty chapel. He opened his eyes, watched the flickering tongue of the sanctuary flame for a moment, but there was no answering sigh, no word. The walls, the hour, the night, the swoon of his heart that the sweep and the hurl of the great God bore down with a horror of height, and the midriff straining. It was a terrible moment for Reynolds. He bowed his head, closed his eyes again and spoke fluently to his God, offering his life, in however humble a capacity, to His service, whether it be in the ringing of the Angelus bells, in the dusting of the chapel aisles, in the gathering of fallen apples or the tidying of already tidy graves, but that his life be of some use to the great Creator of all. He would become a Brother; he would garb himself for ever in the service of the Lord. Then he breathed heavily again, but felt no relief, no satisfaction. When he stood up and turned to walk back down into the monastery cloister Reynolds had never felt so much alone; he stood, he felt, on a deserted shore, and all the boats had put out to sea, had disappeared already over the dark horizon, leaving him alone, quietened but alone.

TWENTY-ONE

It was Big Tom came laughing and gabbling into school, his mockery sharpened and moistened for Doctor Weir and the evening he had been called out to the dying Wally MacNamara. Big Tom told them all about it, his ugly words directed mainly towards Reynolds, the foolish, untouchable, protected Brother Reynolds. Everyone had heard how Doctor Weir had spent three hours with the old man who did not want to let the doctor go. He was over ninety-five years of age and had worked about his little farm all his life, and had made extra money out on the trawlers during the good weathers. He did not want to let go of life. Half of him, the doctor said, was eaten away already and it was a miracle that he could still breathe and speak, that he had such a strong grip on the doctor's sleeve. The priest had come and gone, several times over the last few months, and Wally was wonderfully prepared for that last ploughline up beyond the top of the field. 'I feel about twenty-five years old, Doctor,' the old man said. 'Feel no different from back then. Sure, I cannot jump a fence like before, but there's loads I have still left to do.'

All the doctor could do was soothe him, keep him peaceful, give him the stuff that would make his dying easy for him, and for his family. The old man kept asking for whiskey, and the doctor saw no harm in a glass or two. The doctor, unfortunately, joined him. In one glass. Then in a second. And a third. And the night passed on. Time passed. By midnight the doctor, still seated at the bedside, was beginning to doze from the whiskey he had shared, and the old man had tried, several times, to sing.

'He died singing,' Big Tom giggled, 'he died singing.'

Doctor Weir had taken his leave. It was a dark night, some rain. A slithery road. And it was morning before Doctor Weir was discovered, fast asleep still, the dark green Anglia wedged between two tree-trunks in the old wood down beyond the village crossroads. A car severely damaged, a doctor still in the whole of his health.

It was just two days after Wally MacNamara had been laid, sozzled and content, in his grave. Doctor Weir was in disgrace and now young Deirdre Weir was seen as fair game. Big Tom sniggered, and pointed at Reynolds. 'Watch out!' he said. 'No wee skirt to save you now.'

During lunch break they were all out in the yard. A dull day, a fine mist barely touching the small bodies clustered here and there under the shelter of bushes in the yard. The gable wall of the school a dark green under the wet and dusk of years. The smell of chalk and of damp clothes reaching out into the air of the day. Deirdre Weir standing with another girl under the far reach of rhododendron branches. Opening the paper bag that held her lunch. And it was Big Tom again, along with Nora McGreil and Doreen Murphy, who came sidling over to her, and stood at a little distance, watching.

Deirdre took out a fine red apple along with her sandwich. She left the apple down on the low wall under the rhododendron. Then she took out a bar of chocolate and left that down too. She was chatting to her friend. She bit into her sandwich. It was time. Big Tom moved slowly forward, grinning, and picked the bar of chocolate and the apple from the wall. Deirdre snatched at them but Big Tom was too quick for her. He stood back then, Big Tom, a giant faced with a small, tidy girl, and handed the apple to Nora. He began to tear the paper off the bar of chocolate.

'You have no right ...' Deirdre began.

'I have too!' shouted Big Tom. 'Your daddy's a drunkard, and that gives me every right.' He bit into the chocolate bar. Nora bit into the apple. Big Tom took two squares from the bar and handed them to Doreen. 'Here, Doreen,' he said. 'Your daddy's not a drunkard. But you have no chocolate. So here, you deserve this, too.'

Deirdre stood watching them. What could she do? She spoke very quietly. 'My father is not a drunkard. He was out late, helping Mr MacNamara. He was very, very tired.'

'He's a bloody drunkard, that's what he is. So there!' This was Nora McGreil. And then the three of them began to chant: 'Doctor Weir's a drunkard! Doctor Weir's a drunkard!'

Deirdre grew very pale. The girl beside her had begun to move away. And it was just at that moment that Reynolds rushed forward and snatched the chocolate from Big Tom and the apple from the hand of Nora McGreil. He pushed Big Tom away, held the food in his hand and saw that it was destroyed now for Deirdre. He picked up the paper bag and dropped the apple and chocolate into it, and handed the bag to Deirdre.

Big Tom was grinning. 'Right!' he said. 'So! It's Brother Reynolds who thinks he can get away with it now that he's sponging off the Brothers. After school, Reynolds, at the gate!' and he wet his right index finger and rubbed it against Reynolds's cheek. He turned triumphantly towards the two big girls. 'Let him off too easy last time,' he sneered. 'This time I'll make a floodin' jelly out of him. You wait and see. It's the end of Reynolds, that's for sure. I'll break the eejit into little pieces.'

Reynolds turned to Deirdre and tried to speak. She was pale and trembling.

'No, Reynolds,' she said. 'You mustn't do it. Big Tom is too big and strong. It's not fair. I could manage. I was all right. But I thank you, very much indeed.' She bowed her head over her sandwich and Reynolds grinned, standing up very tall. She looked up at him again. 'This time,' she said, 'I know they won't pay any heed to me. You better go straight back to the monastery after school. Please. Don't get hurt for my sake. They won't do anything to me. Not really.'

Reynolds smiled at her, shook his head slowly, and moved back towards the schoolroom door.

Afternoon in the classroom passed with particular slowness. On the wall over the old fireplace the big clock swung its pendulum, over, back, over, back, slowly, slowly, slowly. The monotony was destructive. Over all the classroom hung a fug of tension and excitement. Big Tom sat up straight and proud in his desk, anticipating victory. Nora and Doreen, as well as Joan Macken, glanced at Reynolds often to sneer.

At first Reynolds wondered if Brother Leo noticed something amiss in the class. There were moments of inattention alternating with moments of pure concentration. Did he notice Deirdre, above all, who sat pale and anxious in her desk?

There was a new poem that day, a poem by Shelley, called 'Ozymandias of Egypt', and Reynolds relished it, sounding it over and over within himself, sucking inwardly at the sounds while Brother Leo spoke it out several times.

> I met a traveller from an antique land
> Who said: Two vast and trunkless legs of stone
> Stand in the desert ...

Oh that was rich to Reynolds's soul. And that stirring ending:

> 'My name is Ozymandias, king of kings;
> Look on my works, ye Mighty, and despair!'
> Nothing beside remains. Round the decay
> Of that colossal wreck, boundless and bare,
> The lone and level sands stretch far away.

Leo could see Reynolds's mouth working on the word, *O-zy-man-di-as*. And his heart went out to the boy once again, that he could not speak the word into the air.

When they raced out the school gate at last, everybody, including Reynolds, turned away from the monastery towards the road. The smaller ones ran more quickly and took up their positions on the grass mound where this battle would take place. The bigger boys and girls moved more slowly, certain of their places, sure of what was about to occur. Only Deirdre hung back beside Reynolds and tugged at his sleeve, begging him to go home, to go to the Brothers, that it did not matter, that she was all right. Reynolds smiled at her. What he wanted to say was: 'Look on my works, ye Mighty, and despair!' but even if he could say it, he wasn't sure that Deirdre would follow his meaning. There were tears in her eyes when they reached the ring the boys and girls had formed. There was laughter and a high buzzing sound of excitement. Big Tom was already in the centre of the ring, his jacket off, his sleeves rolled up. He was prancing about, posturing, making shapes, breaking great monsters out of the air and felling them to the ground. He was cheered on from all sides.

Reynolds moved deliberately into the circle, having to shove his way past several of the students who stood, indifferent to his fate, eager only to witness violence. Reynolds left his schoolbag down beside Deirdre. He did not bother taking off his jacket. He strode forward and faced Big Tom.

'Ha! Reynolds! The eejit. Brother Reynolds. The fool! The jackass! Prepare for death! Prepare to be blackened, flattened, laid out along the grass in bits and pieces!' So, Big Tom, and each name, each phrase, followed by a delighted shout from the small mob about him. 'Come on!' Tom yelled. 'Hit me!'

Reynolds's fist shot out with incredible speed and caught Big Tom straight on the chin. For a moment Tom stood, astonishment colouring his face, and then his head jerked back and he fell backwards onto the ground, stunned. Reynolds stood, waiting, and the sudden silence about him was wonderful.

Big Tom breathed heavily, picking himself up slowly. He turned to his audience. 'He cheated! He hit me before we had started! He's yellow!'

Reynolds waited. Big Tom raised his fists and moved forward slowly. He made a few jabs at Reynolds, who bent his head back from the blows. Tom made a few more feints, then suddenly put his head down and charged. Reynolds stepped aside nimbly and Big Tom blundered into a small group of boys on the rim of the circle. They pushed him back. There was silence still. Reynolds waited. Slowly now, and with caution, Big Tom advanced, his fists flailing, his face scared. He hit Reynolds once, lightly, on the chest and Reynolds's fist flew again, and once more Big Tom was on his back on the ground, blood beginning to flow from his nose. After a few moments Tom picked himself up again, holding his hand to his nose, watching the blood with terror and then he began to cry, reached for his jacket and turned away.

It was a terrible and quick humiliation. Mumbling and muttering among themselves, all Tom's friends moved away from the beaten boy as he tried, while still holding his nose, to put his jacket on. Deirdre came and picked up his schoolbag. She took out a small handkerchief and gave it to Tom, without saying a word. Then she stood up on tiptoes and gave Reynolds just the gentlest kiss on his cheek. She stood back from him and smiled. He blushed wildly. She took off a silver bracelet she was wearing on her left wrist and moved to take his hand. He backed away from her, shaking his head.

'Yes,' she insisted. 'Yes, you must have it. It's from me. You must keep it. For ever.' And she laughed a little mountain-stream laugh. She caught his left hand and tried to fit the brace-let around his wrist but it scarcely came halfway. 'You're too big,' she said. She laughed again, pushed the bracelet into his hand and smiled up at him. She moved quickly away. Several of the bigger girls were waiting for her and they welcomed her loudly.

For a while Reynolds gazed in astonishment at the lovely, simple bracelet; it was not marked; the ends were joined by a little silver chain. He lifted it to his lips and kissed it softly, then put it away in the inside pocket of his jacket. He had never felt so happy.

That evening, when he was undressing for bed, Reynolds's heart soared again as he took out the bracelet. He fingered it for a while, then he hung it up around the crossbeam of the little wooden crucifix that was hanging over the head of his bed.

TWENTY-TWO

Reynolds lived for many years with the Brothers, and his life was peaceful, ordered and content. The days passed, coloured with the natural hues of the seasons and the sacred rituals, eased by the regularity and certainties of the Brothers' way of life. Time for these men was a special thing; the wholly uniform yet varied and always surprising turn of the seasons, the days, the months, the years, moved with a perfect mirroring of the human being's misery and greatness. And outside the confines of that special place the lives of the island people moved with their own rhythms, the tides rising and falling, the sun and the stars and the moon moving in their perfectly structured way, their goings and their returns, and the endless, terrifying and gratifying accidents that change, at times, that onbearing order.

For Reynolds, time seemed to have ceased to matter. It was a question of following the orders of the Brothers and of the seasons. And always he attended, waiting patiently for the moment when he would go to Brother Angelo Maria in the office and ask to be admitted into the monastery as one of the Brothers. He knew what the people in the great world beyond had to suffer: their slow and tedious lives filled with recurring and monotonous tasks that served merely to keep their slow and tedious lives in motion. And the slow brightening of the fields under their growth of heathers, and their slow easing back into the dullness of russet and brown and black. He saw the Brothers with their slow and leisured certainties, their unambiguous choreographies, and his heart lurched to become one of them, and at last, when time for him had come to a halt, to be laid down in his own ordered plot in the graveyard under the trees, between the gravel paths, beyond the laden orchard.

He spoke with Brother Leo, the one he liked most. It was a day when the sunshine bathed orchard and garden and cemetery in a soft and warm silver aura. They were sitting on a garden bench, under a huge yew tree that had been growing for decades in the corner of the cemetery. Reynolds pointed to himself. 'Mmmmee,' he managed. Then he pointed to the brown soutane that Leo was wearing, pointed to the white knotted cincture, the large rosary beads hanging from it. Then pointed to himself again.

'You would like to join us?' Leo interpreted, and Reynolds nodded happily.

There was a pause. A thrush flew down into the cemetery, landed on the concrete surround of a grave some small distance from them. Its wide eye watched them a while. It pounced and they saw it wrench a snail from under some half-dead leaves that had fallen on the grave. Head high the thrush watched again towards the two men. With the snail in its bill, the bird hopped up on the surround once more and started hitting it hard off the concrete. Reynolds could hear the sharp smash of the shell. Several times the thrush lifted and thumped the snail, then picked the whole, broken creature and flew off with it some-where. A quick sadness flung across Reynolds's chest, like a pain. He had to remind himself, again and again, that this was God's way, this the flow of necessity, this the pitiless earth in its essential mechanism, making its way towards perfection.

'I don't know what Brother Angelo Maria would say to that,' Leo said quietly. 'We will have to go and ask him. I'll come with you, if you like. I think you would make a perfect Brother of the Holy Angels. Perfect. And sure you know our ways and lives and prayers so well already. I'll talk to Angelo and we'll fix a time to go along together.'

Some few days later Brother Leo brought Reynolds to the office. Leo knocked gently, waited until he heard the answering call, then he ushered Reynolds ahead of him. 'Mind if I join you?' Leo said to Brother Angelo. 'I can perhaps best interpret what Reynolds wishes to say.'

The room was dim in the afternoon light; a small green lamp was lit on Angelo's large table and he was visible in a small ball of light behind piles of papers and books scattered everywhere over the table. Reynolds saw him nod distractedly, as he tried to gather up some papers and leave them carefully to one side. And distractedly he waved Leo and Reynolds into the room, pointing vaguely to a chair on the other side of the table from him. For a short while there was silence, Reynolds feeling so nervous he thought he could hear the ongoing fall of dust across the dryness of the room. Angelo Maria looked annoyed, sifting his materials, preparing his mind for this interview. Then, quite suddenly, he looked up.

'Brother Reynolds, eh?' he said archly. 'Brother Reynolds of the Holy Angels. Sounds good, don't you think, Leo?'

Leo laughed quietly. 'I do think our Reynolds would make a wonderful Brother,' he said.

Reynolds knew he was grinning widely, and he tried to fasten his face into a more serious aspect as Angelo's two strange eyes turned and focused on him. As usual Reynolds's gaze was drawn to the glass eye, drawn, held and teased by it. He looked down at his hands in his lap.

'I have given the question a good deal of thought,' the Superior said. 'I have also wired our house in Rome and given an outline of what we are thinking. And I have had an answer back already, from Brother Bonaventure, in Rome. He suggests that it would be impossible, quite impossible.'

Angelo paused, began to straighten out some papers before him. Reynolds felt his whole being sag with emptiness. Angelo looked up again and held Reynolds's eye. The Brother leaned forward, his two elbows on the table in front of him, his hands joined as if in prayer. He looked severe. Reynolds suddenly remembered some of the times he had held his hands out before this man to receive punishment. He shivered.

'However,' Brother Angelo said, and Reynolds's heart lifted again. 'However. I am not sure I was able to convey to Brother Bonaventure exactly what kind of a boy – what kind of a man – we are dealing with in the person of Reynolds here. You cannot speak, truly you cannot speak. You are not of the brightest, that's for sure. Yet I look around me and I see the Brothers with whom I live and work and I would have to say some of these, too, are not the brightest.' Reynolds heard Leo chuckle a little. There was a smile on Angelo's face. 'And again,' he continued. 'What is speech? I know, Reynolds, that you speak well with your God, with our God. I have seen you in chapel, I have seen your homework when you write on cate-chism and bible stories. And in our monastery there will be tasks to be carried out, like the ones you are already doing, and doing well, might I add, that do not require the gift of speech. So.' The Brother scrunched his neck, shrugging it inside the half Roman collar, shaking his head for comfort. He sat back and began fiddling with a ruler on the desk.

'Quite so, Brother Angelo,' Leo said very softly. 'If I may speak on behalf of Reynolds, he has been exemplary. Exemp-lary. As if he were an angel come from out a heavenly fire to spend his days amongst us. Exemplary. As good a Brother as you might want to find. Truly.'

There was silence. Reynolds felt his whole being swell a little with satisfaction.

'There remains the problem of Brother Bonaventure,' Angelo went on, 'of Rome, in fact.' He leaned forward again on the desk. 'How to convince the Brothers there. Well, I have decided. When the school year ends, this July, that's just six weeks or so away, I will send Reynolds to our house in Rome, to spend a month there under the supervision, indeed under the very eyes, of Brother Bonaventure himself. And you will go with him, Brother Leo, you will attend him. As you know, someone from here was going to have to visit the Mother House soon, quite soon, with our reports, and with the reports of the Bishop, so I am entrusting these reports to you. The financial statement, the parish statement, our good parish priest's words, such like, such like. And Reynolds. Reynolds will go, too, will see a little of the great world beyond these fences and bogs, and will convince Brother Bonaventure one way or the other. A trip to Rome, how does that sound, eh Reynolds?'

Leo leaned across and grabbed Reynolds by the arm, grinning hugely at him, shaking him happily. Reynolds's mouth was open in shock and delight.

'But one thing I would add,' Angelo said, his eyes bright with merriment. 'You should try and keep that mouth of yours quite closed, except perhaps when you are eating. You will not have to speak a great deal, but it would not be too beneficial to drool and dribble on Brother Bonaventure's spotless marble halls in the Mother House in Rome.'

Reynolds stood. For a moment he looked at the Brother sitting there in the glow of the small green lamp. He was happy beyond belief. Then he stumbled forward, leaned over the great table and reached for Brother Angelo's hand. His elbow knocked several books from the pile they were in and they fell onto the floor with a great clatter. But Angelo Maria only smiled and shook Reynolds's hand warmly.

TWENTY-THREE

There were strange noises coming from old man Reynolds now, especially in the night-time. He could not lie still. His dwindling body shifted and jerked and spasmed in the bed, as if the very weight of the sheets was too much for him to bear. And he cried out, too, in his pain, and this pain was becoming established all over his body, in every joint, every bone, every extremity. The suffering was worst in the darkness and he cried often through the night, suffering not only the physical pain of his deteriorating condition but the far more serious pain of his own self-awareness.

There is a point in the night when the world appears to come to a halt, its turning, its motion, even its light or darkness, a point somewhere beyond midnight, before the whole thing turns again towards the day. That is the deepest, the darkest, the most abandoned moment, the moment of dying, or of yielding to the void that underlies all our actions and our being. There comes a silence that is terrifying if you fall into it, a sense of self that is irksome and calling on the body to give up all its efforts. There comes a widening of the eyes into a wakefulness that is hopeless of ever finding rest or sleep again, and that night Reynolds halted in his living, and dropped heavily down into that void.

He was lying on his back, his hands, now little more than dried sticks, holding the sheet up under his chin. His eyes came suddenly wide open under the darkness of the ceiling and of the great excess of heaviness above the ceiling. He was aware of that silence that is not, and is, an external silence but one also that comes to the body and to the brain, allowing all bleak and bleary thoughts and emotions to enter. He could sense distant shiftings and slight rumblings in his stomach that were, and were not, pains, because he knew there was little in his stomach to keep the juices active and they would need to feed on the lining of that stomach. The sensation was one of gnawing, as if some slothful, large creature were determinedly eating away his internal organs. With great difficulty Reynolds pulled his body together, garnered any energy he could find, and climbed out of bed.

He drew an overcoat over the dressing gown that clung over his pyjamas, his vest, his underpants, and made his way to the window. He drew up a hard wooden chair, pulled back the frayed and stained curtains, and gazed out onto the night. There seemed to be stillness. The sickly yellow lights of the street sent a sickly yellow reach against stars and moon but the moon was there, high and distant and incorrigibly other. Clouds moved lazily across the sky, making little difference to that sickly light. Reynolds leaned his elbows on the window ledge, leaned his head on his hands, and watched.

He could see out over his own back garden, across the back garden of the house opposite that was in peaceful darkness, and beyond that to the tips of other houses in Heatherfield. To his left the back garden of Genevieve's house lay dark and empty. As if that darkness and emptiness were some form of reproach to Reynolds. He sighed deeply. There was no stir of life now in his own back garden, no pigs, no hens, no shifting of comfortable bodies. All was empty, and still.

For a long moment Reynolds knew some kind of peace, in spite of all his pains and hopelessness. It was the peace that came from this most illusory and most threatening of periods of darkness, the peace that suggests that maybe everything has indeed come to a halt, that time will not move on into the impossible demands of another day. Because as soon as that day's dimmest first light began to show itself, then surely would the demands of the future make themselves felt. And for Reynolds his hold on the future was now utterly tenuous. We live always under the illusion that the body has a grip on that future, that when the flesh is hungry it will be fed, when it is thirsty it will find solace in drink. Reynolds had yielded all of that up, all the illusions, all the actual power over the future. When the body screamed out of its hunger it would not be fed. When the spirit faced out into the light of another day and demanded its own satisfaction, its energy to grow, its motives for that energy, they would not be there. There were no more longings to be met, no desires to be fulfilled, except the ending of it all. What Reynolds had done was to rip away, like the chain of a rosary, the binding power of both the past and the future. What he was trying to do was live in the present, merely, and man can only survive that way by becoming a vegetable, a prune, a raisin.

Without glancing back Reynolds could see his bed, the sheets and blankets tossed and pulled away, and he felt as if the person who had spent time in there was now dead and gone, and that that person was once beloved, and now, already, Reynolds was in deep mourning for that being. An intolerable grief hit him then, as if he had lost to death the one person whom he had ever loved and loved without hesitation or condition, that that person was irretrievably lost to him, and therefore nothing on earth, under the earth, or over the earth was worth breathing for. Without shifting his position at the window ledge Reynolds wept. The weeping was silent but intense, the tears real and falling down his cheeks, down his arms onto the window ledge. How did he have enough moisture left in his body for tears? For he was nothing now, nothing, neither living nor dead, neither there nor not-there, he was nothing. Empty. Void.

But time does pass, we know it well. The moon came with a small surge of light as a thickness of cloud passed from before it and a big black cat came from the wall of Genevieve's garden onto the wall of Reynolds's. The cat moved slowly, but there was movement, a darker black against the darkness of the night. It passed along the top of the wall and disappeared amongst the leaves and branches of the hawthorn bushes of the house next door. Life, after all, goes on. And Reynolds knew a different weariness in his mind and body, a pleasant weariness, as of vegetable or stone in its utter lassitude, and he laid his head down on his arms along the window ledge and he slept a deep, long, unrestorative sleep.

TWENTY-FOUR

There came a day when Reynolds was out gathering eggs at the back of his house in Heatherfield, the sun warm on the old garden. There was a gentle buzzing of bees from the glorious growth of clematis he had on the trellis between his house and Genevieve's. The flowers were large and white and there were streaks of dark blood-purple on the sepals, the long yellow sepals covered with pollen and reaching out towards the enquiring bees. On a branch of the plum tree were several blue-tits, hopping along the branches, among the leaves and among the tiny growths that would become plums, nipping away at greenfly and blackfly and all sorts of other wicked things.

Three cats were dozing in the sunlight at the back of Reynolds's garden, their half-shut eyes watching Reynolds with a certain degree of carelessness, for they almost trusted him, among humans, as being kind to cats, as being reasonably safe to be around. For a long moment Reynolds eyed them, the marmalade pair, and the botched tabby, all of them free agents in this difficult world. Reynolds had a piece of old ham; he went to fetch it.

Cats. There was a night, not all that long ago, when Reynolds lay in bed, half a-doze, half a-dream, and the cats set up their symphony on the back wall of his garden. Reynolds listened to the cacophony with some pleasure. The noise was huge, filling what was otherwise a quiet night. There were at least two toms, he knew, and several females, and the night being warm and long they would play on their cat guts for some time. The howling rose and fell and was punctuated by an occasional wild screech. Then silence for a short while but soon it would start again, always close by, always distant, always loud and always filled with the living notes of cat-being. Reynolds found it soothing.

He was just dozing off when he heard a strange and disturbing sound. He thought at first it was a gunshot fired from some distance away. There was a sharp crack, high-pitched, followed at once by a pained screech from one of the cats. Then silence. Nothing more. Reynolds decided some car in the distance had back-fired, that the noise had frightened the cats, that they had moved away. He forgot about it. He slept.

But the following morning there was a large black-and-white cat lying at the foot of the wall of his back garden. It was dead. Reynolds picked it up and examined it; he could see at once that there was dried, black blood on its shoulder. Reynolds put down the cat, found a small stick and probed the fur. He found a hole in the cat's flesh; there was a pellet lodged deep inside the hole. The pellet was grey in colour as Reynolds poked at it, it was leaden and covered now with the blood of the cat. Reynolds knew at once that it was an air gun of some kind that had fired the pellet. He looked around and up at the back bed-room window of the house next door; Randy, he thought, it had to be Randy. From the size and weight of the pellet Reynolds knew the gun must be a strong one, the cat's wound was serious, though it may have taken it some time to die. Reynolds was angry; after all it is in the nature of a cat to produce its cat-music, it is in the nature of love to sing to one's would-be lover, it is in the nature of a lover to howl down a rival. Carefully, Reynolds wrapped the cat in an old blanket, dug a deep hole in a corner of his garden and buried the creature. He murmured a few prayers over it but his thoughts were filled with anger against the slayer and would not rise towards God.

TWENTY-FIVE

Two nights after the slaying of the cat Reynolds again heard the caterwauling and sour-note musical serenading of the cats. They appeared once more to be on the back wall of Reynolds's garden. Quickly he got out of bed, opened as softly as he could the back window of his bedroom. There was a faint light from a quarter-moon away in the distance. With that light and with the weak orange glow of the streetlamps, Reynolds could make out three cats on his wall. There was one large cat, a tom, on the left corner of the wall; two smaller cats were crouched on the other corner of the wall; the play was underway, the instinctive urges and fleshly demands of the world were at work. The wailing and wauling rose and fell; Reynolds was entranced.

He noticed the bedroom window of the house next door open out. He could see the barrel of a gun carefully moving out from that window; it was Randy's house, that was Randy's room and Reynolds did not doubt that Genevieve was there with him, perhaps not urging him on, but certainly aware. There was that sudden crack, louder and more powerful to Reynolds's ears than the first time. Again there was a sudden skreeking shout from the cats and they disappeared at once. Reynolds waited; there was silence. Randy's window closed quietly. Reynolds closed his own window, leaving the curtains drawn so that the moonlight shone softly in. He went back to bed.

There was no cat-corpse in his garden next morning. Reynolds was relieved. Randy must have missed. Then Reynolds thought that perhaps he had not missed, that one of the cats may very well be creeping in the secret places of Heatherfield, hurt and bearing in its body the torture of a heavy leaden pellet embedded in its flesh. Searching for a quiet place to lay down and die. Searching for some release from a pain not understood. Reynolds felt more sad than before. He had to do something about it. He had to call next door. Perhaps he could speak to Genevieve. He tidied himself as best he could. He pressed the buzzer on Genevieve's door, very conscious of the small camera that was trained on him. He waited. Fidgeting. But it was Randy himself who opened the door, and Randy was big, big and threatening.

'What do you want?' Randy asked, making no attempt to invite Reynolds in.

Reynolds worked hard. 'Ca ... cats!' he managed, then shook his head, mimed the act of aiming a rifle, shook his head again.

'Ho!' said Randy. 'The cats, well, well, well. I should have known. You with your pigs and hens and that awful perpetual stench coming over into our garden ... I should have known you'd have cats too. Those fucking cats screeching and scrawking and keeping the whole neighbourhood awake all night. Your cats, are they?'

Reynolds again shook his head. 'But ...' he managed. 'They're ... cre ... cre ... creatures too!' It cost him a great effort but the words came out. Along with spittle and dribbles, but they came out.

Randy laughed. 'They won't be creatures for long, I can tell you, I'll see to that!' He began to turn back into his house, began to shut the door in Reynolds's face.

Reynolds needed to make one more effort; he stepped forward, putting one foot in the door. Randy waited and watched. But Reynolds was incapable. He stammered and no words came out. He held the jamb of the door and tried to force the words but they would not come.

'You're pathetic, do you know that?' Randy said. 'And keep your bloody eggs to yourself. We don't want them. Genevieve has to fling them into the garbage every time. Stick those fucking eggs up your ... and your hens and pigs with them!' He shut the door firmly.

Reynolds stood at the door a long time. The glum and iron face of the knocker stared back at him.

Reynolds did find another cat dead in a corner of his back garden a couple of weeks later; he did not know for sure how long it had been there, hiding itself away to die in a sweet corner, amongst dandelion clumps and nettles, behind a clump of bricks and garden stones. There was a small army of maggots busy in the sodden flesh. Reynolds heaped the bricks and stones over it. He felt sad, he missed the great open spaces of the fields where the heather had grown freely, where the kestrel hovered, where even the odd hare could be seen, its ears raised like watch-towers over the battlements of itself. He missed the people who took the things of nature as they presented themselves, part of the world in which they, all the creatures, took an important and accepted part.

His pigs were rooting away contentedly in their corner. There was the occasional murmuring from the hens at ease. The sun was warm, mid-morning and Randy's giant Russian sunflowers were peering in at him over the dividing wall. Prize sunflowers; must be at least six or seven feet high now, the flowerheads like great patterned plates. Without hesitation Reynolds went back into his kitchen, fetched his scissors, stood up on the edge of his chicken coop, drew the heads of the flowers towards him and fed them, one after the other, to his pigs. The sun continued to shine. The pigs grunted with happiness. The world did not stop. Reynolds felt no guilt. Sadness only, that it should have come to this.

TWENTY-SIX

The end-of-school days came, for Reynolds and his class. They held their sports on the sandy banks, down by the ocean. The sea was wonderful in its vastness, the ease of its roar at that noontime, waves coming in with a gentleness and beauty that were uplifting. And at the far end of the long, curving beach were the cliffs, majestic utterly, high and sacred, a haze hanging about them from the day's warmth. And elsewhere the green fields stretching away to the mountains, and the heathers giving the lower mountain reaches a radiance that was somehow godly, a rich lilac colour pervading all, with here and there patches of golden furze stippling the panorama.

They had fun, all of them, and Reynolds was deeply glad in himself. There was Rome to think of, that challenging adventure. There was a life ahead that was braced in security and peace. There were friends on earth; there was a friend in Heaven. He took part in the sports with a great heart. He was treated with respect and complete tolerance, as if everybody knew this was a special boy now and this was the last chance they would have of seeing him as a boy. He was on a donkey in the donkey race, his weight ensuring, of course, that the animal stood completely still as Reynolds shook and laughed and urged. The distance to be covered was the width of the beach itself at high tide, but the first donkey that actually crossed the winning line took the best part of twelve minutes to get there. Reynolds's animal never moved.

There was the slow-bicycle race and Reynolds mounted an ancient machine that belonged to the monastery. There was a dignity about that bicycle that suited a Brother in full regalia moving down a rhododendron lane but Reynolds atop the saddle was a different sight altogether. This time Reynolds was first across the line, the winner being the one who did not stir from the starting place. Again Reynolds collapsed in laughter. He stood and watched as Deirdre Weir was doing well in the girls' egg-and-spoon race and he instinctively moved forward, his hands out, when the egg fell from her spoon and dropped slowly, hopelessly, onto the grass. Deirdre was out. For a moment Reynolds's face mirrored tragedy but when Deirdre herself broke into laughter Reynolds was happy again.

So that afternoon passed, in laughter, sunshine and bliss. The last race of the day was the hundred-yards dash and Reynolds was in that too. To use the word *dash* of Reynolds's progress was to misuse the English language utterly. He wobbled and enthused and more or less collapsed forward and came in last of all, but he came in to a great cheer from the crowd. And at the end of it all they gave him a special prize, a beautifully bound copy of Virgil's *Aeneid* in translation, and it was perhaps a prize for making it this far, for succeeding in still being alive. But Reynolds longed for one of those small mock-silver cups that the others had been given, something to put on a shelf, a token that would remind him of having achieved something in his life. The parish priest, however, praised him highly, his work, his enthusiasm, his fortitude, and the people sent up a loud cheer that vanished like a breath into the seashore air.

TWENTY-SEVEN

How many days had it been? How many nights? Years. Months. Hours, long, countless hours. Under his weight of bedclothes Reynolds suffered. His limbs were the slender, hard branches of thorn bushes. His stomach was sometimes bloated with the volume of nothingness within, sometimes sunken like a centuries-old wreck. He was almost too weary to get up any more. Yet he suffered a continual, gnashing thirst. By now his sense of what it was to be hungry had left him; it had settled into an ongoing ache that was somewhere between agony and oblivion, and that seemed to lie like muddy water all through his body.

He decided he would work to fetch a jug of water, bring it beside his bed so he could suck from it now and again. When the thirst became intolerable. As it seemed to be almost all of the time. It was with enormous effort he hauled himself out of the bed. For a long time he sat on the edge of the bed, trying to gather energy, afraid his limbs might snap, like matchsticks, if he moved them too quickly. The old pyjamas were like great sacks about his wasting body.

He made it as far as the bathroom door. There were unusual noises inside. When he pushed the door open he saw Mother. She was kneeling over the toilet bowl, gazing down into it. She scarcely glanced up at him as he stood there, almost a spectre himself, watching her. She hum-humphed at him. She was wearing, for some reason, her Sunday best, that once-smart grey-black suit with the minuscule pinstripes through it, that once-white blouse with the frills at the neck; in her buttonhole she had a pin with a large pewter shamrock on it. And she was wearing that cocky black hat she wore when she felt cocky, that had a glossy blue feather in it, from some unfortunate peacock or other strange bird.

'Is it Patrick's Day?' Reynolds asked.

She looked up at him and laughed sarcastically. 'Not at all, you eejit you. How could it be Patrick's Day? Isn't it autumn? God help me but I dragged up an eejit. Isn't this wonderful, though? This.' And she reached and jerked the handle of the toilet, letting a flood of water from the cistern go shooshing all about the bowl. She jerked back with a little call of delight. Watching it. Then she looked up towards the ceiling. 'Don't need one of them old chains these days. They were awful, anyway, always rustin'. Breakin'. And then swingin' and swingin' till they left a bloody brown line on the cement of the wall, in the shape of a half loop. Do you remember?'

'Every house has these modern things now, Mother,' Reynolds said. 'For decades really. I remember the day Father was sitting in the outside toilet, at home, and he ...'

She wasn't listening to him. She had stood up and was looking at herself in the mirror over the sink. Touching the wisps of grey hair that slipped out from under her Sunday hat. But her eyes met his in the mirror. 'You're not lookin' your best, you know,' she said to him, and she laughed. 'No, you're lookin' a bit shook. But you're takin' your time with it. Can't hang about in these good duds for ever, you know. Waitin' for you. For the celebrations, like.'

'Sorry, Mother.'

She moved to the bath and turned the taps quickly. Reynolds hadn't often used the bath and there was a line of scum halfway up and all around the porcelain, and a long brown stain leading to the plughole.

'A sort of a dirty son you were, always, and are still, God help me,' she said. But she was impressed with the way the water came from the two taps into the bath. 'What's this third tap for?' she asked, reaching and turning it, then leaping back when a spray of water came from the shower spout above her. 'Well glory be to Christ!' she said. 'What on earth's that for?'

'That's a shower, Mother, for when if you don't want the trouble of having a full bath. You stand in under that. Like a shower of rain, like – '

'I can see it's like a shower of rain, do you think I'm daft or somethin'?' She turned off the taps, shook herself as dry as she could, looked Reynolds up and down a bit more, then headed rapidly for the door. Just as she left the bathroom she turned and said to him: 'Get a jerk into yourself now, there's a good lad, and don't take all year about it.' Then she was gone.

Reynolds took a large enamel jug from the floor; it was white, chipped here and there, but it served. He poured water into it from the bath tap until it was almost full. He found, however, he could not lift it out over the edge of the bath. It was too heavy. He was too frail. He emptied some out. Then he hoisted it carefully and left it on the floor of the bathroom. For a moment, he turned on the shower and put his head in under the spray, his mouth open. The water chilled him for a moment but he was able to take in some of the drops. He closed his eyes, imagining himself back on the heath in the old times, enjoying the slow beauty of the rain as it moved past in high, unhurried caravans, the world beyond it flowing in its own mirage of beauty and wonder. For a short moment he knew again what it had once been like, to be young, and free, and almost happy. Joy, he knew, can raise a man towards thoughts of eternity. Suffering, like he was knowing now, plunged a man into the cold and swirling waters of time. Can a man die before his death? Reynolds thought so. He thought he was dead now, just going through the motions still, the motions of corporal and spiritual pain. A man must die before his death. And, carefully and painfully heaving the jug from the bathroom to the side of his bed, Reynolds made his way back onto that space that would become his resting-place, until some unfortunate eventually found what was left of him. With a great sigh of relief he lowered himself back onto the bed.

TWENTY-EIGHT

They gave Reynolds an old suitcase that had belonged to one of the Brothers who was now lying at peace in the monastery graveyard. It was none too large but contained enough space, and more, for the few pieces of clothing Reynolds owned. He was warned: Rome, it will be warm. But the sea-crossing will be cold. Bring several different kinds of clothes. Reynolds only had one suit, now too small for him, the suit he had worn to the funeral some years before, short now in the sleeves, in the trouser leg, and he had to keep the top button of the fly open and wear braces, not one of the modern belts, so that the trouser would fit about his waist. Then he had an old pair of trousers that Brother Leo had cast off; they were frayed, but clean. He had two shirts and he figured he could wear his vest if the weather got too hot. Brother Angelo Maria was kind enough to buy him a pair of open sandals and a fine, light green, modern T-shirt with short sleeves and open neck. He packed his Virgil; he packed his *Golden Treasury* and he placed in a pocket of his jacket the bracelet that Deirdre Weir had given him. He was ready.

Brother Leo Mason and Reynolds set out early on a July morning on the great journey. Each carried one suitcase, Reynolds's was tied about with strong fishing-twine. They walked side by side up the laneway from the monastery to the main road. The sun was brilliant, though the chill of early morning hung in the air. The larks were already filling the sky above the heathers with their warm pouring of song; thrushes in the hawthorns offered their perfect lyrics. Reynolds had never felt so happy. They stood together at the monastery gate, waiting.

Between Leo and Reynolds there had grown an understanding. If ever a man could become a second father to a boy, then it had happened in this case. Little needed to be spoken between them, a look, a smile, a glance, even a stuttered beginning of words, sufficed. They left the suitcases down on the roadside and Leo walked out onto the centre of the empty road and leaped up in the air, clapping his hands in glee. For him, this was a special pilgrimage. He liked to get out of the clinging and heavy soutane and rope and rosary and feel more free in the black suit, the white shirt, the half-collar, the black stock. He liked the fine black hat that would leave its tidemark of sweat about his brow. Reynolds grinned with pleasure.

There were few passengers on the big green bus that morning; the conductor stepped out jauntily and climbed the steps onto the roof of the bus; Leo and Reynolds handed up their cases and the conductor fitted them in under the canvas cover. The bus journey was a short one, to take them to the ferry and then another bus on to the city. The island bus stopped at almost every laneway and isolated cottage and at times the conductor stepped out and chatted easily with someone at a gate or a doorway, before picking up some piece of luggage or produce and storing it away in a space at the back of the bus.

There was an old man and an old woman sitting in front of Reynolds. The excitement in Reynolds's stomach soon settled and he relaxed into enjoying the journey. Except that the two heads in front kept distracting him. There was a great red wen on the back of the old man's neck and a few stained-yellow hairs failed to cover it. Reynolds was smitten by the small folds and wrinkles on the man's skull and he imagined he could almost see the movements of the brain within. The old woman was small and wizened-looking, from years of labour and strain, and the knot of grey hair she had fixed at the back of her head with a brown hairpin kept coming undone; she reached small patient fingers to fix it back in place. They had shabby black coats about their bodies even on this warm and sunny morning, small brown packages held carefully on their knees, silence between

them, their rheumy eyes staring straight ahead. Reynolds tried
to turn from his thoughts to the passing fields, the geese at the
side of the road, the few cars, the fields with their fences and
their desultory herds of cattle, and he knew that without the
rare sunshine that lit up this particular day, the world would
look a totally inhospitable place to live in. He forced his mind
to think of Rome: of the excitement of the rest of the journey;
of the hopes he had for his own life.

They crossed England by train in the middle of the night, the
boat arriving into Holyhead bearing a young boy who was
neither fully awake nor fully asleep. He had a vague memory of
bustle and crowds, of trains shunting, of a huge shed where
someone asked him questions he couldn't answer. He depended
wholly on Brother Leo, to take his hand and guide him, to
speak for him, to produce passports and tickets and to explain,
to lead him to a hard seat in a crowded train that jerked and
shifted through the night, across a country and landscape he
could make nothing of until, early in the morning, he came
awake to a slowing train, to a vista of high and dirty brick walls
hemming them in, tracks crossing and recrossing each other,
and Leo smiling at him from a seat on the other side of the
compartment.

'London!' Leo whispered with satisfaction.

Reynolds later remembered a hauling of suitcases through
streets he had never believed could be so crowded. There was
hustling and shoving, people in greatcoats and suits even though
the day was hot and dusty and he and Leo were sweating. He
remembered sitting in a black taxi that took them through
impossible windings and tiny streets, horns blowing, huge buses
passing, until at last they drew up in front of another station,
hauled and heaved their suitcases again and were, at last, once
more sitting in the carriage of a train.

Leo disappeared for a moment, leaving Reynolds alone in the
carriage. He savoured the quietness. There was almost peace,
somewhere in the distance an engine shunting, somewhere a
sharp whistle blown, beyond the windows people moved as if

they were ghosts, most of them hurried and anxious-looking. His train idled, with perfect indifference, occasional sighs of steam escaping from somewhere. Reynolds leaned his head back against the seat, looked up at the suitcases on the rack overhead, then closed his eyes again, and dozed. Almost at once great floods of memory washed over him: he was back again in the heather field, alone in sunlight in his hide-out amongst the furze and its lovely blossoms, a book in his hands, wheatears scolding in the distance, a lark in the absolute blue of the sky and at home his father and mother waited for him, everything in order, settled and serene.

A carriage door banged shut and Reynolds was back again in his train. There was a sepia-coloured landscape opposite him, in a small black timber frame; it was a photograph of Kendal in the Lake District and for a short moment Reynolds's heart fluttered with recognition: Wordsworth! Coleridge! Southey! He was in the land of the great poets, of Shakespeare, of Milton, of Keats. He jumped up and slid across the top part of the window of the carriage but all that could be seen was another train idling alongside, and if he squinted hard upwards, he could catch a glimpse of a blue sky with a grey cloud moving gently across it.

Reynolds sat down again. What on earth am I doing here, he thought? Heading for Rome, questions of joining the Brothers, of spending all his life in a monastery, if ever he got back safely to the island. What on earth am I doing here? What on earth am I doing on earth? And where is Leo? A sense of panic shot through him, as murderous as a knife-jab; what if he had been abandoned, here in a station somewhere in London, with no address to go to, no money in his pocket, no speech in his mouth, anguish in his heart? He opened the carriage door and stepped down onto the platform, holding the door open behind him. The same hustling and rushing and shoving went on all along the platform; there were porters pushing trolleys covered with small and large and medium trunks and suitcases; there were women searching in purses while walking distractedly along, men clinging to small black briefcases as they moved rapidly by, their eyes watchful; hawkers calling out their news-papers, their sandwiches, their teas, and there, at last, coming slowly and thoughtfully along the platform towards him was Leo, Brother Leo, his own Brother Leo Mason.

As the train moved speedily and gently through the rich pastures of Kent, Brother Leo gave Reynolds a long talk on trust and faith. They were the only ones in the carriage and both of them sat at the great and dusty window, watching out over the fields, the houses neatly kept, the gardens gently trimmed.

'You will remember Peter,' Leo said. 'Jesus invited him onto the waters of the lake, to join him, and Peter at first stepped out without hesitation. And he walked on the water towards his Friend. But he lost trust, you see, his faith gave out and at once he began to sink. Jesus had to reach out His hand to him, to hold him up. Now, my dear Reynolds, you must keep faith, too, because we are living in a world that is enormous, difficult and demanding but we know with certainty that we have a God who loves us without hesitation, without undue demands, all we have to do is live our lives to the best of our abilities and know He will sustain us, no matter what. Be assured, my dear Reynolds, if you have faith, you will walk out on the waters and you will not drown.'

Reynolds felt a warm glow move through his body. He was happy now, and this big, gentle man in front of him had all the golden keys that he would ever need and he would trust him, absolutely, always. And of course he would try and trust to his God, to that same God of the louvred belfry at home, of the quiet and whisperful chapel, of the still and sun-drenched graveyard. And here he was, travelling in the great world, safe and secure, and a great adventure opening up in front of him.

'We are passing through a world where wars have been fought,' Leo went on. 'And not all that long ago. These fields were cowering under fighter planes, bombs were falling on them, the sons of these homes were in foreign countries, suffering and dying under the most awful of conditions. Because although we have a God of love that underpins all our lives, our being, our doings, yet within us all there is a great curse, a curse that we call original sin, the curse of time that we must spend working our way across this world into God's eternity. And we fail so often to live up to that love that our God offers us. We are walking on water always, my dear Reynolds, trusting in our God, and not in human ways, because human ways lead to death and selfishness and destruction. We know that underneath our cautious tread there is a great void, and that those who fall through because of their own utter contempt for the great love offered us by God fall through for lack of faith, and their souls will not survive, they will be annihilated and will not live again. Trust in life, in love, and above all in Jesus, Reynolds, trust in him, step out boldly on the great ocean that is life and remember always that down under the waters there is darkness, emptiness and despair, but above the waters there is warmth, and sunshine and love.'

Reynolds thought of these words as the ferry left the harbour in Dover and moved out onto the waters of the English Channel. He watched, with awe, the great white walls of the cliffs fade away into the haze of day; he watched the gulls follow the wake of the ship, crying for scraps; he watched the wake itself, becoming, as he did so, a little dizzy; he imagined the world of fish and darkness and strangely different plant life that must be down there below the waves; he imagined the ship going under, his grasping for breath, for land, and he turned away quickly, the terror of drowning, of losing hold, overwhelming him.

They boarded another train that evening, Reynolds still overcome, but now by the bustle and strangeness of people in another land, talking in another language. He felt an utter stranger on the earth and without Leo's strength and certainties he knew he would have folded himself away into a ball and hidden in a corner until he was either dead or someone would come by to rescue him. Leo seemed unperturbed by this strangeness, this shifting from train to ship to train to ship to train. They waited a long time in the station and the carriage grew crowded, Reynolds finding himself squeezed into a corner opposite Leo. The people were confident, alert and perpetually busy, chatting away in loud strange words, fixing their luggage, unfolding newspapers, opening magazines; many of them had sandwiches folded away, one man had a bottle of wine sticking out of each pocket of his greatcoat and he sat leaning forward on the seat, winking at Reynolds, grinning at the world.

From the moment the train jolted into movement Reynolds lost all sense of reality. The train moved slowly at first through the back yards of Calais, then out onto a wonderfully rolling pasture-land with trees planted in neat rows, the fields all carefully cultivated, while the people in the carriage settled down to a shiftless silence, reading, munching, dozing. Every now and then Reynolds glanced over at Brother Leo, for assurance. The man with the greatcoat had taken a cork out of one of the bottles with his teeth and was drinking his way through the contents, grinning at Reynolds, though he never offered anyone the bottle. Dusk settled over the fields of France, a faint yellow and glimmering light came on in the carriage and Reynolds fell into a deep and dream-ridden sleep.

He woke in a darkness that was heavy with his own sleeping and dim under vague lighting, yellow and old, that shone through the now-grimy window of the carriage from the station where they had stopped. Paris! He sat up suddenly. The carriage was emptying itself, though Brother Leo remained fast asleep on the seat opposite him. He could hear voices, the strange sharp sounds of French spoken loudly or shouted along the platform; the banging of carriage doors, the seeming silence of the train that had settled itself to a kind of panting restfulness, the movement on the corridor outside, all of this disturbed Reynolds but left Leo asleep. Paris. The very name aroused the strangest of emotions in him, a curiosity mingled with dread, the vastness of the city, its history of violence and its gatherings of art, its music, its river, churches and night-haunts, all of this he had read about, all of this intrigued and terrified him at the same time. Cautiously he stepped out onto the corridor and leaned his head out the window over the platform.

There was a great deal of bustling about the station; porters shoving their carts and hauling trunks, passengers greeting friends, people hurrying like souls lost in some underworld, while here and there passed along the platform offering for sale, from trays tied about their necks, strange-looking breads and sausages, strange-smelling coffee and cakes. The dome of the station was not very high, the iron girders holding up a filthied glass darkened utterly now by night. A lazy, ochre glow came from the lamps placed fitfully here and there and all the time the train itself seemed to sigh irregularly, as if utterly tired of its task and exhausted already at the great demands still ahead of it.

The strangeness and difference made Reynolds turn back quickly to share his feelings with Brother Leo. He turned from the opened window and went back to the carriage door but Leo was still fast asleep in his corner. Reynolds watched him for a while, affection welling up within him. When Reynolds put his head out the window again he was startled. The platform was completely empty. An eerie silence had descended everywhere and only a few pigeons bumped themselves about in dark and dusty corners of the rest rooms and offices. All the passengers had gone. All the porters, too, and all the officials. Only a few scraps of paper were shifting about in the desultory occasional breezes. And then, down at the far end of the platform, Reynolds saw somebody, a figure that appeared quite familiar to him, a man moving very slowly up along the platform in his direction. It was the sense of familiarity, as well as the sudden emptying of the entire station, that riveted Reynolds's attention on the man. He was big, not well dressed, he held a small and battered-looking suitcase in his right hand. He wore a cap, the peak of it falling down before his eyes, and his face was turned down towards the platform floor. Reynolds heard, distinctly, the slow, hard clunk of the man's boots on the platform. Slow clunk, slow clunk, familiar and vaguely upsetting.

When he was within two carriages of Reynolds the man looked up a moment, as if seeking some explanation of where he was, and where he was supposed to go. He hesitated, gazing to his left, towards the offices and rest rooms and exits, and suddenly Reynolds called out, 'Father! Father! It's me. I'm here. I'm here!' The man glanced once in Reynolds's direction, then seemed to decide and moved quickly towards a door that led out of the station into some room or hallway or vestibule. He disappeared. For a moment Reynolds was stricken. Could it possibly have been his father? It could not. Oh it could not.

His father was dead. Long dead. And yet, that shape, that
hangdog self-conscious awkwardness and guilt in his bearing,
even that old battered suitcase, the clothes, the face, the cap ...
all of it, how could it be other than his father? Who else could,
in this strangely lit and echoing and now empty landscape,
move Reynolds into such a sudden paroxysm of loss and
sadness and misery. He began to cry. Silent tears, at first, as he
stood, his hands holding the rim of the window, his face
outside, his body within, eyes turned to where the figure had
disappeared; then shuddering sobs and sighs, deeply rooted
moans of sadness and loss until Reynolds's whole body shivered
with a sense of anguish he had not known for years and he
drew back from the window, back from this strange world,
stumbling back into the carriage where he flung himself down
on the seat opposite Leo, curled himself into a ball, and wept
bitterly.

He had fallen into that deep hole over which all human
beings walk at all times, into which they can fall at some un-
guarded moment. Anytime. Anywhere. His face, though he had
it hidden from the world, from Leo lest he should wake, was red
and swollen with his tears. Reynolds scarcely noticed the noises
beginning to happen about him, a new bustling, new move-
ments, until somebody touched him on the shoulder and he
jerked upright, suddenly. The same dim light was on in the
carriage; Leo seemed to be still deeply asleep in the corner op-
posite him, but now the carriage was filling up again and a man,
big and kindly looking, was standing over him, gazing down at
him and murmuring something, in French perhaps, or in Italian,
solicitous, eager to help. Reynolds knew what he was saying to
him and he shook his head and tried to smile. He pointed to Leo
in the corner, then to himself, he smiled again, then settled back
down into his corner, willing himself to go into the comfortable
darkness of insensibility.

It was in that moment of folding his arms against his chest for
comfort that he felt something in the inside pocket of his jacket.
He knew at once what it was and he reached in eagerly and
brought it out. He relished the coolness of the bracelet in his
fingers, the silver chain joining the two delicate ends. Idly he

tried again to fit it on his wrist but he had grown even larger, the bracelet seemed even smaller. But it brought an unusual warmth and comfort into Reynolds's breast and he settled back more peacefully to sleep.

TWENTY-NINE

Reynolds wondered if, indeed, he had actually been asleep or had floated away on a small dinghy of pain, floated on the current of his own weakness and hunger, every bone in his body begging him for pity, for sustenance. He simply opened his eyes and knew he was back in his own miserable room, his suffering body, his aching soul. For a long time, he lay in an absence heavy with slowly shifting dust-motes, his eyes half open, uncertain of where he was, uncertain even of who he was. He felt the earth shaking beneath or about him, as if he were in a railway carriage, or on the open sea. The pain he was suffering, all through his body, held him numb.

At last he moved. He shifted his body, trying to rise, and the pains combed through him, everywhere. He was too weak even to moan. He succeeded in sitting up in the bed. Even the clothes over his knees seemed too heavy now but he was cold, very cold. He sat for a while, vaguely aware of the dimness in the room, of the half-closed curtains, dimly aware of Mother, too, who stood, arms akimbo, just inside the closed door, watching him. He forced a wry smile and turned his eyes towards her. He closed his eyes again, in mute acknowledgement of his foolishness. She shook her head. She knew all about his foolishness. He moved his legs, cautiously, over the edge of the bed, touching his feet to the floor. Now he sat on the edge of the bed, exhausted already with the effort.

His eyes were taken by the pillow. It was grey with dirt from his head, he knew that, but now there was more than dirt there, there were small tufts of hair. His left hand reached slowly and picked some of the hairs off the pillow. He felt quite indifferent to this added loss, though his right hand moved onto his scalp and he knew a vague sense of sorrow. How he must look now, bald patches in his already balding hair, the skull, no doubt, shoving through, and ugly. His left hand squeezed the pillow in a sudden surge of anger and anguish and the pain the effort caused him forced him to shout.

'What do you expect, you kind of a species of an idiot?' his mother muttered angrily. 'Give a fish a worm and he'll swallow it whole, and relish it, the fool, hook and all. Oh you fool, you permanent, ejaculatin' fool!'

Reynolds was too far gone to pay any attention to the rantings of his mother. The pillow slipped from his hand and fell off the bed onto the ground. And there, he had almost forgotten it, he *had* forgotten it, lay the silver bracelet given to him decades ago, centuries ago! by Deirdre Weir. And he was back again, suddenly, in that train, just after it had begun to leave the station in Paris, that black night, that grim and ugly night of loss and loneliness, and he was curled up in sorrow in the corner of the carriage, shuddering with his emptiness, and in his curling he had felt that bracelet in the pocket of his jacket. He had put it in there to be company to him, to have its hardness and softness against his heart, and now he had taken it out, still hiding it from the strangers on the train, and he had held it, like a soother, like a hand, and it had stilled him, and he had slept.

Even in reaching for it now, there on the stained sheet, Reynolds felt an almost unbearable spiritual pain as well as the physical suffering he was going through. How easy it would be to stop this suffering, a simple descent into his kitchen, a cup of reviving tea, sugar in it, and perhaps a stale biscuit, nothing more, and he would be on the way back into his life again. How easy that would be, and how good. But he knew that even then the spiritual suffering would merely increase, now Leo had gone, and he did not know where Deirdre Weir was; he had not known for years. And in any case, she would be wholly other now, indifferent to him, no doubt, possibly hostile to the memory of her childish foolishness years ago.

He would have cried again, but there were no tears left, and he did not have the energy to cry. Holding the bracelet in his hand he managed to make his way once more into the bathroom. A small sip of water from the cold tap, to keep him from impossible agonies. That was all he would take. Then he would get back into that train beside Leo, and doze, and wake up in Rome, and everything would be good again. Into the train? he tried to laugh. Now even time was leaving him, his head was becoming like porridge, dull and creamed and wet. Into bed, of course, into the bed, where he would continue his journey until it ended of itself. Naturally.

THIRTY

When Reynolds woke the train had stopped somewhere in a lush and steep valley. He felt Deirdre's bracelet pressing hard against the palm of his hand. He was cramped, every bone in his body stiff and sore. But he sat up, slowly, and gazed out the window. The train was hissing quietly. But otherwise there was a great silence. Reynolds suddenly realised there was nobody left in the carriage. He jumped up, hurting his bones, and he gasped. He rubbed the laziness from his eyes and tried to shake the sadness that still hung heavily about his heart. Then he stepped out of the compartment onto the passageway, out and down the steep steps of the carriage.

Many people were gathered on the grass verges near the railway line. For a while all that Reynolds wanted to do was find Brother Leo. But there was already a sweep of warm sunshine that bathed his body in gentleness. There was a delicate and lovely scent on the air. He knew he was standing in the midst of wonderful beauty. The railway line ran along the lower slope of a hill; there was a long slow curve of the line behind them and on the hill-slopes above the line Reynolds could see row after row of small shrubs, neatly tied and staked. Vines! he knew it. Grapes! Higher up the slope the trees were rich and varied and also planted in neat rows. Down and across the lower slopes were fields of flowers of many sorts, with houses here and there, quaint-looking, with black-and-white gable ends and tall chimneys. And further still, down near the valley's core, a river flowed and sparkled in the early sunshine and there, breathtakingly beautiful, was a large meadow of sunflowers, huge heads bowed gently, the golden glow from them touching his being towards praise.

For a long time Reynolds gazed at the beauty of the place. Then he turned. The people were all standing, too, enjoying the sunshine. And there, further ahead, away in the distance, Reynolds could see mountains, endless ranges of them disappearing into a haze of cloud or distance, and many of them against the bright azure of the sky rose high and white with snow. Something happened then in Reynolds's soul, a great lift of joy and a breathful sigh of release, as if the cleanliness and loveliness all around him were enough to bathe in for ever. His whole body relaxed in delight and every sense of loss and heaviness lifted from him, like a wet, heavy blanket being taken off his entire body. He stood and, though he wasn't aware of it, he worshipped. He heard then the high and challenging hoot of another train and saw it coming from the south, on the other track, coming from that distant and overwhelmingly lovely country of mountain and snow, coming with a great pride of white smoke and a roar of power. He put his hands to his ears and called out in delight as it pounded past on the other side of their train, the rattling and shaking of the world being something shocking and gratifying to him. Then it had passed, away into this world of strangeness, vastness and glory that made Reynolds aware of how small he was, how tiny his concerns, how helpless his own being.

And there was Leo, moving towards him, smiling, a large sandwich in his right hand. 'Switzerland,' Leo said, nodding in the direction from which the other train had come. 'And beyond it, Italy. Isn't it glorious?' Reynolds nodded his head and took the sandwich, biting into it with appetite and gratitude, and smiling broadly at the wise head of Brother Leo. He felt happy, wildly happy, and alive with a new certainty and determination. They heard a commanding hoot from the engine of their train and a guard came down along the embankment, waving a green flag at them, ordering everybody back aboard.

Reynolds spent the whole of that day with his face pressed against the window of the train. Vast landscapes, riverscapes, mountainscapes glided past, strange trees, tall and proud, rivers that seemed swollen with melt-water and flowed with a splashing, spraying greenish-yellow foam over rocks and boulders before they eased into a lazy, wide blackness among fields and towns; he saw wide fields of sunflowers, brilliantly bright and vulnerable; there were high slopes, where cattle, large bells about their necks, seemed to browse at a severe angle, near the dark entrances to woods, near wooden shacks that had a strange and irregular beauty about them; and always, coming into view and disappearing again, high snow-covered peaks backed by a turquoise sky.

At last the train seemed to come down from higher slopes and paused on the borders of Italy. There was a long stop while the engine was changed, and the station, its great number of tracks spread out over a large area, rusted and gleamed under the sun. A train, high and haughty and puffing roundly, came from the south and stopped just two sections of track away from them. Reynolds watched the drippings of moisture onto the already blackened ground about, he marvelled at the dark green though shabby-looking vegetation, straggly unflowering plants that survived beneath and beside the great trains and there, suddenly, he noticed a lizard, its dark olive colouring, its slightly curved shape, its absolute stillness keeping it almost invisible. But it had laid itself down across the rail, just in front of the first wheel of the engine, and was indifferent to the puffing, the steam, the hissing, unaware of the danger. Reynolds watched, petrified; he jerked back from the window and drew Leo's attention to the delicate creature and its peril. Leo was dozing and not too pleased to be brought to his senses. He cautioned Reynolds not to worry, that God's creatures were in God's care and everything would be all right. Leo laid his arm back across the window ledge, laid his head back against the rest, and closed his eyes again. Reynolds watched the lizard closely. He heard a high-pitched whistle from the far platform, he saw the great engine emit a huge and sudden cloud of steam and instantly the lizard had disappeared, as fast as thought, as sudden as the click of a finger, and Reynolds smiled broadly out on the lovely, sun-filled world of Italy.

They arrived at Stazione Termini in Rome in the late evening. Leo bustled and fussed about in the carriage. The other passengers, too, were shifting and organising themselves. Reynolds held onto his one small suitcase and waited. When they stepped out onto the platform he was astonished at the size of the station. There were lines upon lines of railway tracks, all leading up to the low buffered wall at the end. The high roof above was girdered and covered in glass that was shattered here and there and dark with years of dirt and dust. Pigeons flew about up there, swooping and gliding. And everywhere the passengers hurried and talked and bothered as if every moment's delay was to be a catastrophe, every other person out to get in their way and thwart them of their purposes.

Leo and Reynolds moved slowly along with the crowd, presented their tickets at a desk and came out onto the streets of Rome. For Reynolds it was a special moment. The late evening was darkening but the heat was still heavy on the air. It struck Reynolds the way a thump on the back would strike him and he staggered in astonishment. Almost at once he could feel the sweat breaking out on his forehead and he had to lay down his suitcase and rub his face with the back of his hand.

Leo dived. 'Reynolds!' he said sternly. 'Never, never must you leave anything out of your hands in this city. It's Rome, the holy city, but not everybody in the city is holy. I promise you. There are thousands of young lads like yourself who are clever and fast and always on the watch. Thieves. Vagabonds. Professionals almost. So watch out. And keep any money you will have close against your body so you'll know where it is at every moment. Now, take up your suitcase again. We have just a little walk and then we'll be home.'

Reynolds was watching all the bustling on the street outside the station. There were cars and buses all making as much noise as they possibly could. People were shouting and gesticulating and at the crossroads near the station there was a policeman standing in a kind of pulpit in the centre of the road, waving his arms and blowing constantly the most shrill and piercing whistle that Reynolds had ever heard. There were young boys everywhere, and Reynolds could see how they watched, not just him and Leo, but everyone. They chatted easily amongst themselves, laughed, punched one another playfully, but Reynolds, being warned, saw the glint of watchfulness in those dark eyes.

They walked slowly down a very beautiful street. 'Via Tiburtina,' Leo pronounced proudly. There were a lot of people strolling along the street; the shops were still open, gallantly lit and cool-looking with great marble floors and huge, overwhelming candelabras. The men were mostly in dark jackets, in spite of the impossible heat of the evening, the women in long and elegant dresses, arms bare to the elbows. Reynolds clung to his suitcase. He was sweating profusely. He tried to avoid bumping into anybody but it was almost impossible, several times men, young and old, and sometimes even women, came shoving by at a great speed. Reynolds had not believed the world was so great; he had not believed there were so many people in it, and that they all seemed in haste to achieve something.

After a short while Leo turned into another street. This one was darker, the houses on either side were high, five, six and even seven storeys high, and it was difficult to see the dark grey sky high above. There were swifts and swallows, Reynolds thought, house martins, too, perhaps, streaming through the air and in and out amongst all the electric and phone wires strung out above; in the confined spaces of the street their high-pitched calls and screams added to Reynolds's sense of confusion and noise. 'Via Serena,' Leo announced. They stopped suddenly outside a massive door of dark wood. It seemed to be a house much as any other house in the street though directly across from it Reynolds noticed a church, its vast porticoes and enormous doorway in complete darkness now, looming, its spire rising away into the awful darkness above. They had arrived: Convento San Francisco, Via Serena, Roma.

THIRTY-ONE

In Heatherfield estate a marked police car was an unusual thing to see. But one had drawn up outside Reynolds's door. Someone knocked.

'A few questions, if you don't mind, sir,' a man said when Reynolds answered. He showed Reynolds some sort of badge and gestured towards the police car parked outside the gate, a uniformed policeman leaning against the side.

The detective, friendly and understanding, dressed in a light blue suit, dark blue shirt and purple tie, sat and had coffee with Reynolds and patiently waited while Reynolds answered his questions by writing his words down on a piece of paper. The detective copied them down into a notebook. Reynolds had told this man – Eamonn, he insisted on being called – about the cats, about the shots he had heard in the night-time. He did not mention Randy, he did not write where he thought the shots had come from. Eamonn seemed only vaguely interested, though he wrote and nodded and chatted on encouragingly.

Eamonn seemed more interested in the eggs that stood in a bowl on Reynolds's table. He picked them up, rubbing gently at some tiny feathers still adhering. 'Rather fine eggs, these,' he said. 'Free range, too, I suspect.' Reynolds nodded proudly and gestured towards the back yard. 'Can I see?' Eamonn asked, rising slowly.

He went out into Reynolds's back yard, moving non-chalantly, inviting Reynolds to accompany him. They stood a while outside the back door, Eamonn with his hands carelessly in his pockets. Reynolds gazed around his small demesne; in the fenced-off area his pigs, Venus, Cupid and Juno, were all three lazing on the hard earth, half a-doze. The hens were pecking desultorily here and there, their gilded colours soft and warm in the easy sunshine. Plums on the tree were beginning to colour nicely and under the far wall the apples were plumping too.

'Lovely, lovely,' Eamonn murmured. 'You have your own life here, Reynolds, and it's rather unusual, if I may say so. Pigs. Hens. Cats and pigeons and perhaps an odd fox or two, I suppose?'

Reynolds knew it wasn't really a question. There was something rather cautious and hard in Eamonn's voice that disturbed Reynolds. He came and stood in front of the detective, gestured towards the yard and tried to say 'Well?'

Eamonn moved quickly away from him, out a little further into the garden. 'I will have to say, Reynolds, and I say this reluctantly mind, I will have to say there have been complaints. Yes. Complaints.' He stood a while, sniffing the air. 'Hmmm,' he said, his head raised, his eyes watchful. He glanced towards the upper windows of the houses on either side of Reynolds's. Then he turned firmly towards the fenced-off area and moved close to the wires. Lazily one of the pigs got up and moved forward to investigate. 'It's the smell, you see, Reynolds. It's pervasive. And not too pleasant, you know, none too pleasant at all.'

Reynolds, too, sniffed the air. To him it was pure, filled with life-giving scents, fresh and healthy. He shoved his neck out quizzically.

Eamonn continued to gaze, as if abstractedly, into the pen. 'There have been several complaints, down at the office, you know. About the smell. It's the pigs, I reckon. The pigs.'

Reynolds went back in the house and came out with his pen and paper. 'The pigs are clean,' he wrote.

'Then it's the chickens,' Eamonn said. 'It must be the smell of the chicken-shit. I can get it myself and I sure as hell don't fancy it. And then there's the noise, it must be the cockerels. Crowing. And the pigs grunting. That kind of thing. Not natural right here, you know. Not natural at all.'

Reynolds wrote on his paper: 'There are no cocks. All hens. They don't crow.'

'That may be,' Eamonn said. 'Hens, pigs, foxes, geese ... who knows? But the fact that there's so many complaints. Something will have to be done. Something.'

Reynolds was getting very worried now. He wrote: 'WHO?'

Eamonn turned away from the fence and began to move slowly back towards the house. With his right hand he gestured towards the house next door. 'The beauty,' he said quietly. 'I expect she has a delicate set of nostrils, you know, as well as a delicate everything else. A real beauty. She is. And needs nought but beauty about her.' He paused. 'Wonderful eggs, as you say, and pigs and geese and stuff. Right. Thank you, Reynolds. You'll be hearing, I say, you'll be hearing ...'

When he had gone Reynolds came back out into his yard. He opened the gate into the pen and stood sadly amongst his animals. Cupid came and rubbed his snout gently against his trouser leg. Several of the hens came lazily towards him, anticipating grains. Reynolds squatted down amongst them. He touched the hirsute hides of the pigs, he tipped the feathers of the hens. There was, at least, some comfort in the touch.

THIRTY-TWO

Together Brother Leo and Reynolds took the long walk from Via Serena towards the Vatican. It was hot. And very crowded. Reynolds sweated. He had sweated all night and had slept badly. But he was excited; a visit to the Vatican today, then the meeting tomorrow with Brother Bonaventure, a meeting that would decide his future, then a walk on the famous Appian Way the day after that and a visit to the Catacombs. Reynolds's stomach churned in anticipation.

The windows of the glorious shops were packed with goods: clothes, bags, jewellery. People jostled and hurried, but they all appeared to be in good humour, all of them with destinations, dreams, tasks, money in their pockets, or money assured. Reynolds dragged behind a little, fascinated and overwhelmed. Along the Corso Vittorio Emanuele Brother Leo became a little frustrated by the heat, the people and the laggard on the sidewalk behind him. He took Reynolds by the hand and ushered him along as if he were a little child. The world too big for Reynolds, his place in it uncertain.

At last they came to the river and crossed on the Ponte Umberto. Leo paused on the bridge and leaned over; 'Tiber!' he murmured with extraordinary reverence. Reynolds, too, leaned over to look down into the famous river. He was disappointed; there was little water flowing and what there was seemed greenish and dirty, a trickle like you'd see along some hedgerow back at home. Here and there rubbish was thrown and stuck in the muddy bottom or was held amongst the small stones that were at the sides of the water; Reynolds could even see small bushes

growing where he had expected a mighty flow. The boy point-
ed, wordlessly, and Leo understood. 'It's summer, Reynolds. It's
hot. There's no rain. The river dries up a little, but you can be
sure in the winter it'll be a torrent. The Tiber, boy. We're lucky
to be here. Lucky indeed.'

Leo was admiring the great spread of the city as it rose now
to their left, and to their right the city of the Vatican itself could
just be seen. They hurried on. Eventually they came into the
great square before St Peter's and Reynolds stopped, over-
whelmed by majesty. The space was busy with people, so many
different coloured people, in different coloured clothes, in all
sorts of clothes, in hats, caps, shirtsleeves, every possible and im-
possible combination, all the world, it seemed to him, wander-
ing in awe about the vast square that was open to the heavens
where pigeons wheeled and flew, yet all of it leading inevitably
to the massive church at the top of the square. Mouth hanging
open, hand in Brother Leo's hand, Reynolds eventually entered
the church itself.

It was enormous, terrifyingly high, filled with awesome
echoes, dwarfing every human thought. The decorations ap-
peared to Reynolds to be sumptuous beyond belief, beyond
necessity. People moved about the empty apse that appeared to
Reynolds to be as large as the seashore of his island, and as full
of whispering sounds, and as hopeless of access. Away in the
distance he could see the altar with a magnificent canopy of
gilded bronze, huge spiral columns, and he thought that here
must be the dwelling place of God Himself. Together Reynolds
and Leo had moved, as in a dream, up along the apse and now
stood under the spectacular dome with its pictures of saints all
gazing down from impossible heights onto the small and foolish
human beings on the marble floor beneath. They gazed up, as if
they were gazing in through the window of a difficult and
demanding heaven and suddenly Reynolds found himself sitting
hard on the floor, dizzy and dismayed.

He sat a while, Leo standing still beside him. He looked
down then at his own shoes, scuffed and greatly in need of
polishing, the laces tied in a knot that could never be undone
because they had broken so often and had shortened. And his

stockings: Reynolds could just see the tip of his heel on the left appear above the shoe, only a few tiny frayed threads holding the stocking in place. And the knees of his trousers, so scuffed and frayed and greyed with washing and ironing, all hopeless and worn and unholy. He found the tears flowing silently down his cheeks and he brushed them away with his hand. He got up then, and despite all Leo's pleas and blandishments, Reynolds walked slowly and determinedly, his eyes cast down, out the door that would have allowed a herd of elephants through, and onto the sunlit piazza.

Without Leo, he began to move towards home, towards the monastery of Saint Francis on Via Serena, where at least he could gaze on the modest statue of the poor friar, and smell ordinary kitchen smells, and touch the ceilings if he jumped high enough, and sleep in a room small enough not to cow him into terror. And he wished, at once, to move further than that, to get back to his own island, to his heather fields, to that small belfry with the slightly hoarse bell that would ring its call for simple prayers to simple people across simple fields.

THIRTY-THREE

It was coming close to the end of October. Leaves were already strewing the streets of Heatherfield. Gutters were beginning to be clogged and sudden breezes sent delightful scattered packages of golden and red and red-golden leaves scurrying down Heatherfield Gardens, and to gather in a neat pile against the end wall of the street, to be scattered back in the opposite direction as soon as the wind changed, sending the cats wild with the pleasure of the chase, creating small glorious whirlwinds of rusty beauty in unexpected corners. Reynolds gathered them when he could, for composting.

He was sweeping up the leaves in his back yard one evening when a sudden bang not far from his back wall startled him. It was loud and challenging, louder and more echoing than Randy's air gun, and almost immediately he saw a rainbow of white stars shoot up into the sky. Soon, he remembered, it would be Hallowe'en, and all sorts of bangers and clatterers and sparkers would be set off day and night around the estate. Reynolds had his rituals to deal with the influx of willed terror. His hens would be quickly distressed by the noise and would flutter and cackle and cease to lay, some of them would moult a little, all of them would be frightened out of the tiny ganglion of wits that they might own. So in the early evenings Reynolds would lock them up in the coop he had made, high enough off the ground to deter any roaming fox, comfortable and safe enough for them to worry that bit less about the strange and terrifying lights and explosions around them. The pigs would be happy enough to snuggle in onto the straw he left for them under the coop, where there would be shelter and warmth and safety. Or so Reynolds thought.

On Hallowe'en itself Reynolds enjoyed answering the door to the wandering gangs of children who dressed themselves up in all the tissues and shrouds of dread and horror, as if by becoming themselves the marauding dead they might obviate all possibility of terror in their own young lives. And all over the estate the sounds rang out, like artillery fire, like precision bombing, with the rainbow fireworks, the Catherine wheels, the bangers. It was a precious night and Reynolds indulged himself in nuts and chocolates and grew sad and forlorn when the children had done their rounds and had disappeared to divide their booty. Who would there be now to knock on his door?

Later that night, as Reynolds sat in his front room, reading from his *Golden Treasury*, the explosions and gunfire sounds grew more desultory. But every now and then a report sounded that came to Reynolds's ears as being too close for comfort; three times he went to his front door and looked out, wondering at the noise of it, startled, a little perplexed. And then, taking some of the left-over fruit, he headed for his back yard to offer his pigs the treat of fine sweet apples. As he crossed his kitchen towards the back door he was astounded to see the brightness of the yard outside, as if a whole galaxy of fireworks had been set off, bathing the estate in a bright and shifting light. Reynolds opened the door into his yard and stepped out.

The usual lemon-yellow glow from the streetlamps struggled with the darkness of the night, but great flames were rising from the hencoop halfway down Reynolds's yard. For a moment he stood motionless, stunned. He had suffered a great life-change before as the result of fire. Strange and terrible images and memories came shooting through his mind. His yard was brightly lit by the fire. There was a strong smell of petrol. His first thought was that some fireworks had come hurtling in over his wall and had set the coop ablaze. But could that be?

He moved. He turned quickly back into his house and found a basin. He turned on both taps in the sink and the basin filled.

He rushed out into the yard and flung the water onto the coop. There was a great hissing sound and the flames hesitated a moment, then took on again as if they were mocking his efforts. He went for another basin. That, too, seemed easily absorbed by the flames but in the moment of their dying down he caught sight of his pigs, of Venus, Cupid and Juno, and they lay without movement at the edge of the fence underneath the coop. Reynolds staggered. They were not burned, but they lay in the stillness of death.

With four or five more basins of water Reynolds managed to douse the flames. An uneasy, fraught darkness settled over the yard. A slow, lazy smoke lifted into the night sky. And suddenly Reynolds noticed the open window of Genevieve's house next door; the light was on and Randy stood in the window. Reynolds could see for certain, there was a rifle in his hands. Behind him Reynolds could see Genevieve herself, tugging lazily at Randy's sleeve.

Randy shouted down at him: 'Death by misadventure, you dirty scumbag! Death by misadventure!'

Randy closed the window and drew the curtain, and left Reynolds to the destruction of his yard. He went indoors and brought out a torch. The coop had collapsed now onto the earth beneath and all his hens were dead, burned alive, their feathers almost completely scorched off so that they lay tortured and naked, as if they had deserved the most severe punishment man is capable of thinking up. And Cupid, Juno and Venus had several open wounds in their heads. Reynolds could see the pellets, some of them clinging to the tough skin, some of them buried deep inside.

Reynolds allowed his body to sink down onto the ground of the yard. His mind was wholly empty, save for a terrible sense of suffering and an overwhelming weight of sadness. He glanced up at the darkened window. There was no movement now, a faint light could just be seen through the curtains. The bangs and screams of fireworks still going off came desultorily from here and there about the estate. Reynolds sat on, shivering. The hencoop hissed a little now and then from the water he had thrown on it. There was no stir at all from the hens nor from the pigs. He put his head down between his knees and tried to blot out all thought, every image, every memory. If only he could become a stone, unfeeling, unthinking, unyielding. But he could not.

THIRTY-FOUR

The great room in Convento San Francisco, where Brother Bonaventure received Brother Leo and Reynolds, was polished to within a centimetre of flight. There was an enormous table down the centre of the room, its mahogany surface reflecting the sparse light that came in from the street outside. Around it were plush, high-backed chairs, all fitted neatly in underneath the table, waiting. At the very head of the table sat Brother Bonaventure, a tall, angular-faced man, clean-shaven, with short black hair neatly cropped. His face was pale, his eyes dulled, as if with a sense of the terrible duties he had to carry out on behalf of the monastery and the brothers.

When Leo and Reynolds came in he motioned with a wave of his hand that they should come and sit on either side of him. Reynolds tried to close the heavy door behind him; it, too, was great, shining, and had an enormous brass door-knob that frightened him. In his anxiety he banged the door too quickly and the noise seemed to shake the monastery to its core. Reynolds hung his head. The floor was wooden and his old shoes squeaked uneasily as he crossed it. As he pulled out the heavy chair to the right of Brother Bonaventure, he could hear the scream of the chair-legs across that polished floor and the Brother looked at him irritably. At length they were seated, Brother Bonaventure arranging papers before him. He looked at Leo.

'So, this boy wants to become one of us. Eh?'

Leo smiled and nodded. 'He's been with us already for some years and has filled his position in the monastery with exemplary credit.' Leo glanced encouragingly at Reynolds.

'Parents?' Bonaventure asked.

Leo hesitated. 'I'm afraid his parents, both of them, they were, em, they were both killed in a terrible accident. After that Reynolds came to us. We took him in, as it were.'

'Of course, of course. I have all that here before me. I have read all of that. Yes, yes. That is very sad, very sad indeed. But it is relevant, you know, Reynolds' – and here he turned his severe, gaunt face towards the boy – 'as we would need to have permission ... eh? But in this case, of course ...' His voice trailed away as he dropped his head again over the papers.

Reynolds shifted uneasily. He was sweating profusely again and was too nervous to take out his handkerchief and wipe his face. He kept his hands tightly clenched under the table. He glanced at Leo. He could see that his friend was sweating, too, but had his handkerchief in his hand and occasionally raised it to his face.

Brother Bonaventure hummed and humphed a little as he turned the pages. 'What I don't understand fully is why Brother Angelo Maria Spenser has sent you out to me. Cannot he make that decision himself? Locally, I mean. It's not really a question for me. Eh?'

Again Leo responded quickly. 'Reynolds is wonderful about the monastery. He's extremely obedient, he prays well, he works at the tasks he's given and acquits himself wonderfully. He has expressed, himself, a desire to take on our life in its fullness. Indeed, Reynolds has nowhere else in life to go, should he ever wish to leave our walls. But there is the problem of his speech. Reynolds, as you will see ...'

Once again Brother Bonaventure gazed towards Reynolds. Reynolds shifted in his chair and tried to look away out the high window that showed only other windows just across the street. There was silence a moment as Brother Bonaventure looked Reynolds up and down.

'Well, Reynolds. How do you like Rome? Eh?'

Reynolds glanced at the Brother. Then he looked down at the table and was smitten to see his own very red face gaze back up at him. He looked over at Brother Leo but Leo remained silent, nodding his head slightly with encouragement.

Reynolds looked at Bonaventure and shook his head.

'Eh?'

'No ...' Reynolds managed, then fell silent.

'You don't like it, then. Don't blame you. Too hot, surely. Too crowded. What do you think?'

Brother Leo intervened. 'This is the problem, Brother Bonaventure. I think, as a result of the accident to his parents, to which Reynolds was a witness, indeed at which he acquitted himself like a hero, he has suffered, and suffers, a speech impediment. But he can read and write and pray, and he is a great lover of poetry.'

'Poetry, eh?' Again Brother Bonaventure turned towards the squirming boy. 'We have Dante, of course, in this country. And Leopardi. And Boccaccio. And several more. Can't say I ever read them myself. Haven't time. But I hear good things ... So, Reynolds. You would like to join us. Eh?'

Reynolds again looked appealingly across to Leo. Then, taking sudden resolution, he shook his head and pronounced 'No' again.

Brother Bonaventure looked quizzically at Leo.

Leo, somewhat taken aback, spoke up on Reynolds's behalf. 'I think Rome has been too much, too sudden for Reynolds, who has never before left the island. And the Vatican, well, we both found ourselves somewhat overwhelmed, dwarfed, physically and spiritually, you might say. But I have to say that I have never seen anyone more reverent, thoughtful and prayerful about the altar. I see Reynolds, perhaps, as sacristan, a post he would fill with distinction. And I see him offering our monastery a great service, for he knows our ways and our rules and constitution, he tends our living and he tends our dying, and he calls us to prayer with the greatest devotion in the ringing of the bell.'

'I see, I see. But what about acolyte? Can he manage that? Eh?'

Leo was silent.

Brother Bonaventure said to Reynolds, 'At the Mass, when the priest turns to the people and he says, *Dominus vobiscum*, and you're there, serving his Mass, what do you reply? Eh?'

Et cum spiritu tuo, Reynolds sounded at once, in the depth of his brain. He opened his mouth and only his tongue protruded. He pushed hard at the words wherever they were stuck but his silence had never been so definite, so final. He sat like that for a while, staring, mouth open, at Brother Bonaventure. And suddenly the whole size and shape of the room about him, the dark oil-portraits of Brothers and saints hung about the walls, the huge mahogany sideboard with its vast mirror doubling the room, and its silver trays and coffee-pots, this hard Brother before him, with his collar and his immaculately black soutane, his long El Greco fingers, the half-moons of the nails, all of it, all of it ... And Reynolds lifted himself quickly from his chair, shoved it back in under the table, ignoring the squealing, then he looked over at Leo and shook his head sadly. He stood a while, trying to say 'Sorry', but only a long, slow hiss came from him. He moved away slowly, opened the heavy door and stepped out onto the darkly overwhelming corridor outside.

Seemingly from a great distance the rumour of Rome's busy and impatient traffic could be heard. Somewhere within the walls of Convento San Francisco a door banged. A faint scent of nourishing soup came from beyond the walls. Reynolds sat, waiting. He had his head down between his hands but he did not feel unhappy. Indeed, there was a kind of certainty in his mind. At least now he knew, he knew how much he was capable of, and how he must stop reaching beyond his own limited strength.

In a quiet corner of the convent, in the near-dusk, just as the long hot day was beginning to be more bearable, Leo tried to reassure him. Bonaventure had said there was no possibility of Reynolds joining as a Brother, but he saw no reason why he should not continue in the monastery as he had been doing. Leo sighed a long and heavy sigh. 'Yes, yes. We shall keep you,' he said. 'You are, in fact, a treasure to us. And there is no reason why you shouldn't continue with us for as long as you wish. We can offer you a very small stipend. But everything else we can provide. Indeed, seeing you here, Reynolds, and in the Vatican, I am certain that you would not be able for this great world and will need shelter and care.' He leaned forward and touched Reynolds on his shoulder.

They sat together in perfect quiet for a while, and then Reynolds managed an almost perfect 'Thank you.'

THIRTY-FIVE

They had one day left in Rome. They both rose that day, somewhat relieved that it had all been settled. They set out mid-morning to see some of the oldest parts of the city. It was already hot – roasting, Reynolds thought. They walked to the end of Via Serena and caught a bus across the city. The bus seemed as old, to Reynolds, as parts of the ruins of ancient Rome that they passed; it juddered and jangled as if some of its essential joints must fall apart. The benches were made of wood and were uncomfortable and Reynolds and Leo stood most of the time, gazing out the open windows at the city.

Then they caught a second bus and were soon set down at the end of Via Appia. The heat was great as they began to walk along the edge of the famous road.

'Sulla and Augustus,' Leo explained, 'were carried along this road to their burial places and, of course, it was along this road that our own dear Saint Paul was led into the city a prisoner.'

Cypresses grew high and dusty on either side of the road and, idly, Reynolds broke off one of the lower branches and held it to inhale its strange, rich and ancient scent. There were birds flying amongst the high reaches of the trees and here and there they passed great family tombs with busts and urns and names inscribed in strange writing. Reynolds heard the familiar cackling of magpies and once two beautiful doves, their plumage a silken grey, their beaks a delicate pink, with a small white mark, like a medal, on their necks, flew down and landed on the old cobbles just ahead of them. The birds proceeded to

pick at grains among the cobbles and utterly ignored the two
travellers.

Soon, on either side, were fields baking in the sunshine and
signs here and there along the road pointing to the Catacombs.

'Under these fields,' Leo went on, 'there is a whole maze of
catacombs. Roman citizens were buried here in those long-ago
times, buried outside the city, and when the Christians were
being persecuted they came and hid in these places. Among
the dead.'

Reynolds shivered. And they were going to visit such a place?
He stopped and looked at Leo.

'Don't worry,' Leo laughed. 'There's no one been buried
here since those times. We won't bump into any of the dead.
No fear of that. Or maybe, no such luck!' and he chuckled to
himself.

A little further on they passed a small church, the church of
Domine Quo Vadis, Leo said; that was where Saint Peter is
supposed to have met the risen Christ when he was running
away from Rome, trying to escape. But he turned back, pre-
pared for anything, after that.

Soon they came to the entrance of one of the most famous
of the catacombs, those of San Callisto. Reynolds was
expecting to see a cave, with its black mouth gaping onto the
world, but there was only a shingle path in through the
cypresses, then a small hut where Leo bought two tickets. He
handed one of them to Reynolds; it was large, its writing in
gold-leaf, and it had a picture of a tomb with bas-reliefs of
some old gods on it. Reynolds shoved it into the pocket of his
jacket and he stuck the small cypress branch in alongside it.
They passed through a turnstile and entered what appeared to
Reynolds to be a hall, like one of the dance-halls on the island
at home. But it was dim inside; there was a musty smell and
Reynolds could see that some of the timber beams about the
building were cracked and moulding. An entrance led into a
deeper dimness, and the track began to slope downwards
almost at once.

Reynolds was scared. He reached out and held Brother Leo's
hand as they left the wooden flooring and began to walk on the

hard, trodden earth. There were dim lights set up along the walls as they descended.

'Don't be afraid, Reynolds,' Leo encouraged. 'Nothing here can harm you. Anyway, it's the living that are the dangerous ones; the dead are already in the arms of the Lord and know only love and care.' Leo was whispering and the sound seemed like a flight of wings through the still air.

They descended into the gloom. Soon they reached a long passageway that appeared to stretch off into endless darkness before them. The lights were dimmer still, though small niches in the dark clay were visible on either side. Reynolds glanced in apprehensively. In the first of them there was only an old, empty box of matches; the second held a crumpled sweet paper, and the rest of them were wholly empty. Reynolds began to gather courage. He was grateful, too, for the feeling of cold that surrounded him everywhere, after the overwhelming heat of the city.

They came halfway along this first passageway and found another track, where the bulbs on the sides of the walls seemed stronger. They turned in and found themselves going down steeply once more.

'There are layers of passageways,' Leo whispered. 'Thousands and thousands of people were buried here.'

Reynolds clutched him and pointed to a small arrow near the low ceiling, pointing back the way they had come. USCITA was written on it.

'That means exit!' Leo explained. 'We can't get lost. But in those days the Christians were fairly safe down here, they kept moving ahead of any soldiers that came searching for them and they could easily ambush them in these narrow confines.'

Dimly through the shadows and the dark solitudes of the place they moved. It was almost like a path scarcely lit at night by a half-shrouded moon through a forest, and off at either side were holes of blackness. The air was unpleasant to breathe and Reynolds found himself panting a little. He stopped. He had suddenly thought of Father and Mother, and their death, and how other and utterly different from living it all was. A great gasp of grief overcame him so that he reached out and held to

one of the edges of the tombs. The volcanic stone was rough
and holed and Reynolds imagined a certain warmth remained
in it.

'Are you all right?' Leo asked and Reynolds nodded his head.
But he sat down on the ledge of a tomb and breathed heavily.
He shook his head and smiled at Brother Leo.

'I want to go on down to the next level,' Leo said, 'just to see
how deep it goes around here. You can stay here and wait, or
you can come with me?'

Reynolds looked up at one of the bulbs burning dimly just
above him. He glanced back at the sign on the wall, USCITA,
exit. There were no other visitors in the tombs at the moment.
He felt safe. He pointed to where he was sitting, then to himself.
He pointed to Leo and waved him on. It was all right. He
would stay here. He knew he had seen enough.

Leo grinned, leaned forward and tapped him gently on the
shoulder. 'I'll just be a few minutes. Then we'll find a café
somewhere and have cakes and coffee. And maybe a big Italian
ice cream. How about that?'

Reynolds grinned and nodded. Leo moved away and was
soon lost in the dimness.

A strange silence settled around Reynolds. He wondered
how far underground he was. What if there were a landslide
now, or a volcano, or an earthquake, and the opening to the
catacombs was closed? What then? He thought he heard a tiny
rustling behind him and he jumped up from the niche where he
was sitting. A rat darted quickly away, across the path and into
another niche and disappeared. Reynolds had been chilled
through with dread. Then he laughed at himself and sat down
again. The silence returned. The buzzing from inside his brain
seemed loud to him, and he knew the silence was the same as
that he had often known before, without the richness of his
furze-bush hideaway, without the resonance that was merely
waiting in the belfry of the monastery at home. But he was, for
the moment, glad to be away from the hustle and noise, the
blaring of horns and the grinding of gears, the rushing of people
and the demands of the great shop windows along the streets of
Rome.

And then he heard footsteps, slow, gentle footsteps, coming from the direction in which they had just come. Descending that same slope. Heading towards him. An icy coldness seemed to tickle his back and lodge somewhere under the hair at the back of his neck. He tried to stand up and move towards where Leo had disappeared but his body seemed to have become rigid; only his face turned slowly towards the dimness from which the sound was coming. He tried to convince himself this was only a tourist following the trail but the sound was a strange one, a hushed, hushing and shushing sound coming intermittently along with a slow, shuffling noise. Reynolds wondered if the dead still haunted this place, and if they would resent him being there, now that he had decided he would never become a Brother. He was cold. His body frozen in place. Terror overcoming him.

Then there was a sneeze, followed by a low murmuring and complaining sound. That second sound seemed vaguely familiar but, in this place, in this dimness, he could not register what it meant. The shuffling, the shushing, continued. And then he saw something small and white shifting haphazardly through the faint light, coming down the passageway through which he and Leo had come. It appeared, seemed to dash at something, then disappeared. The shuffling sound continued and at last a figure appeared in the dimness, a solitary soul, shuffling slowly towards him. Reynolds leaped up off the ledge where he was sitting when he recognised the figure; he banged his head against the wall on the other side and moaned with the fright of it, and the blow.

'Well, well, well!' he heard the old familiar voice. She had a goose-wing in her hand and was brushing and dusting at the ledges of the catacombs as she came along. Reynolds stood watching her, his mouth open, his hand massaging his head. She was as she always had been, a small sour look on her face, her kitchen clothes on underneath that old apron, that dark navy blue with its myriad of tiny white stars. And she was wearing those old slippers, also a dark blue, with her big toe bursting through on each one, adding that awful shuffling sound to her every step. 'What brings you down here?' she asked him, in her usual complaining tone. 'Have you nothin' better to be doin' with your time than pokin' your lumpy body down where it don't belong? Gettin' in everybody's way. Every body. So to speak.' And she laughed, a dry, half-hearted laugh.

'I'm over with Brother Leo,' Reynolds began, and his voice sounded loud and echoing in the confined space. 'I was thinking I might join – '

'Yeah, yeah, yeah!' she replied. She kept darting the white goose-wing towards the niches, scattering specks of dust onto the passageway, into the thin air. 'What an eejit! Who on earth would want you to be a Brother? Sure you can't even talk proper.'

'I know, I know. I've changed my mind.'

'Or had it changed for you.'

'How are you, Mother?'

As soon as he had asked he knew the question was a foolish one.

She stopped and looked at him, and her face took on that old, sarcastic stare. 'How am I, is it? Can't you see for yourself? They have me down here, dustin' and mindin', and it all gets into me nostrils and makes me sneeze. Bits of the old dead, you know. Can't be healthy for a body. So to speak. Mind the way.' She shuffled closer to him, dusting wildly.

Reynolds pressed his body back against the passage wall but his mother went by without touching him. Reynolds, too, sneezed from the risen dust.

She stopped and looked back at him. There was the vaguest sense of residual tenderness in her voice when she asked him, 'And how is everthin' up above, with you, I mean?'

'Fine, Mother, fine. I'm happy, I think. I work in the monastery, they have given me the ...'

But she had moved on as if she weren't listening to him. She was already fading into the dimness. She paused and half-turned back to him. 'And himself? How's himself?'

Reynolds answered her quickly. 'He's fine, I think. I mean, he's dead, you know, in the fire.'

'Ach you oul' eejit, sure I know that well. I mean, how is he, like?'

Reynolds hesitated. 'I thought I saw him the other day,' he offered, and stopped.

She seemed to be scarcely listening to him; she was peering into the darkness of one of the empty niches and poking in with the goose-wing. 'Well?'

'I mean, I'm almost certain I saw him. In the station, the train station, in Paris. And he seemed to be heading somewhere. He had a bag or something. He didn't see me, I think. He just moved on.'

She sneered. 'So that's where the old bugger got to,' she said. 'I bet he thinks he's a hengineer or somethin' fancy, workin' on them trains, I'll bet. Travellin'. The oul' bugger. Ach but sure it's hopin' to bag one of them nudey women does be paradin' their bodies up in that place, what's it called? there beyant in Paris, what's it called, Piggle, Piggley, or something like that. Fat chance, the lazy oul' bugger. An' him dead an' all. Fat chance. Hah!' Then she chuckled and turned fully back towards Reynolds. 'And you, son, any sight nor light of a mad wee slip of a woman lookin' your way yet? For bein' married, I mean. Havin' a chile, a babby, to carry on the ridiculous name of Reynolds? Hah? What about that big bushty one you used to know, what's her name, Nora McGreil wasn't it? She'd be a bit of a thing now in the bed all right. She'd do fine. Good hips I'm thinkin', make a fine bolt of a son for you, mightn't be such an eejit as you neither, or there was the other one, another fine lump of a girl she was, what's her name too, was it Doreen something or other, almost as big and as stupid as yerself, but I'd say she could make a baby for you, too, if you could get yourself into her. What are you doin' about it? Time doesn't go on for ever, you know. I've found that out be meself. Hah!'

In the dimness Reynolds knew it didn't matter that he was blushing fiercely. His face burned, his hands fidgeted hopelessly with his jacket, his pockets. He felt the little branch of cypress tree in his inner pocket and he drew it out, to have something in his hands to distract his thoughts. 'Nothing, Mother. There's not much chance, I think. They didn't like me. Always bullied me. But there was Deirdre ...'

'What? That little twig of a girl of the doctor's? Of the

drunken doctor's? Sure she wouldn't have a notion of you, you oul' eejit, even though her father was a drunkard. Keep your eyes lower down, boy, lower down – if you can get down as low as your own daft self, that's where you'll find somethin', if you're lucky. If you play your cards right. An' joinin' them Brothers! For God's sake, how could you ever think of it, are you right in the head at all? What chance is there of producin' your own flesh and blood again, or havin' a chile, and you locked away in them walls, in them britches the monks wear, in them habits? Not a chance. Here, gimme that!' She moved swiftly and grabbed the cypress branch out of his hands. Her swipe of it felt as if a cold breeze moved by him suddenly. She examined it; felt it, turned it in her hands, smelt it. 'So,' she commented quietly and somewhat sadly. 'Must be summer or spring up there, is it?'

'It's summer, Mother. And it's awful hot!'

She looked at him then, long and steadily, as if for the first time. There seemed to be some tenderness in her eyes. He stood, waiting. All sense of fear and hesitation had left him and he felt a strong sense of companionship, of affection, even of love. She moved her hand slightly towards him, as if to touch him, but stopped, and held it some distance from his cheek. She seemed to sigh a little, then dropped her hand again. There came a sound from a distance further down the passageway. Reynolds heard Leo's voice call his name and he tried to respond, but no sound came out. His mother had turned quickly away and began to move in the direction where Leo was coming. In her left hand she held the branch of cypress; her right hand brushed away with the goose-wing at the walls. She half-spoke, half-whispered, back to him. 'I'll be keepin' my eye on you, mind, I'll be watchin' for them women in your life. Be sure now and find a good hoult of a one, a fine big bushty woman that'll give you a chile to carry on the name. And if you see himself, in Paris or wherever, tell him to get his arse down here fast till I tell him what's what. Remember that now!'

'Pray for me, Mother,' Reynolds spoke after her disappearing frame.

She seemed startled. She paused. 'Pray!' she said back at him.

'What the hell ...' and her voice faded quickly as she disappeared into the gloom of the passageway.

At once Brother Leo appeared, moving rapidly up the passageway towards him. Reynolds pointed and Leo turned a moment, then continued on his way.

'Seen a ghost, Reynolds?' he laughed. 'It goes on for ever down there, it's quite wonderful, you know. Quite wonderful. But I think it's time we headed out now, right? There's that ice cream waiting, you know. Would you like that?'

Reynolds tried to speak. There was dust in his mouth, and rocks, but no words.

THIRTY-SIX

Early in the morning, after Hallowe'en, Reynolds walked slowly down Heatherfield estate to the public phonebox. He rang the number and Leo Mason answered. Reynolds did not have to speak. The voice on the other end of the line said, 'Reynolds? Right. I'll be over shortly.'

Reynolds went out into his back yard. He had a shovel and a spade. He began to dig at the end of the garden. There was devastation in his yard and though the day was dark, there seemed little breeze and it was not cold. He and Leo would dig a great hole. They would bury the pigs and the remains of the hens. Then he would see. Then Reynolds would decide.

The monastery in the heather fields of the island lasted another seven years after Reynolds and Leo came back from Rome. Brother Sebastian had died and was buried now in that neat little plot. In the kitchen of the monastery Brother Juniper had one day gone a little berserk and had tried to set fire to the walls. He was screaming, charging at the walls and the cupboards, and he had a box of matches with which he was lighting bundles of newspapers and trying to set the whole place alight. It was Reynolds who had pacified him, Reynolds who had come in and grabbed him around the shoulders and had cried with him and hugged him until they both sat down on the floor together, wearied. Juniper was taken away that evening and Reynolds never saw him again.

In the new Ireland everything appeared to swerve towards economy and wealth and physical wellbeing. The word everywhere was rationalisation. Jobs were shed at the quay;

several of the larger trawlers had to sell up and the fishermen moved away to the mainland. Soon the monastery school had to close and the monastery itself had become redundant.

Brother Leo insisted, when the monastery and grounds had to be sold, that Reynolds be allocated one of the new houses that were to be built on the large site, so that when he and Brother Angelo Maria were to move into a smaller building on the mainland, Reynolds would be able to look after himself and survive. Heatherfield estate had been built. Reynolds had been given the house. Leo and he stayed in touch.

They knocked down the old monastery gate and rubbled the field where the boys had fought after school. The rhododendron hedgerows were dug out, as were the furze bushes and haw-thorn trees. The heathers that gave the area its name were torn out and the whole land levelled. The road down from the monastery gate became Heatherfield Avenue and the little turn into the school, with the old playing fields, became Heatherfield Drive. The monastery buildings themselves were demolished, although the chapel was left, and the tidy graveyard, with its yews and gravel walkways, was enclosed within a high wall so that it could not be seen from any of the windows of Heatherfield. It was tended, lovingly, by Reynolds, and Leo came sometimes and prayed there. Other parts of the old heather meadows became Heatherfield Road, Heatherfield Walk, Heatherfield Meadows, Heatherfield Gardens (where Reynolds was given a house) Heatherfield Moors and Heatherfield Close. Then there was The Heathers, the biggest houses, all detached five-bedroom, two-garage homes, not overlooked. And away at the other end were the shops, the supermarket, the gardening centre (where you could buy a fine variety of exotic heathers incapable of withstanding the island winds), the salons, the hardware shops and all the other addenda and pudenda to a great estate. And Reynolds had lived quietly and reasonably contentedly in the Gardens for many years.

When Leo arrived and saw the devastation in Reynolds's garden he could find no words. He and Reynolds stood a while, and Reynolds only shook his head. Leo took a spade and started to dig.

After a while, as they paused and entered the kitchen for a coffee, Leo said: 'When we're done, Reynolds, we'll head out to the harbour, take the boat out for a while, get away from all this misery, this new world, out on the freedom of the open sea. How about that?'

Reynolds nodded his head. Then he shook Leo heartily by the hand.

THIRTY-SEVEN

Reynolds felt as if he had been lying for ever on a bed of fire. He could not tell whether it had been days, or weeks or perhaps months, since he and Leo had headed out that fatal day on the sea. Reynolds was unable now to rise from bed. He did not have the strength. He could scarcely reach to the side of the bed and take a sip of water. If he moved at all, daggers jabbed every part of his body and a hammer struck against the side of his head. If he opened his eyes, he could see no more than a faint glimmer of light somewhere, and he could not tell if this was a mere memory of light, or if he had a tiny piece of his sight left to him. Every breath he drew was painful, like drawing an enamel bucket up along the sides of a dry and jagged well and dropping it slowly down again. He knew that all his hair had fallen out and must lie in grey bits and lumps about the bed. The teeth in his head had loosened and come out gradually, and he thought he had swallowed some of them while he was asleep or in a fever. And for all that length of time nobody had come to see how he fared, nobody had come to tell him how they cared for him, how they missed his company, how they were watching out for him.

Once more he seemed to surface into some small form of consciousness. Even the sheet that still lay over him on the bed pressed on him with hurtful weight and the mattress underneath him seemed to push hard against his bones, burning them. He shifted slightly, and the extra pain sent red lights flashing across his blindness and a tidal wave of suffering along his body. The fingers of his left hand touched something hard in his pyjama

top pocket and he groped with extreme difficulty to take it out.
He could not see but he knew it was the bracelet Deirdre Weir
had given him lifetimes before. He pictured it, how it scarcely
fitted over three fingers together, how its silver ends were joined
by a beautiful silver chain. Slowly then he brought it up over his
fingers again and it slid softly onto his wrist. He tried to laugh
but it would have caused him too much pain. How slight his
frame must be, he thought, now the bracelet fits so easily. It
brought him comfort, and the thought came to him that if ever
anybody found him – police, fire brigade, anybody – then all
they would find of him would be his skeleton, and a lovely
delicate bracelet lying against the bones of his wrist.

He lay back, utterly exhausted from that effort. He closed his
eyes, shutting out even the slightest memory of light. But soon
he opened them wide again for he knew there was a presence in
the room. There she was, standing over his bed, her arms across
her old apron, shaking her head and looking down at him.

'Well, well, well,' she said, but kindly enough. 'There you
are at last! All done in. My poor eejit. My poor son. There you
are now!'

Reynolds found he could just sit up in the bed, without
any real pain. He lifted his left arm and pointed to the bracelet
that hung loosely there. 'Deirdre Weir gave me that!' he said
proudly.

'Sure she did, sure she did,' Mother answered. 'And that's
about as close as you came to it in your foolish old life, isn't it?
But sure maybe it wasn't all your fault. You lie back there now,
like a good boy, and rest yourself. You need a good rest. Indeed
I suppose you could say you deserve it.'

Reynolds lay back down in the bed and his mother tucked
the clothes in about him, expertly, gently. He gazed up at her
and felt truly happy.

She grinned at him. 'There you are now, all tucked in. All
done. Close your eyes now, and I'll be seein' you. You
blitherin' old eejit you!'

He smiled and closed his eyes again.

THE LONG GOODBYE

The door, banging itself shut, startled her. It was a small clap of thunder in the house. She always left the hall door open, expectantly. Ghosts could move in and out quite freely but a human being would like to see the door open before him. She was sitting by the dead stove, absent. She could see that the first green-golden leaves of the sycamore had been blown into the kitchen. The earth, weary at its labouring, was beginning its long, easeful outbreathing. She got up, laggardly, and opened the door. There was no one there. The hall door remained open; she kept it back against the wall, an old anvil from the days of busyness holding it. Draughts, those invisible trickster-spirits, made their presence felt without message or comfort or release. They touched her skin, thin as an autumn leaf itself, with small, chilling fingers.

She could see the road curve gently away towards the wood. The trees and hedgerows were moving slightly, making soft, sighing sounds in the morning breeze. Young trees, planted in neat rows across the hillside opposite, scarcely yet showed above the summer grasses and untamed growth of the marshy ground. The grasses now were turning straw-yellow. The trees would grow, and tower, and beautify the ugly old hill but she would not be there to see it. She knew, and was glad that it was so.

There was no movement on the road. As usual. She sighed and closed the kitchen door softly.

'The road,' she whispered to the ghosts in her kitchen, 'the road over the wold.' When she laughed aloud at her own foolishness she was taken aback, the voice sounding where no voice ever sounded now, unless it was the postman, or the priest on his occasional, reluctant visits, or sometimes the electricity man, coming to read the meter.

She sat down again. Idly her hand picked up an old cloth and she began to rub, abstractedly, the black-iron edging of the stove. Her hand was wrinkled, 'Ugly,' she muttered to herself, twisted bones and hardened skin from so many years of effort and dismay. But the stove edge shone, buffed and buffed for years until she could almost see her reflection in its surface. As if such friction, such frotting and rubbing, could reduce the absolutely stolid presence of the stove to a sylphlike being. And when the stove was lit, these later years, how it sang, a piccolo-music, a skylark-flight of contented efficiency. Unlike her, her darkening body, reflecting nothing but grey and saddened light, suffering a heaviness of spirit in proportion as the body lightened into fragility.

She jumped up suddenly and moved towards the kitchen door. She had to hold her hand to her back where she had jerked it into pain. Had there been a knock? Perhaps there had. She opened the door again. There was no one there. The light of late summer, early fall, as if hesitating on a threshold, as she was, too, filled the hallway with its threat and promise. She sighed deeply, stood a while, gazing into that light; outside the sunshine, weakening, shifted on the stipple-wash of the garden wall. The pain in her back was exquisite for a while, taking her breath away. How the years wear and wear against a body until it is thin as dried stalks, and as brittle.

Another summer dying away, and still she had not heard a word. Eight years now since John had left, gone to see the great turning world, he had said, where life has more lift and fall to it than here in this backwash of a place, where he would find work to give him importance, to make him shine out more than just another glistering haw in the hawthorn hedge. For a few months the occasional card had come, bringing the post-man's hurrying green van to her door. Glasgow. Then Madrid. Then Nairobi. Miami. Cities of light and air. New York. Boston. And finally, Montevideo, the messages always little more than a small bird's chirping, but that he lived, and grew and was doing well. And ending always, 'All my love, dear Sparrow-Mother. John.'

Some day, she knew, she knew with an absolute certainty, some day she would hear the quietly powerful noise of a strange car turning into her driveway, the gravel shifting under its wheels, the engine dying. She would sit shivering with anticipation, she would hear the car door shut, footsteps approaching, unhesitating footsteps. She knew, too, there would be no knock on the door, it would be opened, simply opened, and he would step blithely into her kitchen, big, smiling, her son, a stranger. Home. For ever. Or for a season, like the migratory birds.

She stood at the door a long time then scolded herself for her foolishness. She could go on like that all day, getting nowhere, doing nothing, allowing the world to speed on without her. She sat again, musing how the house had emptied. Almost imperceptibly, from the crammed and jangling noises of the early years of her marriage, the bustle and braggadocio of jobs to be done about the yard, the fields, from the arguments and gratulations, the shared prayers and the raucous gatherings – to this, this silence, this emptiness, this disappearance. As if she had closed her eyes gently one day in the sweet ecstasy of her first full embrace and opened them suddenly on age and loneliness. All passes, in the space of a long inbreathing, with nothing left but a long and easeful exhalation.

She stirred herself. It had been Christopher who had had that love affair with labour, with chores, saying that to be idle was to allow the earth to wheel along without you and wasn't God Himself the Master-craftsman, the Labourer, not only building the universe but permanently sustaining it? And Christ, too, wasn't He the carpenter, the labourer who worked His way to the hill on which His final, most difficult, chore had to be carried through? Thus, Christopher. Husband. Gone. The world grinds on, season by season, day by day, minute by minute. And what difference had he made to it, after all? Or herself, for that matter, what difference? She must not allow herself to fall outside its scope and become a useless burden to it.

She raked out the ashes from the stove. This was one of the

negative tasks that she hated, a wasting task, essential but un-
productive in itself, as if you were taking a step backwards,
against the flow. It was a tiny memory of that feeling she had
when she stood over Christopher's opened grave and watched
how they lowered him with their long, thin straps, gently,
gently, yet horrifically, down into darkness. And worse still when
her other son, her young and willing yet self-indulgent son
Brendan, had driven himself into the blank wall and had been
lowered, too, into that same darkness. That second time she had
stood, shaking but dry-eyed, promising silently that she would
yield herself to that darkness, too, step willingly aside from the
light of day and join her menfolk, soon, inside that darkness.

She shuddered now, remembering. It had been so long,
already, and still she stood on the surface of the earth, breathing,
a burden to herself, and no great use to the seasons of the world.
When she stepped outside a light breeze caught the biscuit tin
that she had filled with ashes and a wistful, fragrant smoke
moved off over the lawn, coating her navy-blue apron with a
light dust. She was grateful, suddenly, for the labour, and for
those other dull, repetitive tasks that stretched ahead; grateful,
too, for the end-of-summer sunlight that gave the countryside a
delicate glow, between the demands of sunshine and the nega-
tivity of shadow. She moved slowly, heaviness ever present in
the stiffening bones, yet almost light enough to feel that a
sudden wind could whip her away into the air.

The short path up to the ashpit had been worn hard and
smooth over the years. How fresh and virginal everything had
seemed when she and Christopher first settled here. How
quickly, how stunningly quickly, everything grew tarnished, as
if the labouring of humans did little more than infect the earth
with lassitude. And yet she would stand astonished that the
thistle could still lift its lovely, unloved and insistent crowns over
the grasses, or that the row of poplar trees between the back
yard and the meadow could still whisper the same old stories,
about winds and rains, about the constant straining upwards.
She sighed, contented.

As she emptied the ashes into the pit the wedding ring slipped
off her finger and dropped, with a slow whoosh of ash, into the

heap, and sank. She gave a little animal cry of distress and fell to her knees, her hand at once up to her elbow in ash, the old sweet-sour smell of the ash-dust almost choking her. She knew that time was fretting away her body but this loss, so dreadful to her loneliness, was yet too much to be permitted.

The tears began behind her eyes and her hand moved blindly in the silken softness of the ashes. Christopher had worn himself down too quickly, working, always working. Day and night in the fields, in the meadows, wearing himself down, fretting and frotting till his skin had hardened and then grown stretched and well-nigh transparent. And when he had fallen ill he had no reserves of strength left to fight, leaving her lost, with her children, the house, the ground, and more labour than she had ever dreamed of. And, of course, the ring.

Her fingers sifted the ash. Down a little way the smoke-soft stuff gave way to a slightly firmer substance that was old and damp and when she felt the hard touch of the ring she cried out with the relief of it. But what matter? there was nobody about who could hear. Her hand came out of the ash with a grateful, whispering sound, the white and ochre tininess of the dust particles clinging a while and falling away from the gold-grey hairs on her arm. She put the ring back on her finger. How loose it was! She, too, beginning to shrink away from the big-ness of being into the tininess of death. Soon, she whispered, soon, please God.

She looked towards the front door of the house. What if he did return and there was nobody to welcome him? The migrant. Returned. And the house abandoned, the nest cold. She stood a while, present, and absent. The sunflower, the solitary sunflower she had planted, had grown taller than she was herself. That great head was already blackening, like a clenched heart gradually letting go to the world all the warmth and colour and life of which it was possessed. The sunflower, its slow and inexorable acquiescence to the forces that were present already in its seed, the forces of growth and expansion and decay, offered her its being and she accepted it, every year, in the absence of her own, dear son.

The old woman shook herself out of her reverie. She was

grateful again for the tissue of small tasks that held the fabric of these slow, empty days together. Grateful, too, for the forces working with her, forces that made her part, however small, of the same onward roll of the universe.

The swifts had nested again in the high angle of the gable wall, and the purity of the whitewash had been tarnished by them over the summer weeks. What matter? she was happy with their company. Always they were there, the swifts, swooping, scything the air, children exulting in the first-found power of their limbs, exquisite, masters and mistresses of the element. And there was Jonathan, the swift that, the year before, came last out of the nest and fluttered down, like an autumn leaf, landing on top of the small cock of hay from the side-field. She had watched how it sat there, how the others flew fast and challenging above it, how its tiny cries spoke already of a world of fear and insecurity and unwarranted challenges. Then she had taken it gently into her hands, known the warmth of its body, admired the perfection of its head and beak streamlined for flight, the eye so perfectly sheathed against speed, felt the heart within, pumping and urgent. She held the bird high and urged it free but it fluttered again, down onto the grass at her feet. It flopped along the ground, ugly and pathetic, out of its element, and she could sense the indifference of the world that everywhere threatened it. Undone was the word that came to her, undone, unmade, incapable. As one day she, too, would be undone; God the maker being also God the unmaker. The undoer. The uncreator.

Once again she had lifted into her hands that tiny body, with whatever flaw in its making that had brought it so soon to this pass. Again she held it high and urged in out onto the air. And it flew, wings beating perfectly a while, a short while, down over the side-field, towards the garden fence, before it flopped again as if it had flown against some solid wall of air. With sadness in her heart, she gathered it once more and once more urged it out onto the stream of living. It flew, confident almost, grateful it seemed, and gained a little height that took it out over the fence, across the road and away over the wild bottoms of Timmie Marron's land until it fell, somewhere down amongst the thickened undergrowth and marsh grasses. Silence about her, the small bird's landing-place inaccessible. She could but hope, pray even, that it would find a way out of there before rat or fox or peregrine tore its fragile flesh to shreds. Jonathan. That was last year. Now she looked up. Perhaps, she thought, it is one of those soaring and swooping through the air, grateful for its being, made, unmade and made again, indifferent now to the woman that gave it a new life, a new start.

She walked, this afternoon, her chores all done, slowly, up and down the lane beyond the house, her head turned towards the sky, her fingers following the beads along her rosary. Her thoughts moved on the swifts and the swallows that were twittering loudly, ranged like indecipherable letters along the wires above her head, gathering. She kept forgetting which mystery she was on, which great wonder she was to contemplate. She was waiting for the end of the prayers, when she would go on to speak for the poor souls in Purgatory, souls waiting, too, for the great migration. So many gone, she was thinking, unmade by death, undone, uncreated. Like Christopher, unmade and gone for ever, the winds and rains already insistently erasing his name from the stone. Again her thoughts were interrupted by the birds above her, their messages to one another becoming stronger and more rapid, here on the quickening edge of autumn, on the very borders of departure. They would stay for a few days more, she knew, the music of their compline growing louder and more urgent, the long lullaby of their farewell to this place leaving her shaken and more alone than ever.

Later that evening, as she reached to the mantel shelf to take down the black-and-white wedding photo in its darkening frame, her elbow knocked over the old blue willow-pattern clock and it fell crashing to the floor, its shattering loud and frightening in the silence of the kitchen. She stood, shocked, a while. Then she shook her head gently, brushed the pieces into the biscuit tin and emptied them into the bin outside the door. She came back into the kitchen, closed and bolted the front door, closed and bolted the door into the kitchen. Then she began to build a fire in the range, and her thin, cracked voice was raised in a soft humming tune; she was working, slowly and determinedly, building warmth against the cold, building light against the coming darkness.

THE PHOTOGRAPH

I had lost something of vital interest to me. In my best recollection it had rolled away out of my hands, along the rust-flagged floor, rattling woodenly, along the skirting board, and had disappeared in under the bookcase. I had been on my hands and knees, reaching in to see if I could retrieve it. I could not feel it anywhere. My hand came out soiled with dust and old gluey cobwebs, such filth, all the more sickening because it felt slightly moist. I shuddered and gave up the search for the moment. Until I knew the time had come when I must go back and search for it again.

I was sleeping those days at the very top of the old red house. In considerable ease and comfort. There was a small skylight that allowed me to see nothing but blue, with occasional dark or milky clouds passing over. That was enough for me. Everything below seemed to be of less importance, except, indeed, what I had lost. It took me some time to get up the courage to go and search but eventually I set once more about the business.

There was a trapdoor in the floor of my room. I lifted it and it came up with a loud squeaking that hurt my senses. The wooden steps down to the landing below were well-nigh vertical but I got down without trouble. Something whizzed past my head with a sense of wind and speed and I ducked instinctively. There were cold breezes on the landing, too, and I could see that the windows at each end were famished, the frames hanging broken, several panes of glass missing. Through these windows there were swallows coming and going, their high cries piercing through my inner ears to my very soul. There were nests up under the ceiling and indeed the rafters up there were host to several nests, the whitewash hanging loose like old scabs. I was astonished.

I took a few steps towards the top of the stairs, only to notice that the floor of the landing seemed particularly dangerous. The carpet, once bright red with large purple flowers in the patterning, was threadbare and here and there the wood of the floor showed through. I was disgusted to see the bird shit that lay scattered all over floor and carpet; the high corners of the landing were filthy with old cobwebs, husks of bluebottles, butterflies and harvesters. And there, right at my feet, was a tiny bird foetus, soft-beaked and naked. I shuddered. The swallows kept flying past my head, whooshing by as if I were not there, and I had to duck continuously to avoid the speed and hurtle of their trajectories.

I stepped out onto the first stair. I noticed that the winds were creaking everywhere in the deep stairwell, that the high striped green-and-white wallpaper was hanging in tatters, and that great brown wet-stains were showing through the old walls. I shivered, as if the very dampness of the air had got through into my bones. I turned the angle of the stairwell and there was the old cabbage-green door that opened into the kitchen; it was broken, and the winds were banging its half-hanging shape half-to. The noise was quiet, but irritating, its irregularity, its insistence beginning to fray my nerves. Once, such care and concern were put into every moment and every metre of this house that I could not understand or accept its current neglect.

The smell of must in the kitchen was overpowering. The old green oil-cloth on the table was filthy and there were cups and saucers in a state of utter dirt, dust and mould and all sorts of unnameable and unidentifiable things crusting everywhere. I hurried through into the old flagged hallway. Facing me was the door into the parlour, a room we kept sacrosanct for special visitors, like the priest, the doctor, the aunt from London, or for special days like Christmas Eve and Easter. The furniture in here had been heavier and darker, there was an old piano that we never used and the wallpaper had always been of a heavy plum colour, contributing something special to the sense of separateness and richness the room had always been meant to convey. Now I could see that the door was almost eaten through by rot, even by rodents, and it was falling open of itself. I crossed the hallway and went in cautiously, feeling – in the strange silence pervading the old red house – that I was little more than an intruder, an unwelcome guest, a spectre.

All the furniture was gone. The carpet had been taken away and the wooden floor was holed and gapped in many places. There was a smell of rot and decay and the richly kept fleur-de-lis plum wallpaper was hanging off the walls, like old hands hanging down helplessly in despair. Even the small lamp in the ceiling had disappeared, the bulb, too, leaving only a wormlike and dead wire hanging in the tainted air. Over in the corner stood the old piano, scarcely recognisable now. It seemed more like a pile of wooden planks strung together with wire, yet every now and then its own internal decaying, or some stray breeze, produced a faint note from it, a moan, almost a slow howl of sadness and loss.

I stood, shocked and dismayed. I was standing in a world of dust and decay, of neglect and abandonment. I could scarcely remember what I was doing in this old house. And then I heard them – footsteps that, in the rare silence of the house, seemed loud. They were coming up the gravel pathway towards the front door and sounded strangely hesitant, sometimes scraping, sometimes soft, and quite erratic. I felt a terrible chill come over my whole body; I was petrified, as if this presence were to be a ghost of some kind, haunting this old and abandoned house. I moved, crossing the hallway again as quickly as I could and moving back into the kitchen towards the staircase. Then I paused.

It sounded as if the intruder had clumped his body against the front door, bursting it open instead of lifting the latch. I heard a gasping sound, as of somebody in pain, there were muttered words, indistinguishable, as if they were badly articulated calls for help, or cries of pain. A kind of shuffling sound ensued, and I imagined that the intruder, the visitor, was hauling himself along the wall, towards the bathroom at the end of the hallway.

It was clear he, she, or even it, was not heading for the kitchen so I was not going to be noticed, for the moment. I crept back to the door of the kitchen that was still hanging ajar. I peered out.

There was a man in the hallway, on his knees on the rust-flagged floor, his left hand raised to the wall for support, his right hand clutching his throat. He was elderly, but firmly built, and his white hair was almost completely gone. He had the remnants, too, of a white beard but it was his face that frightened me, the paleness of it, and how drops of blood were coming from his nose and mouth, and even, if I were not mistaken, from his eyes. He was gasping for breath, trying to drag himself along towards the end of the hallway, towards the only door that seemed perfectly intact in the house. He was making strange, half-strangled sounds and it was very clear that he was in a terminal state, and suffering greatly. I did not know what to do. The man was vaguely familiar to me and yet I knew an overpowering dread of him; some ill-defined sense of terror held me fixed to where I stood, useless, helpless.

He made his way, with extreme difficulty, along by the wall, his left hand falling lower all the time, his upper body drooping forward, the blood coming more freely from his mouth. And then he had reached the bookcase and his hand was clawing at it for support. I felt astonished that the bookcase appeared to be in perfect condition, that the books looked well aligned and clean, all their spines facing outwards. I was surprised, too, that the bathroom door seemed in such perfect shape and the flags of the hallway clean and scrubbed. I had little time for such thoughts, however, as the poor man made one final, violent struggle to keep himself upright, both hands flailing at the bookcase so much so that he fell forward on his face, dragging down the bookcase on top of him. It all happened so very, very slowly; I saw some of the books first, one by one, then several at a time, tip forward over their shelves and begin to fall. The old man was already face down on the flags, his throat making a horrible, choking sound, his whole body twitching slightly. Before the bookcase itself came down on him, after the individual fall of the books, I could see that his body had gone still. Very still.

The crash the fall made seemed to make the old red house shudder to the stones that were its flesh and the beams that were its skeleton. I closed my eyes with the fright of it, and the whole horror of what I had seen. For a few moments, an intensely emotional sense of what the whole of humanity has to suffer in its straining for life passed through my soul, a sense of sorrow at our grief and loss, a sense of anger at the necessity for decay and pain, and a sense of wonderment that I was still able to breathe and move about, though scarcely aware of where I was or what was happening to me. I inhaled deeply and opened my eyes again. By the old Rayburn, now cold and rusting where once there had been great heat and the heart-warming scents of bread baking, there was the leathern corpse of a rat, flattened almost, in the mire and dust of the kitchen floor. I moved away quickly, out into the hallway. Wondering if there was anything I could do.

You can imagine my astonishment when I found there was no trace of anybody in that hallway, no trace of the old man who had come stumbling through a moment before, no trace of the old bookcase, nor of any book, and even the old door at the end, the door that once led into a fine bathroom, was dirty, broken and hanging loose on its hinges. The very floor, the old rust-flagged floor, was filthy with the scatterings of blown leaves and the wings of butterflies and moths. A soft breeze was blowing in through the shattered front door and I could see the front garden beyond, what had been the front garden, but was now a tossed and tossing wilderness of weeds and hawthorn bushes. As I moved, in a kind of dread-filled trance, towards that front door, I could see an old photograph still hanging on the wall. It was a black-and-white photograph of a young couple, holding hands, eager, facing out into the world they were about to tackle together, smiles on their faces, the whole of existence at their feet. I knew I ought to be able to name them, that young couple, I knew them well but for the moment could not remember who they were.

On the wall opposite, and lightly reflected in the untainted glass of the photograph, was an old painting, framed, dusty and hanging at an angle, a painting of the God of ages, white-bearded, the face lined with care, the eyes darkened and filled with pain, and slow dribbles of blood were coming from that face, from the mouth, the nostrils, and even, I thought, from the eyes, moving slowly down the wall onto the hallstand, onto the frames of the walls, onto the wainscoting.

THE EYE OF THE BEHOLDER

Augustine Honeywell was a small man. About five feet two and a half inches tall, and made to match in every way; a pole, thin legs, thin wrists, thin body, thin face. And his ground was thin, his small farm just a few acres of thin topsoil and thick undersoil. His cattle were thin, his sheep small. Even the eggs his hens produced were small, mealy, watery eggs. You could say that Gus was a hangover, even though it was a century and a half later, from the Famine in Ireland, as if all his ancestors from that awful time forward had suffered famine of mind and body, and of luck. For Gus, as well as the tendency in his whole life to remain small and thin, had a thin mind, too, a small one given over to bitterness and anger. For the world about him mocked and parodied his being, finding little room for one who did not seem capable of taking his place in the great economic drive of the newly prosperous country. Ireland. Going forward. Indeed. Life had not dealt Augustine Honeywell a hand with even one trump in it. Not an ace, not a king, not a knave; and above all, not a queen.

The evening of the closing dance of the Loughmeen traditional fiddling festival, Gus sat long over his supper, thinking. He lived alone. His parents, thin and small as he, had passed away and were lying in their thin, small grave up behind Loughmeen church. Gus had his best suit on; it was grey, stylish, with a certain gentle sheen to it that would look very well indeed in Loughmeen Parish Hall. He had a fine blue shirt and he would wear his new pink silk tie that he had paid good money for. Later, as the night progressed, he could take the tie off, pop it in his inside pocket, and dance on. Later still, he could take the jacket off and dance the dance of the free, as good as any of the blue-shirted, open-necked lads, with their hairy chests and the slinging-down things, who skipped and loolaed among the girls.

Gus's aim was to put an end to bitterness and begin to live the fuller life. After all, there was a millennium just gone through and a new century beginning. The world out there was rich in possibilities. Why should he let the old tradition of patient suffering and misery-hoking stay with him and mar his chances and his life? Self-expansion would be the name of the game from now on. He would eat plenty, drink plenty, find plenty of women, know and savour the beauty that was to be found in a man's one lifetime. Gus sniffed loudly to himself and Martin-O, the mongrel dog, looked up warily from his corner. Gus could already boast the modernisation of his small farm-house kitchen: fridge, washing machine, television, video. He was thinking of buying a microwave; perhaps even a dish-washer. Appropriate, expand, build the self into something strong and dominating, that was his task in life.

Gus, at the beginning of this year, had written out his new-found urges on a piece of cream-coloured vellum paper, paper that sported the most delicate watermark in the shape of a love-heart. 'I will live tall and proud,' he had written down; 'I will offer my hand, my life, my house and farm and all of my trust and truthfulness to the woman who will offer to love me and give me all of herself in return. And as I achieve my fullness of spiritual and economic stature I shall find contentment. Children shall run about my house and land and I shall grow immortal.' He signed his letter to the future with a fine flourish, folded it carefully and put it away into the inside pocket of the jacket of his fine grey suit. Next and over his heart. His thin, but beating, heart. That morning he had skipped about his farmyard, something being achieved, Martin-O the mongrel dog barking with excitement.

Gus finished off his ready-meal of lasagne, threw the carton into the bin, and went upstairs to wash his hands, put on aftershave, don his tie and straighten himself to conquer. He watched himself in the mirror. He was only twenty-nine, in the full of his health and being. He was a real man. He had a real life. He would find a real woman, a real beauty. He would work hard with her, they would build a real life together, expanding their holdings and visiting the wonderful places in the world he knew all about from American television shows. Gus had been to Torremolinos, to Paris, to Madeira. With a beautiful woman on his arm, he would be better able to relish the real life of such wonderful, and even more exotic, places. He rubbed his chest and stomach with his two hands, up down, up down. He would show them tonight. He was Augustine Honeywell. Expanding.

It is important not to show up too early. The disco began at ten thirty. Gus sauntered into the hall at eleven fifteen to find that he was amongst the very first to arrive. The hall was still brightly lit, the disc jockey desultorily playing something at the far end, in his little glass cage. Several young men were at the bar. Slouching easily. Pints in their hands. Smirking. Gus joined them.

'Lads!'

'Gus! How's she cuttin'?'

'Fierce, lads. Only feckin' fierce.'

'Suit, Gus, looks serious tonight. Wha'?'

Gus grinned and drew an impressive thickness of notes from his inside pocket. Ordered a pint. A chaser. Crisps. Entered into the watchful conversation that was proceeding around him. A few young women drifted in and gathered together, with their vodkas, their long-necked bottles, their cigarettes, at the further end of the long bar. The three Coggin sisters amongst them. Around the empty dance floor the multicoloured, multi-patterned dream-world of impossibilities swirled in millions of tiny lights from the slowly turning globe. It would be a time yet before anybody moved out of the safety of the bar area into the searching and demanding world of the dance.

The Coggin sisters: Monica, Maureen and Madge. They were still young, the oldest, Madge, being scarcely twenty-nine. They lived together in the big house at the bottom of Farragher's Hill. Their father had died many years ago; their mother just one year ago. And, like Augustine Honeywell, they were not pretty. In them, too, generations of famine-fraught,

hard-working people, who stuck grimly to their barely produc-
ing acres, had lived lives hungry for everything the world
seemed to offer easily elsewhere, food, money, luxuries. In the
new century the three sisters had jobs, there were three cars in
the old yard of the house. Neighbouring farmers rented their
land. The three sisters had hopes.

'I see the three ugly sisters are all done up, like shite against a
whitewashed wall,' muttered Larry.

All the male eyes turned to the three young women.

Gus tittered. 'Go to bed early, go to bed late, with the three
ugly sisters it don't matter a hate,' he whispered.

'Take Madge out, Gus,' urged the grinning Mikey. 'Remem-
ber what they say about the early bird. Wha'?'

There was raucous laughter amongst the men, a general
movement of drinking and smirking, the way a small shoal of
fishes swirl together in one seamless grouping.

'Early to bed, I dare ya!' said Larry, to anyone in particular. 'I
bet they're good in bed,' said Larry the brave.

'All three of them together might have something to offer all
right, bejaysus!' offered Gus.

At that, all the men's eyes turned inquisitively towards the
women, all the spoiled imaginations tried to cope.

Madge, Maureen and Monica were well aware of their
features. As schoolgirls they had suffered the overt and exacting
comments of their peers. They had quickly learned to live with
the concept of being 'ugly', though they were brightest in
class and kindly towards everyone. Once, when Maureen, the
youngest, was being baited in the school yard by four of the
bigger girls who sang and jeered around her, Monica and Madge
had quietly stepped forward to help her. The bigger girls were
chanting: 'Three ugly sisters went to the ball, three ugly sisters
had a great fall', and as they chanted they jumped in one by one
towards Maureen and poked her in the stomach with a stick.
There was a fight, a commotion, hair pulled, slaps delivered to
cheeks, kicks where one of them fell, until all the other girls had
gathered round, cheering and encouraging, and the Coggin
sisters eventually emerged, hurt, crying, their whole being dis-
arranged, but together, defiant, and at peace.

How was it that their ugliness seemed to be unimportant while their father had been alive? When the family went to-gether to church it seemed acceptable that the ugly sisters could move and consort with all the others. And why, then, did it seem the more ridiculous when the three ugly sisters went to church, or to weddings, or to funerals, only with their mother, who was herself no great shakes when it came to looks? The spectacle of all four together, minus a man, provoked a silent, reserved and withdrawing wonderment among the parishioners. And then when the mother died and the three ugly sisters grew independent and fashionably well-off, well, the world of ugliness seemed destined to be exiled, at last, from the world of everyday, and everynight, society.

'Should ha' bin nuns, all of 'em, bin better in them black skirts an' veils an' things, hidin' everythin' they have got an' haven't got, that's what I say, lads,' from William James Morrissey, ageing bachelor, drinker, wag.

There was a general shuffling of laughter among the young men, a general drawing together of the young women, with their drinks, their make-up, their most casual best clothes. As if the Coggin sisters did not know what was going on. As if the other women did not feel bigger in stature and beauty because of their willingness to stand beside the Coggin girls.

At almost midnight the night began. A few women moved out together onto the floor and began to dance in the flickering lights. The braver of the men moved slowly towards the women near the bar. The dance-floor area began to fill. The world was beginning to come to life. The dreams were turning gradually, very gradually, towards reality. The lights dimmed; the strobe lights flickered. The music grew louder. The revellers grew more happy in their bravado. The bodies moved in jerky, uneasy rhythms. The young people were living lives.

Gus stayed at the bar. Drinking. He was suddenly nervous. Most of his companions had already moved onto the floor, taking a young woman with them. The bodies whirled and cavorted in the artificial dimness, the men intense, the women animated. There were not many women left near the bar, not many men beside Gus. Then several more women came into the hall, chatting together, coming in a group from somewhere else, already merry and assured. Among them was Elizabeth Curley, whom Gus knew well, from the higher street in the town. She was a well-built, attractive woman and she and Gus often passed each other with polite greetings on the street. Gus closed his mind to doubt, left his glass on the bar and walked towards Elizabeth.

He could see at once she was aware of his approach; she turned to her companions with some remark. They sniggered. He pressed on. He touched her shoulder and she half-turned towards him, smiling.

'Will ye dance?' he asked her.

She shook her head, still smiling.

'Ah ye will, go on!'

She shook her head again and glanced towards her companions. Then she gazed out over the dance-floor. 'I'm expecting Peter Berry to be here,' she muttered to him.

Gus looked about too. 'I haven't seen him all night,' Gus said. 'Sure you'll dance while you're waitin'?'

She grew serious and looked him up and down. 'I'm sorry, Gus,' she said eventually, having made her decision. 'I don't want to dance with you. I want to dance with a good-looking man.' And she turned away, back to her companions. They were silent, watching him. It was direct; it was cruel. The women did not giggle. They lifted glasses to their mouths and gulped. Gus stood still a while. Then he breathed in heavily and turned away, back to the bar. The young women huddled together, mocking him now that he had left. He sucked deeply on his dying pint.

The night moved on. Gus drank more and more and grew silent and sullen. He watched while the Coggin sisters waited at the far end of the bar. Nobody had asked them onto the floor. Gus looked away. He was not that desperate. And then he saw Monica, Maureen and Madge make their own decision and walk out together onto the floor. The three sisters started dancing and Gus watched them, scarcely believing how they each seemed transformed, graceful even, dignified, assured, as if this were perfectly natural for them, going with the living force of the music, with the vivid confidence of their own grace and beauty in the dance. They were perfect. Like a mathematical equation, Gus thought, remembering how they were all three of them teachers somewhere up the country. Like a sum that comes out perfectly, as if the whole world about them were in order for this moment, the answer contained deep within themselves, the equation of self and beauty wholly correct. They were a joy to watch, Gus knew, and even Elizabeth and her companions paused to gaze after them.

'A sum,' Gus muttered out loud. 'Ten plus ten plus ten equals thirty. Perfect. Rounded, smooth, lovely. But can you love a sum? Can your body enter the body of a sum and know its pleasure?' Gus laughed aloud, suddenly, and moved out towards the Coggin girls.

Madge smiled quietly as she saw him draw near to them. But he stood back a little, on his own, and slowly began to try and move to the music. He was awkward. He danced as if he had three feet, all three getting in the way of each other. Gradually he began to forget where he was, who he was, and gave himself over to the evening, to the rhythm, the noise, the dancing. He moved fast and furiously, growing hot and bothered, until he suddenly swung his jacket off, moved back to the bar, draped the jacket over a stool and came back out onto the floor.

The music played on. The three girls danced together in perfect and easy unison. Around Gus the whole of Loughmeen parish seemed to be a-swirl in the dance of life. Gus felt at peace. What did it matter, after all? He had his house, his farm, his future. He had Martin-O the mongrel dog who would follow him into Hell. Let them come to him. Let them see he had his own interior wealth and pride. He would do OK. He would survive. He would acquire more land, he would become a big farmer ... He waved his hands in the air, he shook his body through the strange movements only he could fathom, he swayed backward and forward to his own rhythms and suddenly, for no clear reason, he was on the ground, sitting, his legs splayed out in front of him, his hands supporting him on the floor behind. The music stopped. Somebody had screamed. It was one of the Coggin girls. The lights came up quickly. The circle around Gus moved quickly back.

Without undue embarrassment, Gus picked himself up, grinning, dusting himself down. He waved his hands in the air, exonerating the world, and moved slowly back towards the stool. The lights went down again. The music started up. The girls began to dance.

William James Morrissey was standing by the stool where Gus had left his jacket. He was reading something out to his friend Mikey. They were laughing. For a moment, uncomprehending, Gus stood near them, sweating, trying to gather himself together. '*I will live tall and proud,*' Morrissey was reading out; '*I will offer my hand, my life, my house and farm ...*'

Morrissey looked at Gus. 'Well, well, well,' he said. 'We have Gus Wordsworth here, ladies and gentlemen, a poet, a romantic, a lover.'

Gus began to realise what was going on.

'A lover, indeed,' Mikey added. 'Some lover, flat on his arse in the middle of the dance floor. Even the Coggin sisters won't touch him.'

Morrissey began again. 'Let's see. Oh yes. It says here: *As I achieve my fullness of spiritual and economic stature ...*' He looked at Gus. 'Well, we'll skip over that bit ...'

Gus made a lunge at the paper in Morrissey's hands. He grasped it and snatched it but it ripped loudly in two.

Morrissey and Mikey laughed uproariously. 'Lads!' they were calling out. 'Come and hear Gus Honeywell's will and testament to himself. He's going to put us all to shame.'

Several of the men came towards Morrissey and with them came Madge, Maureen and Monica Coggin. Gus grabbed at the paper in Morrissey's hand, missed it and Morrissey leaped up on a chair at the bar and got ready to read.

Gus took his jacket quickly from the stool, turned and strode with as much dignity as he could muster from the hall.

It was almost eight days later when they found Gus's body in the River Teachty. He had tied around his chest the heavy spare wheel from the boot of his car. He had abandoned the car over a mile away, near the tourist car park. He had left the keys in the ignition. The driver's door wide open. He had left a small scrap of torn paper on the driver's seat. By the time a neighbour came across the car, the battery had run down and the car was dead. The scrap of paper remained a puzzlement to the authorities. They placed it in the inside pocket of the drowned man's jacket and they buried him with it reposing next to his heart.

SAINT BUITE:
THE CONFESSIONS

I am blind now, but my body overflows with vision like an old clay jar stooked full with wine. I did not sleep last night, the darkness I know now being a darkness beyond darkness, a blackness beyond blackness, so that it glows with a febrile light. I left my straw pallet in the corner of my miserable cell. All night the straw, so dry these days that it crackles and snaps like the twig-nest of a rook, whispered and cackled against my body as if were on fire. The monks have finished lauds. Their voices came to me on the breeze, heaving a little comfort my way, but I am not one now for comfort and consolation. The chill of terror has taken me body and soul. I will not hear another lauds. Nor matins. There is that so swollen within me I know that this is to be my very last day on earth. And there is that which I must do that will earn me disdain and anger from my Brothers and my Superior. I cannot face it. Though I must.

I can line up all the prayers, from matins to compline, down all the years and they would lay small as fancy shells along the shore of a vast ocean. But over against all of that I can line up the sins, the faults, the pretences, all the great boulders of my failures and they will be a bulwark against the efficacy of any prayers, they will become a landfall so high and massive that the sea of grace must break in futility against it. The good God have pity on my soul.

Perhaps five, perhaps six, Easters have gone by since the day they asked me to copy out the Psalms. Such a privilege was mine, the Psalms! They gave me quills and parchment, vellum and pigments and all the space and peace that I would require. Such a trust was laid on me I felt humbled indeed. I set to the work with joy and enthusiasm, with that urgent excitement only a lot of good wine or honeyed spirit can give the mind, as if at last you have discovered what is to be the great task that will give meaning to your life.

And today I am to present the finished work to Abbot Maonlaigh. I dread to think what he will do or say when he sees the lines going each which way, the scrawls and scribbles and scrabbles; for all I have succeeded in doing is adding here or there a gloss, some little thought that has surfaced out of all my foolishness and suffering, that may illuminate for a moment the darkness of another soul. I do not know if the words are legible; I do not know if they flow evenly on the page. Even Abbot Maonlaigh is unaware that I have been blind for five Easters. Even poor lumpy Lalachán, whom I have used, abused and dishonoured, does not know the secret. I will be so disgraced. I would not be surprised should they decide to burn me for a criminal and hypocrite in the punishment enclosure. Let them do their worst; it will be their best; for what will it be but purification, the final gloss on my own most sordid living and a fine rehearsal of the suffering that must hold me in its fires for the whole of eternity.

I write down this so that you may pray for me, so that Abbot Maonlaigh may come, some day, to understand, and so that he may read it for Lalachán, the good, the foolish, the manhandled, and that she may be exonerated for ever from all blame.

PRIME

I came out this morning into clean air. I stink, like an animal lifting itself at last out of its fouled lair. I can still sense the night hanging over the monastery in little shivers of coolness and comfort, and a gentle breeze out of the west still holds the scent of night-flowering things. I inhaled the day, drawing into my being such a sudden breathing of loss and sorrow it made me stumble and fall onto the sacred ground. When I hand over the terrible failure of the Psalms, this insult to the trust and intelligence of my brethren, it will be clear that all I have done in this world will be as a bucket of wood-ash blown away in the eastering wind. But all I write down here is true, if you should find it legible, for I have nothing now to lose except my immortal soul, and that is already compromised.

In the sycamores rooks were squabbling, their noise so delightful to me after the smooth and accusatory Latin that had lingered after lauds. I lay, where I had fallen on the trodden earth, for a long while, breathing in its cold, damp scent. Sometimes that scent reminds me of the flesh of Lalachán and I knew again, when that thought returned, that I am damned to have my own flesh forever burning off my bones. And yet, lingering on the ear, the lovely words, *Hear me, you roughcast coastlands, listen to me, ye foolish peoples! the Lord called me from birth and in my mother's womb I had found my name.*

I snorted. Buite! What a name! Buite. But this is my monastery, here I came to find a place where men could purify their souls of the inconsequent effects of the world, a place to study God's own story, and to set out in words and pictures the great songs that tell of our God. But now the parchments I was carrying had spilled out from my hands over the earth. Even the order I had them in would be upset. Abbot Maoinlaigh might at least understand how I tried. I have always loved the Psalms and I have known them all by heart for many years. When you are blind it is impossible to find your place on vellum, impossible to get the point of the quill to move where it ought, impossible to know the pigments and dyes you need. Five years. Squiggles and scratches and jumbles, and gobbets of unmixed colours staining everything. Now, too, bits of grass and clay off the wet earth, my life's works a mockery, and the songs I love a torrid mess.

I picked myself up as best I could. There is pain around the middle of my body as if an iron belt were clasping me, growing tighter all the while. Kidney or stomach or something long fallen useless, the fruits of the monastery garden no more than turnip, watercress and hazelnut. I gathered up the parchments, the vellum, postponed my inevitable humiliation and crept back into my cell. I will wait for vespers, wait until the Abbot is placid and sleepy and might not have the energy to cast me out.

I lay down again on the straw; my fingers have grown expert at seeing, my body has been dunted from knocking against stone cross and hard clay wall, dunted too from the sinful pounding sweet Lalachán has inflicted on me. My eyes, I know, look no different, but from the first she could see my whole soul within my eyes and what she saw she relished. I was hard on her at first, a rather dull and stupid orphan girl from the settlement outside our walls, so plump and twisted and ungainly that I believed she would cause the brethren no distraction. So I gave her work, and worked her hard. She fetched and carried, she handled cow and sheep and goat, she cleaned and sorted and arranged, becoming amongst us scarcely more visible than a haze, no more present to the senses than the autumn stillness.

TERCE

It was at terce that Lalachán first discovered me. I had been struggling all night long with my dreams and visions, the devils calling to me, the most desirable of flesh offered in its manifold but insubstantial perfection. I had stripped my poor body bare, down to my pathetic skin, rough as parchment itself, and my twig-thin bones; I had crouched, for hours, in the clump of thistle, scutch and nettle that saved me before from the rank invaders. And that night I had had the victory. That night my hand did not stray towards my sinful flesh, to ease its swollen urging to release. Towards matins hour I laid me down again on the old straw, my naked body stretched and suffering, but unconquered. I slept, the Lord forgive me, for it was the hour of terce when I awoke and I could hear the monks at their chanting. The giggles and wheezy breathing of Lalachán brought me to my senses. She stood at the entrance to my cell, watching me; she was laughing, no doubt at my wretched and naked body, thin and long as a fallen branch. She wore a frayed gown that reached to her ankles, her large body more unshapely underneath the cloth. And yet I could see that her breasts were great and her body round the thighs was full and wholesome.

'They sent me to see was you all right,' she said cheekily, and she grinned down upon me.

I nodded. She laughed again and I knew my member had stiffened and all my efforts in the night had achieved nothing. *Hear me, O God, and judge my cause ...* For some reason her laugh seemed to offer exoneration; it was the sacred music of understanding. I lay there, stiff and trembling. She watched deep into my eyes, and she knew me. Then her gaze wandered down my body as if she were measuring me. *Amongst those who are born of women ...* I tried to myself, but it was no good. I was a bird fascinated by the fox, caught and held, and relishing it.

She turned slowly, until her broad back was over me. Then, slowly and deliberately, she lowered her great body onto my chest, ending by plopping her backside heavily on me. I gasped under her enormous weight. I was lying on thin straw so that her whole weight was upon me. I was crushed, squashed, and loving it. The coarse cloth of her gown itched me but allowed a full sense of her shape and flesh. I breathed quickly, with difficulty. She turned her head and smiled down at me. Her hair was twigs tangled in a thorn bush. She had a small squint in her light blue eyes. Her cheeks were chubby, her teeth, when she grinned, were gapped. I suffered her weight with great pleasure. She, too, must have found satisfaction in simply sitting there, and if she did, then how could I forbid it? At length I felt her hand move, gently but firmly, onto my swollen flesh and scarcely had she grasped it in her strong hand than my whole body spasmed with uncontainable pleasure and I came, spurting my load onto my thighs and across her strong and chubby fingers. She chuckled loudly. I would have died for shame.

SEXT

I have been lying here in my many layers of darkness, remembering. I cannot yet find the courage to approach the Abbot, for after that I shall have the greatest need to confess. I said nothing to Lalachán, not one word that night, nor ever after, nor did she ever speak to me again. We have a rule of perpetual silence here, to be broken only in the gravest need. This rule I have kept. And greater ones than it I have smashed to smithereens. I shall be doused in Hell pits.

That first evening, I confessed. Abbot Maoinlaigh listened to my tearful outpourings and told me that I was confused, my fasting and my prayers had me worn down, all that had happened was in my mind, he said, I was mixing up reality and unreality, it was fantasy, a gentle tickling from the Devil, masturbation was one of the most impossible things to control. His voice sank to a whisper; he leaned his holy head towards me; he whispered sometimes it is good to release the surging fluids of the body, to free the spirit for more serious worship. God would forgive, he assured me, He would understand. I was to say five Paters and I was absolved.

I will make of you a beacon light to the people, that my salvation may be visited to every corner of the earth. It was during our chanting of sext one day, oh several years before this, when I heard Brother Clonclahaigh, from his position on the tower, hammering on the great warning bell. The noise sent fear through us all, dread and terror. Outside the walls a few militiamen, the few we had to take some small care of the monastery and settlement, were blowing their horns madly. We were being attacked. It happened regularly in those times. And Red Rúdach was the most common brigand. A fearless, desperate and idiotic hero, used so often by our rival monks in the monastery by the ocean to steal our treasures, to maintain their own supremacy.

At the very heart of one of my favourite psalms, number 122 – *I knew naught but joy because it was announced to me that we shall go up now into the Lord's house* – at that very moment all hell broke out. Panic in our little chapel, the Brothers racing all which ways to gather up our treasures, the chalices of gold, the silver plates, the patens, our own small stock of living gold, such things the stuff of this bleak world. I made my own quiet way out into the furthest corner of our grounds where nettle and thistle reign among the uncared-for bramble bushes and unkempt grasses. It was not the thought of Lalachán's delighting body that was driving me to distraction yet again; this time the devils, several of them, pranced-danced about me, male and female both, their brown bodies naked and over-sexed, their stag- and doe-heads leering and pouting, and I could not by plea or prayer chase them from my presence. More terrible this to me than those brigands and warriors the monks had sent to prey on us, for not one of them, in their wildest moments, can ever touch our immortal souls.

And I was sure, oh vanity of vanities, that we were strong enough to repel them, to keep them beyond our walls or, at least, to hold them useless beneath our high round tower. All beyond me then was war and chaos, the brothers, the women and children, even the lesser animals, clamouring, climbing up through the high mouth of the tower. Within me war and chaos, too, and I stripped myself naked and fell into the briars, the brambles, the thistles, slashing my heaving body till the devils must take flight and abandon me.

It was, it remains, no small task. I don't know how long I wrestled with my flesh and mind, suffering cut and tear and sting. I howled, but my cries were lost amidst the tumult about our sacred grounds. When, at last, she-devils first and he-devils after, the temptations had left me, I lay still, spent, on the wet, bruised earth, thorn and bramble wrapping me, a thing of mud and blood and spittle-froth, suffering, but triumphant.

Suddenly a man's body came hurtling in across my hiding-place and I leaped up, prepared for a merely physical combat. It was the enemy, a tall man with a long grey beard, wearing bearskin trousers and nothing else, and he was already dead, a javelin through his throat. Gone down to Hell, I knew, down where my devils dwelt.

I looked out on the battle-scene cautiously. There was may-hem about the monastery grounds. There was screaming, men and women were falling, staggering, the soldiers butchering, animals roaring and running hither-thon into bushes, into walls, into our own small clay cells. But the tower was still secure, the ladders raised, the great mouth shut. From above there came a volley of stones and rocks down upon the enemy. It was when I saw the great warrior himself, the leader of the marauders, Red Rúdach, infamous throughout the land, that my heart misgave me. He was a giant of a man, something like that Goliath of my Psalmist's acquaintance, red-bearded, bare-chested, bare-footed, leggings of wolf-pelt reaching to his waist, and a throw of wolf-head strapped over his shoulder.

Around the base of our tower the enemy had built a large pyre in spite of the rain of stone down upon them. The pyre had risen almost to the high door and I knew at once the trouble all inside would face. The fire would reach, burn through the door, take in its maw the wooden floors within and broil and roast all living flesh that had sought shelter in the tower. Naked I was, and thin as a whippet, already a thing for mockery and buffoonery, but I saw the lighting brand in Red Rúdach's fist and I lost all dream of dignity and foolishness, all mystery of love and grace. I drew the javelin roughly out of the soldier's throat, half his jaw coming away in a mess of flesh and blood along with it; I balanced it in my hands. I knew a coolness and strength as if the Lord himself had touched me. *May those who love you prosper! May peace be within your walls, prosperity in your buildings.*

I roared, and came charging like a boar out of the undergrowth. Red Rúdach had scarcely time to turn but I can still see that smirking grin, that shock of red in hair and beard, and those eyes suddenly lighting up with terror. My rage and speed, along with the Lord's guiding hand, carried that javelin, with its gobbet of soldier's flesh, through Red Rúdach's chest, lifting him bodily from where he stood, and impaling him on the timbers of his own pyre. The lighting brand fell from his right hand, his sword fell from his left, his mouth dropped open and I saw a gush of the blackest blood flow down onto his chest. His eyes were yet fixed on me, my quivering naked body with a new and ghastly erection amidst my bleeding ribs and heaving chest.

'Amen!' I screamed. 'Amen and Alleluia!'

I trampled, with my naked feet, the lit brand into a smouldering, useless stick. I lifted the cruel sword of the dead Red Rúdach, the sword with which he had created havoc. It was heavy, but my blood was hot, I saw only devils in the enemies and, calling on the name of the Lord, I laid about me with that sword, creating my own, my sacred havoc. Whether it was that God Himself was at my side and all about me, or whether it was the sight of my skinny frame, naked and scraped and soiled, and sporting a fine erection, I will never know, but the enemy fell back and away before my roaring onslaught. With both hands swinging that dreadful sword, I hacked and swung at any foreigner who was fool enough to come within my reach, scattering blood and shattering flesh, spreading gore across the grasses, the graves and the high stone crosses, spattering me and them with the terrible fruits of slaughter. And all the time, before their eyes, their indestructible leader, Red Rúdach himself, was impaled onto the stones of our round tower. *You have turned back the sharp sword of my enemy, you have not sustained him in battle.*

It was over. The remnants of our foe went scurrying out through the smashed gates of our enclosure and I was left standing, spent, victorious, covered in blood and sweat and spittle, the horrid sword growing suddenly too heavy in my hands. There came an extraordinary silence. An early afternoon blackbird struck up a song. The soft, uncertain lowing of cattle came from the furthest edge of the enclosure and somewhere in the far distance dogs barked feebly. When a cock crowed outside the walls I dropped that sword as if it were a white-hot thing in my hands. I gazed about me. Bodies were everywhere, some still writhing in agony, others in that perfect peace that only death can bring. Slowly the Brothers, the women and the children came climbing down out of the tower and I knew again that I was naked. I could scarcely move, what with weariness and the anguish that only the destroyers of men must know. My people gathered about me, holding a careful distance, whispering, the brothers approaching cautiously until someone opened up a psalm, number 89, and began the chant of none: *I have found David my servant and with my holy oil have I him anointed. Of a stripling have I made a champion, over the nations have I set a youth. That my arm be with him always, that my arm may make him strong.*

I was a slimed, forked thing of clay and spittle, and the tears flowed down my beard for my enormous sinfulness. But some of the Brothers came and held me, in their hands they bore me up, fetching me amidst acclamations, across the prostrated bodies to the sanctuary of my cell. Gently they laid me down upon the straw, pleading with me that I should take my rest. They left me in the welcome dimness of my cell and I dropped away into a dreamless sleep.

NONE

What a day that had been! and what a sinner I! If I had handed them the great mess of my work upon the Psalms that day Abbot Maoinlaigh would have counted it a masterpiece. But here I am again, on that same straw, hopeless and terrified, knowing I have not won over my own flesh and that, burdened with the impossible burden of my failures, I will soon face eternal judgement. I decided to wait – to wait until my soul had eased itself into some sort of real contrition – then I would lay my burdens down at the Abbot's feet, the mercy of the night enfolding us.

As it had enfolded me that evening when I had helped dispatch our enemies. I lay, naked still, my body terrible in others' blood and sweat, in my own blood and sweat, scratched and scraped and sore, when a soft and welcome sound brought me back from sleep onto the hard earth. It was evening; the little light that filtered through from the world scarcely brightened my cell but I knew at once, by instinct now and by the great shape of her body, that it was Lalachán. I was wide awake at once. From our little chapel I could hear the monks: *When kings see you they shall stand up, and princes shall prostrate themselves because it is the Lord who has been faithful to you and you have been faithful to the Lord.* None. I know it was not me they were praying about and I uttered a little ironic moan to the air.

Lalachán moved slowly towards me where I lay. She said nothing, but she was clapping her hands together as if to express her, and the settlement's, delight in my achievements. Then again she was standing over me, the thin gown she wore outlining the great buttocks, the heavy breasts. When she turned and backed slowly over me, my foolish member leaped at once into firmness. She lowered herself, settling her body down on my chest, as she had done before. Oh she was heavy, I thought my chest might cave in under her weight, I thought my lungs would not find breath, but it was wonderful to me, as she shifted her body, finding her own comfort. She sat quietly, offering me this homage, this kindness from her being. I took shallow breaths; I lay in ecstasy. The voices of the monks still came across the grounds to me but I could not now make out the words. She sat perfectly still, at peace; I lay beneath her, conscious of my weakness, my strength.

I think I could have made of that my eternity. I don't know how long I bore her weight but there came a moment when I felt I could support her no longer. I gasped aloud and moaned a little. She laughed softly, lifted herself a little and thumped her buttocks down on me again, a little lower on my body, on my stomach, winding me utterly. And then her left hand touched my face, her fingers probing, one chubby finger pushing its way through my lips into my mouth, and I began sucking on it, sucking loudly and foolishly, like a wayward child. Her fingers tasted of earth and grit and sourness but she had heisted her gown and had slipped my member deep inside her. She began to lift and drop her body softly and rhythmically and I could hear small animal cries, short, high-pitched calls. I held myself back for as long as I could. As long as I could. Afterwards she laid her body down full length on top of mine, her great breasts under my face, her own face next to mine, and she was asleep, instantly. She was still heavy though now the weight was distributed over me. I heard her loud breathing against my ear; her bosom heaved gently on me, her belly lay pressing down on mine. A great mixture of odours swirled about me, her fetid breath, a smell of goat and sour milk from her gown, her sweat, all mingled with my own sweat and the blood I had spilled, my own and others. She slept. She was at peace. At that moment I heard the brothers in the chapel begin the wonderful hymn of thanksgiving to the Lord, *Te Deum Laudámus*, the music swelling in power and joy. Crushed underneath Lalachán's wonderful body, I joined quietly in the song, *te Dóminum confitémur* ...

VESPERS

I have been sitting for a long time now, conscious that the light of day must be dimming outside. I have been imagining how the enclosure must appear, the high crosses casting long shadows, the yew trees gleaming emerald, the sky behind the towers a glorious evening pink. And in the chapel they have been singing the Psalms: *The Lord is by your hand, your right hand; the kings of the earth he shall crush; he will wreak his judgement on the nations, he will heap the corpses high* ... How could I help but weep, my body soon to be one of those corpses, my efforts despised by God and man, my soul poisoned through with sin?

That long and wondrous night I lay under Lalachán, and in spite of utter weariness, I could find no sleep. This heavy creature of flesh and blood and animal excreta crushed me down into the earth, me, a sweating animal creature covered in filth and gore, but whose soul was the more corrupt in all things human. Lalachán shifted and jerked and stirred; sometimes she snored and farted and once, in the blackest reaches of the night, she clambered up and went out of the cell, leaving me to breathe freely at last.

Somewhere before first light I must have slept, I don't know how long, and when I woke there was the merest hint of light in the day. I lay awhile, spent, but strangely peaceful. Then I heard a voice call my name softly, *Buite*. Who dared to speak through this, the most sacred silence, the Great Silence? Then I wondered if I had heard anything at all. I was wide awake now. I listened, heard no footsteps, no rustling. The voice came again, *Buite. Climb*. I thought I must have misheard. *Buite. Climb.*

With gentleness a soft light and pleasant warmth pervaded my cell and I stood up, uneasy. I was surprised to find myself unshaken, without ache or pain, and I moved with ease out into the faint light. Somewhere, far away, a cock crowed in a desultory way, anticipating something. A lazy mist hung just underneath the departing blackness of the night. Even the Brothers were yet asleep, the call for matins had not sounded. Stillness. And quiet. Something blessed about the trees in their lift of utter perfection, something wonderful about the fullness of the silence.

It was some moments before I heard that voice again, so gentle it scarcely sounded at all. *Climb.* And then I noticed it, a thick hempen ladder with hempen rungs gracefully made and gracefully knotted, reaching down to me out of the dimness above. I began to climb. Without thought. Without fear. It was not easy, rung after rung, the rope yielding to my slight weight, and I thought my wearied and earth-roiled body might not be able to mount too high. I scarcely wondered what this was all about, my mind being darkened, my soul dimmed. I obeyed that voice, no more.

In scarcely a few moments I was well above the monastery grounds, high as the top of the round tower, the greyness of the pre-dawn light was shifting, and the rope reached upwards. I reiterate, it was not easy; the rope, unfixed below, swayed and swung with my every effort and, as I rose higher, I clung on the more tightly. I am not one for heights; my preference is the ground, the solid, soiled and lovely earth.

The rope ladder vanished into the grey of low clouds above me. Now when I looked down the cells and tower of the monastery, the huts of the settlement, all looked small and wizened, so far below, so pathetic. I stopped, shivering with fear; should I fall now that fall would be fast and certain, and I could see my body loop and swirl, I could hear that awful thud against unyielding ground. I gripped more tightly, leaned my head forward between the rungs and closed my eyes. I held on, frozen. Stilled. Until I heard that gentle voice again, encouraging, *Climb!* I rose slowly. There was a breeze stirring about me and I felt cool, in spite of the efforts of my climbing.

When I looked up again I was at the base of the clouds. I hesitated. They were swirling and moving and appeared dense and menacing. But then I was rising through them, the ladder still reaching upwards. In those grey clouds I felt a sudden extraordinary exhilaration; there was a chill amongst them, a moistness, I had some small difficulty in taking my breath, but now that I could no longer see the earth below I was light-headed and excited by this adventure.

I emerged, at last, above the clouds. And what a great and wonderful shock that was! Higher still I could see another layer of clouds, white and pure and beautiful. The clouds below me were wrinkled and ruffled, like a vast grey strand where the waves have been. And I could see our world again, laid out in shapes and patches of green and brown, so very small now, and in the distance a dazzling sheen off the sea that was stippled everywhere like chilled flesh. Like lemon skin. My terror grew once more; the ladder lurched as I climbed, threatening always to tumble me and oh! that dread I had of falling became at times so overwhelming I knew the urge to fling myself away from that dread and yield to inevitable destruction, but that gentle voice was urging, *Climb, Buite. Climb.*

By now the world was a silver-blue cloth unconscionable distances below me, patched and folded, threaded with grey; there were the mountain tops and they were flagged with snow, so beautiful I gasped with pleasure. While all about me and above were blues and indigoes and violets that left me breathless with wonder. So many blues I had not thought. So poor, I knew, our illuminated pages. So majestic, so far beyond us, is our God. If we could find such blues, such white-blues, such cobalt-blues, perhaps we might capture the merest shadow of the shadow-image of God.

I had thought – oh foolishly had I thought so many things – I had thought our world flat as a dish and souls went tumbling off the edge of it down into Hell. I had thought it flat as a many-coloured goatskin page floating leaf-wise on the empyrean. Now I thought it might be a ball, or a great and wondrous egg that might hatch us all one day into eternity. I had thought, too, that by rising towards the sun I would feel warmer, I would burn, but it was not so, not so at all. I grew colder as I rose; at times my fingers on the rope became so chilled I had to pause and breathe on them to ease them. Until at last I looked above me and saw a small rent in the deep blue of the sky through which my ladder rose and disappeared. As I continued to climb a strong and naked arm appeared and held me and drew me up into the marvellous.

Behold I tell you a mystery! Indeed shall we all rise up and shall be changed, in a moment, in the twinkling of an eye. I stood, entranced, and a great multitude stood about me, numberless and beautiful. My senses swelled with a pleasure more intense and wonderful than I can express. There are no words ... There are no psalms ... The splendour, the joy, the sheer unadulterated happiness, the peace, the wonder. Trees planted by running water. And in the distance, the glory ... Why do we love what is vain? why seek we after falsehood? There was light. What is man that you should be mindful ... you have made him little less than the angels ...

It was only a glimpse, only a moment, only a savour, but the gladness of it all, the glory and the knowledge that now nothing lacked, absolutely nothing lacked, and suddenly I was outside again, where I had been, my hands and feet on the hempen ladder, the chill of the height I was at taking my body once more, and I clung, bereft, I wept and pleaded, I called, I begged, until I heard that most gentle of voices once more, *Descend, Buite. Descend.* All my senses had been strained beyond supporting by the wonder I had partaken of and I hesitated long, my eyes raised towards the empyrean; I could no longer see that rent in the heavens, there was no hand reaching and then, oh gift of grief, my sight began to dim, as if someone slowly turned down a lamp until I could see no more, nothing but blackness, nothing, nothing, nothing.

I am blind now, but my body overflows with vision like an old clay jar stooked full with wine. And when I had felt the earth again beneath my feet, when I had crept back into my own dim cell, when I had clothed my febrile flesh, when I had knelt on the ground and offered many psalms of praise to my own Lord, I heard the Brothers begin the matins song and my heart trembled within me, in longing, in grief, and in joy.

COMPLINE

I know now that darkness has fallen over the earth. The

Brothers have begun the compline prayers. May the Lord Almighty grant us a quiet night and a perfect end. Recalling my welcome into Paradise, I went at once, braving my fears, to Abbot Maoinlaigh to confess my great sins, to show him the sorry mess that I, a blind man, had made over these five years, pretending to copy out the Psalms, pretending to write my glosses, pretending to colour with glory and accuracy the letters and figures of the work. The vellum, the parchments, were no more than a soggy bundle in my arms.

They had told me, my Brothers, they had so worried about me, for Abbot Maoinlaigh had visited me, during prime, the morning after Red Rúdach's invasion, to find me lying naked and still, in a very deep sleep on my palette of straw; that he had pitied me, my scars, my pains, my weariness. He had covered my pitiful nakedness and left me to sleep. And for seven full days, he assured me, I had slept and had not stirred from my position. They had fretted and prayed over me but there seemed to be an expression of serenity on my countenance so that they simply trusted, and left me. And never had they known, in all my work and prayers and chanting over those slow years, that, after my vision of Paradise when I could no more look on the things of this earth, that there was not the slightest light in my eyes. Lalachán had come, betimes, had wept over me and had brought a small bundle, the Abbot told me, to receive my blessing.

I presented myself and my sad labours, at last, before Abbot Maoinlaigh. '*Correct us, O God,*' I said, '*and turn away your anger from us.*' I laid the rubbish down upon the Abbot's desk and knelt on the hard earth, and waited. There was a pause. Father Abbot gasped. I expected him to belabour me with blows and curses and spittle, but there was silence and a gentle rustling of vellum. At last he spoke, and there was awe and wonder in his voice. '*You put gladness into my heart,*' he whispered, and I knew it was compline, psalm number four, '*more than when grain and wine abound.* A masterwork, Buite,' he added, 'the lettering so perfect, the colouring so bright and wondrous, so much of blue, I had not known there were so many blues, and all your verses ruled and lined and ordered. And not a blot, no imperfections in the text, so wonderful, a life's work, a glory to our God and our monastery, a grace unto your soul.'

There was such sincerity and gladness in his voice that I fell at once onto my face on the ground of his cell and hid my head in my hands and wept and wept for gratitude. He lifted me gently; '*You are in our midst, O Lord,*' he said, '*your name we bear. Alleluia.*'

Now I am waiting, and peace has come upon me. I am lying on my straw on the cold, hard earth and a great weight of pain has taken over my body. It will be soon, Lord, soon. I hear the Brothers in their holiness draw towards the close of compline; *now do you dismiss your servant, Lord, according to your word, in peace.* Soon they will have begun the *Salve Regina* and I know their hearts and voices will rise, extolling the beauty of peace and the silence of night. Mother of Mercy, our sweetness and our hope. I know before the end of this hymn I will be back in that glorious place, and my eyes will open upon light and love and praise. *Turn then, most gracious advocate, thine eyes of mercy towards us, and after this, our exile ...*

FEVER

I had been sleepwalking all day. The streets shone with a glazing of rain and great drops came plopping off the awnings and I counted them as I walked, three hundred, four hundred, five, and still I was not wet. There was the usual frenzy of cars and buses and trucks about the streets but I moved among them as if I were a piece of gossamer, blown safely out of the way at every danger. The people were busy and preoccupied as usual but to me they were insubstantial as mist. I had nothing to do with them. Then I drove as if I were sleep-driving. How I turned into the estate I will never know, but turn I did and drew up safely before our house. The trees along the suburban avenues were children's shapes of dark green. A blackbird sang on the roof-ridge and his music flooded down the chimney and filled the living room with molten gold. I bumped into chair and armchair and table-edge but I was not hurt. I passed from room to room as if there were a purpose and never opened any door. And there was no one, from dawn to dusk, to whom I offered any words and no one, from dawn to dusk, to offer words to me.

I sat in the high-backed armchair and drank whiskey neat and it was nothing more to me than clear and tepid water. Slowly the darkness crept, like packs of silent predatory animals, out of the corners of the room, from the sullen dark-faced TV set, from the bookshelves filled and abandoned, and in from the neglected garden outside. In the grate, over abandoned ash and cinders, there were balled-up pages of papers filled with news of the world; it was history and some day I would wish to burn away all of the past along with those pages as their arms blackened and reached for hold towards the perfectly moulded briquettes.

Once, the piano strings twanged softly from behind me and I rose and ran my fingers over the polished lid and played your favoured tune. The blackbird had gone silent and the music drummed out harshly in my head. The streetlamp lit up slowly, pale at first as any ghost, and its water flowed noisily in to where I was and left me colder than I had been for a long time. The chestnut tree outside our gate absorbed the light into itself and played with it its own rhythmless music, of white and black and green, of bulb and leaf and shadow, and before I knew it there were tears everywhere and I had smashed the crystal filled with whiskey against the empty hearth. I had been sleepwalking all day, but I had made it through and now I did not need to pretend any more, there in the forbidding darkness, in that noisome isolation. I had been sleepwalking all day, but I had made my purchases and added to the accumulating concrete of my stores. Thus, today; thus, for so many days.

I could not sleep tonight. I lay in warmth and did not toss or fret. The city night glowed beyond me, with its stars and moon scarcely visible through the orange sheen of its night labours. A slight silvering touched the curtain and added to the darkness of the room. I was not afraid. I was remembering how your palm had cooled my forehead, how it would caress my face and lead me into stillness. I was remembering how your fingertips would draw the pain out through my bones and dispense it to the air, how your tongue would moisten the hard clay of my mind and make me malleable to the gentler forces of living. Once, you had drawn the bed over against the window so that day and night would be familiars and the laying down in ever-darkness would one day sing release. I was remembering your fingers.

I make promises to God that I cannot keep; I expect nothing in return. I closed my eyes and I could feel the distant light of the moon bathe me in its careful coldness. I was not surprised, when I opened my eyes again, to see you standing beside the bed, your gentling smile, your big brown eyes. You were speaking even before I had greeted you, you were telling of the waterfall, how we had imagined ourselves taken by the flow and lifted by the water out over the edge and onto air. I laughed to recall our game. And then you told me of the lagoon, how the water there is more pure than the purest blue of the summer sky, how we sat all evening under the jacaranda trees and tasted the grilled fish and drank the red wine. I was remembering how the smoke brought tears of happiness to our eyes, how you licked the tears from my cheek and turned them into words of love. You told me how we prayed that this dusk would linger with us for ever.

I was growing quiet, then, under your words. Your hand touched my brow and your fingertips moved on my face as if you touched the stops on a mountain oboe. I felt the hard bones of your fingers as they raked my body, I knew the moistening spittle of your words as again you made that sweet impossible promise and oh how my body hurt under your guidance, how I suffered the fever of my being, and how the exhaustion that you brought me would swiftly lower me into peace.

It was at that moment, when you had left me, when I felt the sleep come gently over me like a breeze, that I came to believe I would open my wrists and let the blood flow out onto the page.

DOWN ON THE FARM

Valentine Kidney pushed hard on the pedals of his bike. He would not let Gowlawaum Hill get the better of him. He was well jointed, his bike was freshly graced with gears. The day was mild. Once he topped the hill he could coast down into the townland of Killnamaine and the settled valley of his future.

He was finding it hard going. He gripped the handlebars, almost lifting himself out of the saddle to stand on the pedals. He was zigzagging on the hill and Valentine Kidney always liked to follow a straight, unbroken line. If he could focus his thoughts on something other than the hill ... the words of a song maybe ... but all that came to him was: *it's a long long way to Tipperary*; and that was no help at all. He forced into his mind the image of Maureen Tuite, naked; not that he had ever seen her in that state, but he hoped to, and he hoped the naked body might be more pleasing than the somewhat lumpy one that graced Main Street, Killnamaine. For a sweet moment a lusciously shaped, full body flitted before his mind till suddenly the chain broke and Valentine was almost flung to earth. He cursed and dismounted.

He leaned the bike a little from his body and looked at it. He had almost made the top of the hill, almost. He kicked the back wheel where the greasy chain dawdled along the ground. He wheeled his bike to the grass verge and laid it down, took off his overcoat and laid it carefully on the grass. He saw that just one rivet had come out of the chain. It was mendable.

'I'm ept,' he said aloud, 'and I'll fix you, you bugger you.'

The thought of his lordly sailing down the hill towards his target spurred him on. He found a stone and bent to hammer the rivet home. Then he stood the bike saddle-handlebars over arse and balanced it, working to get the chain back on. He could see it was slightly buckled but by dint of twirling the pedals and hoisting the links on carefully he managed to get it working again. As he straightened from the task and set the bike on its wheels he noticed there was a scribbling of black grease on the white cuffs of his best shirt.

'Bugger!' he said aloud. The shirt had cost him a day's wages. It was ruined. How can you get such a mess off a perfect shirt? Possible. Impossible. Ept. Inept. A robin began a loud and un-reasoned melody from a nearby blackthorn bush and Valentine jerked the bike towards it. The bird flew off.

For a long time man and bike stood together, impetus broken. Valentine felt that the straight line of his intentions had been blocked. Down in Killnamaine he knew that Maureen Tuite would soon be closing the shop for lunch break; the 'Closed' sign would be hanging on the door and she would be heading to Eden House for lunch. He had intended being there before her, lunch ordered, a glass of white wine for her, a pint of stout for himself.

He bent to recover his coat. It's always the future that fasci-nates, he knew, that draws you on as if you were being hauled by a rope. And if that rope breaks, you are jerked out of your way and thrown aside, till a new way appears and a new rope pulls. Slowly a gentle glow of satisfaction suffused Valentine's day, as well as a sudden awareness that he had been perspiring, what with the haul up Gowlawaum Hill, the mending of the chain and, no doubt, a certain nervousness over what his purpose had been.

He held the bike from him with the left hand; he lifted his right arm and sniffed towards his body. There was a healthy reek of male sweat, which, he was certain, would make Maureen Tuite cringe and frown. Valentine felt a great surge of relief that he had not made it into Killnamaine. He turned his bike back towards his own world and prepared to mount it. Now, he knew that his purposes towards Maureen were not inspired by love. Nor was it lust, Maureen's poor body resembling in its beauty the fine shape of a turnip. Not love; not lust; it was self-expansion – Thady Tuite being elderly and not in the greatest health, Maureen being sole heir to the fine acres that stretched away towards the midlands. Self-expansion. He would have to satisfy his lust some other way. Valentine heisted his coat, threw his leg over the saddle and let the bike take him cruising merrily back down Gowlawaum Hill.

'Disgruntled?' he asked himself. 'Valentine Kidney disgruntled? No, man, no. Gruntled rather, highly gruntled.' He kicked both feet in the air with relief.

At the bottom of the hill was Connors Cross. He cycled lazily to the front wall of Connors's Stores, leaned his bike against the wall and went in.

Thomas John Connors was topping up a whiskey bottle with some cold tea. He slipped the bottle under the counter as Valentine came in. 'Well, well!' Thomas John called out. 'Here comes Bright's disease.'

'How a' ya, Tommy Johnny?' Valentine grinned. 'What's Bright's disease?'

'Sickness of the kidneys, Val, sickness of the kidneys.'

'You're hilarious, Tommy Johnny, that's what you are. Hilarious. Give us out a bag of crisps there and a bar of Cadbury's best caramel. I think I must have seen two magpies today for I almost did something I shouldn't have done and it was surely only the good Lord Himself stopped me from doing it.'

'Away courtin', I'll be bound. Will ya quit! A mug's game, that. The women'll whip the life out a ya before ya can say shite! I see, Kidney son, you're double-wrapped like Donnelly's sausages for double protection. Overcoat, jacket an' all.'

Valentine was handling a pear, and grew conscious again of his dirtied shirt. 'Th' oul' chain broke on me. An' me headin' to town for the lunch.'

'Sure them hotel lunches aren't worth a hatful of skins, in any case. Can't beat a pear, a bag of crisps and a bar of chocolate.'

'And how are you yourself, Tommy Johnny? Well, I hope.'

'Ah sure, only mixed middlin', that's me, mixed middlin', an'
herself, as usual' – he gestured with eyes and hand towards the
world upstairs – 'whinin' an' goin' on an' complainin'.
Holidays, she's after. Sunshine, she says. Spain, she says, Torry
Molinass or some such, she says. Can you see her lyin' out on a
beach in her knickers, Val, an' me beside her, an' all them fancy
women in their thongs an' their nothin' above paradin' up an'
down in front of me? 'Twould be a question of the risen people
all day an' all night an' no mistake. Hah. Fryin' in the sun like
a lamb chop. An' for what? that's what I want to know. For
aggravation, that's what. Aggravation.'

'Sure there would be great gallery in that, Tommy Johnny.
You don't live for ever, you know. See a bit of the big world
man. Hollywood. Florida. They're all out there waitin' for you.
Go an' be appointed, man, bring the missus and her best knickers,
bring yourself an' yer best long johns.'

'Appointed, Val?'

'Appointed. Not disappointed. Appointed. An' I'll fill out
one of them lottery things as well, seein' as the two magpies are
still hoverin' about my head.'

Valentine Kidney's numbers remained constant. They fol-
lowed a logical line: 3, 6, 9, 18, 24 and 36. Week after week
he had marked in his numbers; week after week he had missed
out.

'Numbers,' he said. 'It's like the great steppin' out of time
and the universe. It's the succession, you know, Tommy
Johnny. The run of it. It's the force that keeps us all on the
straight path. The whole universe. Has to happen sometime,
long as the world lasts. But today is something else, today the
chain broke and that was surely a gift. Today I'm goin' to break
my own chain of numbers, the twenty-four looks too rounded
today, so I'm stickin' in my own age instead, twenty-seven. It's
the future, Tommy Johnny, always the future that gives us
hope.'

As he cycled homewards Valentine was in reflective mood.
Go with the events, he was thinking, take life on the hop. If
there's a road before you, follow along till the end; if there's a
lake before you, row across that lake. Look at Tommy Johnny,

stuck where he is and where he will always be. No change envisaged. No hope, for hope is the future and there's a great chain drawing us to the future, else we're the broken link and it all stops. He laughed aloud, thinking how he had escaped the ball and chain that marriage to Maureen Tuite would be. Val's living had always been a circular thing, round and round the perimeter of his small holding, round and round the perimeter of his small town, the perimeter of his country. And that always brings you back to where you started, getting off your bike again outside your own stable door, shutting the gate behind you, locking yourself into your own small field.

The self needs purposes of past and future. And that was Maureen safely scuttled. But as he sounded her name inside himself Valentine felt a sudden uneasiness. If not Maureen Tuite, then who? He had visions inside his head, visions of beautiful women giving themselves to him, to his needs, longings and whims. He had desires, sinful desires. He held the handlebars more tightly at the thought, crouched forward a little. He had longings, more than the nudge and giggle of the disco in The Ferris Wheel once a week, more than the wholesome and disinfected petting that was rarely permitted among any of the local women. He brought the bike to a full stop at his garden gate.

That night Valentine's numbers came up. He watched the television with a growing sense of uncontainable joy. 9 came up first, followed by 36 and by 3. When 18 tumbled out Val knew he had won at least a few good pounds. The God of straight roads was rewarding him. Then came number 6 and Valentine knew his reward would be great on earth. When the 24 came rolling out he screamed for very delight and pranced about the floor of his small kitchen. It was a while before he remembered he had changed his usual sequence. His heart plopped back into the muck of his stomach. But the TV computer told him that those who had drawn five numbers had all won a great sum, over nine thousand pounds. It was, after all, an exceptional miracle, a day that offered him some proof that life must be taken by the throat and shaken, that the longest road would take him out into the lushest valley.

On Monday morning Valentine Kidney booked himself a week's holiday in Paris, France.

Valentine stayed in l'Hôtel Chapelet just off Avenue Hoche, not far from the Place Charles de Gaulle. It was luxury unheard of, although he was a little disappointed in the breakfast. The first day he spent walking slowly along the rues, the avenues, the boulevards, his mouth wide open, and his eyes. Valentine was impressed. 'This,' he kept saying to himself, 'is livin'.'

Keeping his fingers carefully in his guidebook, he walked the straight line from the Avenue de la Grande Armée to the obelisk in Place de la Concorde. It took hours, the perspective shaking him, the miles of it, the buildings, the dust, the shops, the pigeons. And then he walked the whole way back again, under the disarming Paris lights. The second day he came back to the Place Charles de Gaulle and walked slowly round and round the great Arc de Triomphe. He sat on a bench and watched the beautiful people who seemed to be at home in this wonderful world. He walked down the left-hand side of the Avenue des Champs-Elysées and knew at first hand how poor the rushy fields were around Killnamaine. He saw elegance itself stalk in and out of the great, high shops and he knew how dull and unlovely was Maureen Tuite. He bought a sandwich near the Madeleine and then he walked the whole way back along the Champs-Elysées, on the right-hand side.

Late afternoon, to stop himself from such negative thoughts, he headed away from the wealth and show, for he had glimpsed, somewhere in the high reaches of the city, a fine white church he knew from the guidebook must be the Sacré Coeur. Clutching the book, he wound his way through lesser streets, through market-places and bustling squares, and found himself, tiring, on Boulevard de Clichy. Away up to the left he glimpsed the great church, dominating the world, gleaming in late afternoon sunshine. And then the long chain of his ramblings was rudely broken.

'Pictures, monsieur, photos? Some special pictures,

woman, naked, pissing, making love. Cheap, very cheap. You buy?'

A dark-looking man of indeterminate age was walking shoulder-to-shoulder with Valentine, offering cautiously a bundle of black-and-white photographs. Valentine, not wishing to be impolite, looked at the first of them, and blanched.

'No, no, no, no thank you,' he said and moved hurriedly on. But he was shaken. He was distressed and suddenly aroused. He put his head down and continued along the boulevard. And was stopped again.

'Live sex, monsieur, specially for you. And everything is free. Just step within. Yes?'

Here was a burly gentleman dressed in black suit, white shirt and dicky bow, just as the wealthy wear for weddings in Killnamaine, ushering Valentine towards the open door of a shop. Valentine glanced at the doorway and saw that everything within seemed to be in darkness but on the hoardings outside were pictures of lovely women, almost naked, posturing, smiling, welcoming. Valentine hurried on.

To escape such blandishments he turned sharply down a small side street and leaned back against a wall in the relative quiet, took deep breaths and tried to steady himself. His chest was heaving as if he'd ploughed half a field. His imagination was churning, almost noisily. Live sex! naked women! free! Where was he at all? Heaven?

'Live a little, Kidney,' he whispered, 'live a little. Who's to know? There's no Tommy Johnny Connors about here. And if it's free, what have I to lose?'

He dodged back out onto the boulevard and darted in through the dark door of Paradise of Sex without allowing himself any further doubts.

He had to push through a heavy navy-blue curtain and found himself in what reminded him of one of his stables back home. It was dark but over at one end there were shifting red, blue and yellow lights. Val put one hand up before his eyes and just glimpsed a woman, naked? waving her hands in the air, gyrating to very loud rhythmic music that seemed to Val to be nothing more than someone hammering on an empty barrel. Then she skipped to her right and vanished into blackness. Val's stomach was churning; he stood transfixed; he was in a den of iniquity. Thank God.

There was a restless shuffling in the dim room and a small stocky man, dressed in black trousers, black shirt, took Val firmly by the arm and began to lead him towards a small, round table at the front of the room.

'*Viens,*' he said, '*viens vite. Une belle table pour toi.*' He ushered Val to a hard iron chair and sat him down at the table. Then he said, as if it were the obvious thing, 'Some champagne for the gentleman?'

'Champagne?' Val had never touched the stuff. He was not sure he had ever seen champagne, except perhaps on television when the winners of some motor race seemed intent on drowning each other with it. But, well, wasn't he living, so, why not?

The man in black clicked his fingers and nodded. He moved away. Val tried to keep his head fairly low, as the room was lit with a faintly pink glow from some hidden lights. There were a few small iron tables like his own, a few isolated men sitting at them with glasses of beer or wine. A soft music was playing.

It was then that she appeared, a tall, beautifully built, dark woman, wearing a slight pink blouse that revealed her wondrous body. She wore a golden bra and very small panties underneath it and she walked majestically towards Val's table on very high shoes. She held a tray and on it a bottle and two tall glasses. Val was enthralled. She came right up to him and smiled down at him, setting the tray on the table before him.

'Champagne?' she said.

He nodded, swallowing with difficulty.

'English?' she asked.

He shook his head. 'No, Irish.' His throat and mouth were dry and stiff as planks. 'Ireland. From Ireland. Killnamaine.'

'Ahhh,' she said softly, as if she knew the place well. She lifted the bottle, expertly pulled off the covering, untwisted the little holder and pushed the cork with her two beautiful thumbs. The cork exploded into the roof somewhere and with a delightful chuckle she poured two glasses full of the foaming, bubbling liquid. She set down the bottle. And then ...

She bent down towards Val and motioned him to move his knees out from under the table. Then she turned slowly and sat her wonderful body on his knees. Val closed his eyes and let his whole being sense the glory of her buttocks on him. She leaned in on his chest and turned towards him. When he opened his eyes she was holding the glass of champagne towards him.

'Drink, *chéri*,' she said, and her voice was tinged with huskiness and sticky with honey.

He took the glass and sipped. It was cold, and he was hot. It was fizzy and slightly salty. But it didn't seem anything special. He looked at her. She had great black eyes. She was smiling at him as if he were the one she had been waiting for all her life.

She lifted her glass to him. '*Salut!*' she said.

'Cheers!' he responded and they clinked glasses softly. She sipped, a tiny sip. He drained his glass at one go. She smiled and filled it up for him again.

'I will only do to leave your count here beside us,' she whispered, pulling a small sheet of paper from inside her bra. She snuggled into him, shifting her weight about on his knees. 'What is your name?' she asked.

'Valentine. What's your name?'

She put up a long dark finger with its purple-painted nail and moved it softly down along his cheek. 'I am call Sascha,' she said.

He sounded the name deep inside his soul, where it lodged, sensuous and luscious and strong. He took another great gulp from his champagne. It was not great stuff, he thought, but it was wet and cool.

'You're black,' he said to her.

She laughed softly. 'You are very white,' she said. 'I not black. I think you say – cinnamon.'

Valentine was enchanted. He finished the second glass. She still had not taken another sip. There floated a phrase from

Sundays in Killnamaine into his mind, *let us build here three tabernacles*; Valentine had found eternity.

Sascha leaned further in against him and brushed her lips softly against his cheek. 'I go now,' she said. 'I dance. But you stay. And I come back. After.' She wiggled her bottom a little more on Valentine Kidney's knee, then she got up and moved away quickly into the darkness.

Valentine sat up straight. He gazed about him, proudly. He was disappointed to see that none of the men was watching, there was no ooze of jealousy anywhere. He poured himself another glass. He noticed a tiny purple stain on Sascha's glass and he smiled. He picked up the bill.

A cold stream of dread poured through his body when he saw the sum; it would come to almost one hundred and forty pounds, for the champagne, and the company. He was astonished. He thought it said free outside on the door. He was going to complain but just at that moment the pink light in the room went out and a low, exciting jungle music started up on what Valentine saw was a tiny stage at the top of the room. The red and blue and yellow lights started to flash and turn. Out of the darkness hidden ropes drew on stage a large round cage, like a bird cage, except that inside it he saw Sascha, his cinnamon girl; she was wearing only a tiny white bra and a tiny white thong, and around her neck was a delicate golden cross hanging from a tiny golden chain. In her right hand she held another chain and on the end of the chain, and Valentine gasped, was an animal, a large cat of some kind, a panther perhaps, he thought. For a moment he was terrified for her but then he could see the animal was tame and stayed languidly at her side, its eyes half-shut. The music rose in tempo. Cinnamon began to move.

She was incredibly beautiful. Her body was gleaming golden under the shifting lights, her muscles gleamed and rippled like the water in a mountain stream, her breasts and buttocks, generous and shapely, moved and invited and teased. She moved slowly, rhythmically, about her cage, about the cat, bending to the animal, touching it with her fingers, whispering to it. Valentine drained his third glass of champagne.

Sascha turned her back to the small audience, her hands came to the strap of her bra, she opened it, twirled it slowly in the air, drew it over the muzzle of the cat, then threw it from her on the floor. When she turned back she was smiling and her great breasts were pouting and demanding. She gyrated awhile and Valentine was annoyed when the man, dressed in black trousers and black shirt, appeared at his side.

'You like pay me now, please?'

Valentine reached into his inside pocket quickly, took out his money, counted out the francs and handed them over without complaint. The man reached for the bill and tore it softly in two. Val took another glass.

Now Sascha was standing astride the great cat, her legs, in their high heels, long and lovely on either side of the animal. The jungle music grew louder, the beat more frenetic and suddenly, with a scarcely perceptible gesture, Sascha had taken off the tiny thong and stood gloriously naked over the cat. Her hips moved sensually. Valentine was shivering with anguish and delight. All his past and all his possible futures had faded far from him and he felt moist and malleable before the world. He was alive, living in the present moment, now, now, now. He was conscious of his breathing, how it came in rushes, as if he had just climbed Gowlawaum Hill on his bike. And the present, the now, was holy; he was blessed and filled with grace.

Sascha had gathered the chain that was fastened to the great cat's collar, into her hand; she was leaning forward, her breasts brushing the back of the beast, she was whispering into its ears, whispering softly. Slowly the animal flopped its body down on the floor of the cage between her feet. She stood up straight then, mistress of the jungle, and the lights gleamed and shone on the tiny droplets of sweat that made her body more sensual still. Very slowly she began to lower her naked body, lower and lower, each movement answering the rhythm from the music that was loud and powerful. She poised her body a moment over the ribs of the animal and then let herself sink slowly down onto it. She sat up straight then, her body heavily and fully astride the animal, in command; she was beautiful and proud, the beast utterly in her control.

For that sacred moment even all the pain of Val's desires dripped away from him. He was no longer Valentine Kidney, angular and gangly, the go-boy, the tom, he was all being and he loved, he loved simply and purely and selflessly. He loved his Sascha, his cinnamon, with a pure love. For a moment, as she sat astride the animal, Sascha's eyes roved over the audience and met the eyes of Valentine Kidney, and she smiled.

Valentine stood up then and moved forward to embrace her, to tell her he was cured for ever of his unappeasable longings, that he had found eternity, its breadth and its breathing. The floor was littered with the scales of his longings, of his self-loathing, of his hopeless and debilitating masturbation. Before the small man dressed in black was aware of what was happening Valentine had reached one arm in through the cage, just to touch his woman, to let her know. But she screamed and jerked away from him and his hand reached and clutched wildly. Instantly he was seized in the most powerful grip he had ever known and was rushed quickly through the dark curtain and out onto the wet pavement of the Paris evening. The man in black was speaking venomously at him. Valentine was shocked to the depth of his soul but he understood the threat from this small man and he backed away. He turned a corner and leaned back against a wall, allowing the rain to fall fully on his face and body. Of course he had done wrong, he knew it at once, of course he was a fool, but he had lived. In his hand he held the small, broken chain from around the throat of his goddess. The little golden cross gleamed in the rain.

Two weeks later Valentine Kidney was pushing his bike up the Gowlawaum Hill. Not far from the top he dismounted, held the bike from him and walked slowly to the crest. He was taking up from where he had left off, as if nothing had been interrupted. He paused for a while and gazed down into the valley; the sun was shining weakly and in the distance, among the chestnut trees, the spire of the church rose into the sky. Valentine heaved himself more comfortably into his suit and overcoat, mounted his bike again and pushed it off to coast down the hill into Killnamaine.

CASUALTY

Ephraim Boran had spent the last few years working to become invisible. It was quite clear that he had not yet succeeded. As he turned the corner into Springdale Avenue, he could see Mrs Helen Aldridge McEnery bundling herself along the pavement against him. Mrs McEnery did not make any effort in life to make herself invisible, quite the opposite. It was not that she was enormously huge, but she puffed herself up in extraordinary manners to have herself noticed. Her elbows and arms always seemed to be extended, like an ancient urn; her reasonably sculpted bosom seemed to protrude further than agreeably natural; and she moved on the pavement as if she were a googly ball, weaving and bobbing from side to side.

She noticed Ephraim coming towards her and at once her two arms began a windmill-like rotation to warn him out of her way. In the early days, when Ephraim was still merely a curiosity in the estate, not yet to be despised and looked down upon, Mrs Helen Aldridge McEnery had confided to him, on the corner of Springdale Court and Springdale Park, that she lived in Springdale Close and that the houses in there were all detached, four-bedroom houses, with three bathrooms, a garage and a conservatory, and that they, the Aldridge McEnerys, even had gone and got themselves built a form of cellar where the Hon. McEnery stored his collection of vintage wines. 'You must move on the cutting edge of things, you know, my dear Mr Boran,' she had said. 'The cutting edge, where you can be seen to be making a difference, you know. Living.' Nowadays, however, she was a storm on the pavement and blew towards him as if he were a dog turd still moist before her feet.

Ephraim raised his right forefinger to his cap and lifted that item of clothing from his head a fraction of an inch, in salute. The greeting was ignored. Mrs Helen Aldridge McEnery's eyes were fixed on the moon, which still remained strongly visible in the sky on this bright and chilling January morning. Ephraim knew he had to step off the pavement and he did so, sharply.

At that precise moment Dave McGinnity, in his four-wheel-drive Trooper with roof rack and bull bars – his land-rover big and bullying as a train, bright navy-blue body that gleamed in the chilly light – had turned sharply out of Springdale Grove, his left hand mismanaging the steering wheel while his right hand manipulated a mobile phone against his ear. His anger was mounting at a deal that was not going as it ought. Momentarily he lost control of the car and it veered sharply across the avenue, whistling in an arc on the wrong side of the road until it thudded into the shabby figure of Ephraim Boran. There was a dull thumping sound, an irritated squealing of brakes, and Ephraim was sprawled on the pavement on the other side of Mrs McEnery. Dave's weapon of war screeched along the road another few yards, the tyres leaving black burn marks on the immaculate surface. Then there was silence.

Ephraim lay in a sort of comfort at the side of the road. Face down. On the edge of something. Between. For what seemed a good while he lay there, feeling no pain, feeling nothing, indeed, as if he had at last achieved his wish and had become not only invisible, but non-existent. He closed his eyes. There was a pleasing buzzbuzzbuzz in his ears, a pleasant kind of bubbling feeling in his inners and a general notion of wellbeing all through him.

This morning, in the church, he had noticed how the dead man had been housed overnight in a side-aisle. He thought how he must have spent the darkness, secure in his coffin, secure in the presence of the great crucifix that hung on the wall over the side-chapel, and surrounded by the whispering susurrations a side-aisle makes. Waiting, on the great ledge onto which he had fallen out of life. Ephraim knew that the coffin would be kept invisible from the rest of the human family for as long as possible. It was safe there, perched on its high trestle, bouquets of flowers laid on top, all else only absence and darkness. Nowadays even the candles under the crucifix were artificial, electric bulbs moulded in candle-shape that never got any smaller and that found themselves summarily switched off in the late evening, summarily switched on again in the morning, before the arrival of the first mourners.

And he had noticed, too, though perhaps this was merely a trick of the winter light coming through the high windows behind the altar, that the host, when the priest held it high and a tiny bell rang, appeared translucent, as if the very body of the Christ Himself was not there, but held up so that the world might see through it into the watchful blue eyes of God. Or into whatever they wanted to see beyond it. Ephraim was certain that that was the way he himself wanted to be: transparent; translucent; invisible; absent to the world. In any case the world had sidelined him, and here he was now, lying face down along the gutter as well as any scarcely noticed corpse of worm, or dogbody, or cat.

Angry voices brought him back to himself.

'For God's sake, are you all right?' That was surely Mrs Helen Aldridge McEnery.

For God's sake, she had said. Why for *God's* sake? Surely he was supposed, needed, demanded, to be alive for Dave McGinnity's sake, lest the poor young rich man be vaulted with the terrible mistake of killing off another (almost) human being.

'Let me phone, let me phone!' That was Dave the rampant, and Ephraim wondered, from his place of privilege, if there was anybody at that moment trying to stop him from using that wonderful, tiny gadget of his that summoned the world the way, in the time of otherness, one could draw a genie from a glass bottle.

Mrs Helen Aldridge McEnery was pushing at him with the pointed toe of her immaculate shoe. 'Can't you get up, old man? Get up! Get up!'

If only he were invisible now, how good it would be to lie here for ever, just looking at the beauty of the tiny stones in the asphalt, or the minuscule black insect that was making its way towards the shelter of the gutter. But Mrs McEnery's shoe was stabbing him in the buttock. He would have to move.

Slowly and painfully Ephraim drew himself up into a sitting position. When he was at last squatting on the footpath he felt as if his whole body were a flame of pain. Helen and Dave bustled anxiously about him, asking such and so many questions, and there were other people, too, many of them gathering and congregating and gaping.

'I'm OK,' he told them. 'I'm OK.' But he felt a terrific pain in his right shoulder, there was agony in some unknown quarter deep down in his stomach, and he could feel the blood coming from his face somewhere and stealing into his mouth with its taste of salt and misery. 'I'm OK, just help me up and I'll get home.'

Eagerly Dave McGinnity took him under the arms and heaved. Ephraim screamed with the dreadful agony of it and McGinnity, smitten, let him fall back onto the pavement. He lay, in a complete stupor of pain, for a while. As the suffering eased into a dullness he opened his eyes and looked up at the cold, clear sky. How beautiful it was. How he would like to be a gull, or better still a gannet, his plumage of the purest white, so that when he flew high and higher into that blueness that somewhere up there became silver, he would swiftly grow transparent, and then invisible, to any eyes below him.

There were feet, and legs, trouser legs and stockings and skirts, shifting and moving, and a face or two leaned in over where he was dumped and blocked out his sun. He watched their unreal faces, how out of focus and shape they all appeared. And then he began to make out voices, and words. And it was Mrs McEnery's voice he knew first.

'He just stepped out, I tell you, right off the pavement and into the path of the car. There was no way Mr McGinnity could have avoided him, no way on earth.'

Ephraim laughed. How foolish are we, how foolish. But even the small snigger his mouth and throat made caused him dreadful suffering in his side and he held his mouth and face firmly in control. He was in no hurry anywhere; wasn't he just heading home from his brush with the Lord? He would curl up in bed, in his own house, and disappear into the bliss of sleep.

'Like as if he almost wanted to kill himself!' That was McGinnity's insistent voice.

The anguished screaming of an ambulance siren hurt Ephraim, where he lay, and then he heard the powerful sound of its engine. He was being lifted again, more carefully this time, although even then the pain was very great. He moved between two men dressed in white; they were asking him things, 'Can you walk? Where does it hurt? Can you hear?' Questions, questions, questions, but he ignored them all, wasn't he invisible, wasn't he about to disappear?

'He just leaped out, right at me. My God, but if there's any damage done to my Trooper, he'll be hearing from my solicitor!'

They laid him down on something, they hoisted him, he felt almost seasick and was about to laugh but thought better of it. There were faces, many many faces, peering in at him before they closed the doors of the ambulance. The last words he heard before he passed away into blessed unconsciousness were those of Dave McGinnity: 'There was no way I could have avoided him. It looked as if he wanted to jump out in front of me. My car, my lovely new ...'

When he came back into the world of things and noises and pain, Ephraim was lying on a trolley in a small curtained-off bay. The first thing he noticed was a stain of what looked like dried blood on the partition wall near his face. There was a shabby curtain, plastic, with large ugly blue flowers, drawn across the opening. He could hear a lot of noise outside. He lay still for a while. There was a bag of something that looked like water hanging from a pole beside him; a plastic tube led from it and into his arm. There was a small plastic board with a sheet of paper fastened to it laid on his stomach. He did not feel bad. He was tired, there were dull aches from his shoulder and from his insides. But he was peaceful; he was in good hands.

He waited a long time. There was a lot of movement, comings

and goings, outside, an occasional voice raised in command, an occasional call. But nobody came near him. He watched the slow drip drip drip of the fluid down along the tube towards his arm. Somebody had taken his jacket off; it hung on a hook just inside the curtain.

At last a young nurse pulled the curtain slightly aside and came in. She barely glanced at him, touched the drip for a moment, picked up the form from his chest, glanced at it and put it back again. Then she left.

Ephraim called after her: 'Nurse!'

She put her head back in through the curtain.

'Am I all right?' he asked her. 'What's happening?'

'The doctors will be along to see you soon,' she said impatiently, then she vanished.

Ephraim waited again a long time. He dozed for short moments, then came awake with sudden anxiety. What if the drip ran out? He looked up at it; it still seemed quite full. There was an unshaded bulb in the ceiling above him. It must be afternoon by now, he supposed; he had no watch. He tried to make himself more comfortable on the trolley; there was a black plastic sheet spread under him and it made his whole body sweat. He tried to sit up. He was pleased there was no great pain anywhere.

Then another nurse came breezing in. She did not look at him at all. She went straight to a small cupboard in the cubicle and started rooting through it. Then she stood up, examining something.

'Is there a doctor coming, nurse?' he asked her tentatively.

She looked at him. 'Yes, yes,' she said abstractedly.

'What has to happen? Will I be kept in?'

She looked at him, scarcely seeing him. 'How do I know? A few X-rays maybe, to see if there's anything ... I don't know.' Then she, too, was gone.

X-rays, Ephraim thought, his imagination working; he saw his body like something of gossamer, the bones showing like ghostly black shadows, he saw fractures and breakages and then he could see through himself to the dirty wall beyond. He shuddered and tried to think of something else. The noises from outside continued. He was ignored. He could be invisible.

As the day appeared slowly but perceptibly to darken, Ephraim began to believe that indeed he was invisible. He moved his heavy body slowly round on the trolley, and swung his legs, cautiously, out onto the floor. He had no shoes on, just his socks, woollen and holed. He saw his shoes placed neatly together under the trolley. As he bent, again very cautiously, to get them he felt the slight tug of the tube in his arm and it popped out. He almost screamed in panic. Instead he called out, trying to keep his voice calm: 'Nurse! Doctor! Nurse!'

There was no response. Ephraim looked at his arm. There was a tiny bandage that had held the tube in place. There was cotton wool about it. He pressed it tightly over his arm. There was no blood. There was no problem. The fluid kept dripping very slowly out from the end of the tube; he lifted the end and placed it in a silver, kidney-shaped tray that was resting on the cupboard. He got his shoes on.

Ephraim stood up carefully. He shrugged his shoulders, he twisted his neck about. There was a dull pain, but it was clear there was no great damage done. Then he bent his old body, slowly, up and down from the waist; again the pain in his stomach somewhere was a dull one only; even without an X-ray he knew there was nothing awful there either. He took his jacket off the hook. There was a tiny mirror over the small hand basin in the cubicle; he glanced in it and saw there was a smudge of blood across his left cheek. He licked the palm of his hand and rubbed furtively at the stain.

Then he walked very slowly out from the cubicle. There was a kind of large hallway outside with cubicles like his all along both sides of it. Some of the curtains were closed, others were half-open. Nurses and doctors and orderlies dressed in light blue uniforms moved about, like ants, he thought. There were trolleys being pushed, some with people lying on them, others with green covers thrown loosely over them, moving somewhere, somebody surely knowing what was going on. For some reason Ephraim had a quick vision of the seashore on a summer day, crowded with people stirring about between earth and ocean, but silent, awe-stricken, unsure. Here and there were wheelchairs; most of them unoccupied. One with a very old man who was wheezing badly, the chair left at a strange angle to the wall. There was a large desk in the middle of the corridor and two big nurses in navy-blue uniforms, looking as if they were important, bustled about it with various papers and forms. He saw the exit sign at the end of the corridor. He wanted to get out. He would like to pass invisibly down the corridor.

Ephraim Boran assumed an air of nonchalance as he stuck his hands in his trouser pockets and moved slowly down the corridor. He had to step aside as a trolley came at speed towards him, pushed by an orderly in his green coat. On the trolley lay a young man who was grinning broadly to the ceiling as it passed rapidly above him. He did not glance at Ephraim. The old man continued, keeping in as close as he could to the cubicles on the other side of the corridor from the nurses' station. Perhaps they would not see him. Perhaps they could not see him. Then he was past them.

Suddenly a man with a stethoscope hanging about his neck, a big man dressed in an immaculately pinstriped navy-blue suit, came storming out of one of the cubicles. A great and important gentleman, surely, Ephraim thought, as he was quickly brushed aside. The big man was followed by a gaggle of young nurses or student doctors, all dressed in clean white coats, all intent on staying close to the great man. Like a waddle of ducklings behind daddy duck, Ephraim giggled. They moved down the corridor like a snowstorm. Ephraim continued on his way.

He noticed high on the wall over the exit sign a large crucifix hanging. He saw that the right hand of the crucified Christ had fallen loose from the cross beam and was hanging out over the corridor, as if pointing. There was a large cobweb between that broken arm and the crossbeam. The world moved on underneath the figure as if that very crucifix were invisible. Ephraim crossed himself hurriedly, then looked around to see if anybody had noticed his strange action. The bustle and harrying continued the length of the corridor as far as he could see and hear. Ephraim's hand reached the door. He pushed. He was out in another waiting room. The door to the yard outside was wide open. He moved quickly towards it, then he was out in the open air again. He did not dare hesitate. He had no money. He set off quickly towards the great hospital gates. He gathered all his forces. It would be a long walk home.

THE LANGUAGE OF HANDS

The night was perfect. It was crisp, so you could hear the sounds travelling for miles across the country darkness. It was dry too. I was outside the house from eleven thirty onwards, I stood outside the front door and there was scarcely a sound from the old ash trees. But the stars were as beautiful as ever I've seen them. How the mind fails utterly before their numbers, their patterning, their extent. I saw them that night as if I had never seen them before and somehow I felt that it would be up there, among the constellations, that something would have to happen. After all the forecasting and apprehension, surely some mighty event was about to take place.

Who cares about the little glitches that might occur in computers, in some neon-lit functional offices high in the city? Momentary disruptions to business and economies, of no import whatever! Who cares about the little slips and foolishnesses some laptops might suffer here and there in the money-scalded hands of investors? I was thinking about kilter, how the living universe itself might slip in some way, sag or lurch or lean, how a whole galaxy might shift a little across the sky, exposing for the fraction of a second a rent in the blackness, allowing a glimpse – to those who wish to look upward from the earth instead of downward to immaculately soiled hands – of the ultimate God-stuff, the love-matter, that is spread across the whole acreage of eternity.

I know; an old man grows foolish. The more he has learned through a long hard life, the less he knows. The closer he comes to the final locking of the gate at the furthest end of the lane,

the more distant he thinks himself from that gate and the nearer
to the simplicities of his earliest days as he set out upon the lane.
I can scarcely recall what happened last week, last month, but
every detail of colour, smell and sound of my early days over
eighty years ago comes clear and fresh to the front of my mind.

Time is the problem. Time.

Something we master with our clocks, our calendars, our
diaries. Time, that masters us. There I stood, alone in the town-
land with a few foxes and badgers perhaps, some rats and owls,
with the unutterable millennial moment imminent, and I knew
I had grasped nothing at all of life, but that surely now some
great revelation would be at hand, the way the angels must have
rent the darkness above the shepherds and enriched those simple
men's conception of living for ever.

I walked up and down, trying to stay warm, trying to contain
a growing excitement, or trying to urge a full excitement to
possess me, I forget now what those precise emotions were. Was
I dredging up hope or did I really believe something was about
to occur?

I put my hands up in front of my face and held them so they
blocked out my view of the sky. Then I spread two fingers and
looked through the gap; now I could see some of the stars more
clearly. I have never had to wear glasses, the good hard life of a
country farmer has kept all my senses pretty well intact but I
noticed that now my eyesight wasn't as it used to be. Doing that
with my fingers helped a little.

I have large hands, hands that have worked without let-up for
over eighty years. I'm a big man, all of me is big, even now. I
feel as if all of my eighty-and-some years have filled my body,
from my bones outwards, with particles, dense particles, the
same particles that go to make up the universe. And these
particles are time-particles. I am made of time. As is everybody.
As was poor Noel. And we're all made of particles. Even the
stars up there, and the ground on which we walk, and the space
between that ground and the stars.

Thirty minutes or so I spent pacing up and down. Behind me
the empty house. Empty but for several generations of ghosts
that are restlessly moving through every room. Empty, except

for the bottle of whiskey and the patchwork of packets and cans on which I now live. And my radio, of course, my radio that keeps me aware of the broken and breaking world I want no part of; the radio that tells me regularly what the time is, day and night.

Time is a difficult partner but there were days when I have felt master of time, when I thought life was heading somewhere and I knew the lift of love and the swell of success. More often than not, time was mistress and I was slave; all I had built up, all I had traded my breathing for, seemed betimes to crumble and fall away. And all that was left was a burden of sorrow that weighed ever more heavily on my old shoulders.

What a paragon of beauty the millennial night sky proved to be. How could it be possible that the birth of the Christ would not be marked tonight in a unique way? The shifting of one day into another, of one month into the next, one year into the next, of one century into the next and, most especially, of one millennium into the next. Some slip or kink or slide, one moment even slightly out of place or alignment to allow the certainty of hope. That's what I wanted, what I paced up and down for, what I waited for.

Forty-two years ago I had come striding out that door, in a more populated time, a time more worthy. The world then was filled with sacrament and sacramental and the gentle fingers of the Father-God were guiding us along. There was faith. There was my own poor Gráinne, rest her and shrive her ever. And there was Noel. Born Christmas Eve, like a promise of well-being beyond the norm, a gift from the hand of the Christ-child and His blessed Mother. A son given to us, a child born to us. Noel.

I have often thought it was a flaw in the movement of time that had hurt our Noel. To see him sitting there on that mound before the door, rocking himself slowly, for hours on end, as if he could find no connection between all the separate instances that go to the making of a day. I often felt he was searching for some sort of stitching mechanism for those fingers that kept restlessly rubbing against one another, fretting, twisting and un-twisting; if he could stitch time and times together into a coherent whole, he might make something of his life. But then, I suppose, that's what we are all trying to achieve: linking our moments into some sort of coherency, like one of those old tapestries of autumn gold and rust and russet that hung on the walls of ancient castles.

Our little house was always that bit removed from the world, settled out on the cusp of living. That was the way I wanted it: out of town a few miles; off the main road, then off the lesser road a mile or so and finally up a lane wholly off the beaten way. Far from the rush and panic. Snug and self-reliant, certain of beginning, middle and end. That was the way life was. To that belief was I brought up. And when Gráinne and I got married, in our own steady way, and when the fine holding came into my hands, I thought that all was well with the world.

A few cows. A donkey. Sheep. Hens. Our own meadows. An orchard. Outhouses. The cart. No need of a tractor for our damp but productive acres. A stream running by. A small lake down at the end. A patch of bog where I could save my turf. Gráinne in the house, housewifing. Plenty of food, good food. The warmth of a hearth at evening. Market on Tuesdays. A good bike. What need did we have of car or phone or television? Such intrusions. We had the wireless. The Sunday paper. Linking minute to minute under the quiet breathing of the trees by day and the watchful guardianship of the stars by night. Season to season. Growth.

Till Gráinne fell into some kind of brown stupor, some dark despondency not long after we were given the gift of our son. Poor Gráinne. She made valiant efforts to overcome what I had always thought of as nerve troubles. Because Noel was truly a gift of a baby, placid, healthy, a sleeper, an eater. And it was not until later on we saw there was a flaw somewhere, for he was not whole in mind. He was good enough at school, 'adequate' was the word the teacher would use, except for occasional lapses of concentration when he would seem to have slipped away out of time. There would be little use in trying to rouse him, not until he decided for himself to come back out of that under-brush. He would shake himself, eventually, and come back into our world of seconds and minutes and he'd never be able to say where his mind had dandered off to, or of what he had been dreaming.

I'd see him out in the garden, or down along the meadow, just standing there, like a tree stump, eyes gazing away into some otherwhere. Calling him would be useless and I was scared to push or jostle him, just like you wouldn't frighten a sleepwalker in case you'd terrify him into madness.

There were moments of rage that he tumbled into. If you crossed him in something when he had his heart fixed on it, he would rage so that you could almost see him foam at the mouth. He'd jump up and down and his fists would shake, his whole body tremble. I'd be afraid for him then. Sometimes he'd just go down to the little lake at the bottom of the meadows and fling things out into the water, stones, branches, old cans. Once, I saw him leaping up and down in the grip of some fury and he knee-deep in the waters of the lake.

I have to admit I was not good at physical contact. Of course Gráinne and I made love and it was good, too, for a while, though modest, on both sides. After Noel was born even that minimum of physical contact began to fade and we just seemed to go on living at a little distance from one another. With Noel I was always of the belief, instilled in me over the years, that between man and man there is the minimum of touch. I was nervous of him when he was a boy and found myself scarcely able to bathe his little body. As he grew we never embraced; we both found it too awkward. We shook hands, of course, when he came back from somewhere, or when I came back from a week in Salthill or Bundoran, but even that was a distant thing, a sort of embarrassed twisting of the finger and we often made a joke of it, grinning and looking away.

My own hands are big and hard from all my years of labouring with the earth and perhaps they were never sensitive enough to the delicate things. Yet I was good with flowers; they seemed to thrive under my fingers. I could snip and sow and prune as well as any gentlewoman living. I was proud of those hands, hard as boards, powerful as wrenches, firm as fence-posts and tender as the petals of the rose.

Time unfolds, like a fern, or like a stream whose first bubblings nobody has ever seen. It may unfold in a long line like the stream, or in a circular way, falling back into itself in winter, unfolding again in the new year. But there must be a moment of renewal, a moment when the outgoing touches the incoming. And when nothing happened on millennium night, nothing, nothing, nothing, I felt aggrieved. I stood a long while, there in the lonesomeness of the front yard. The shepherds had a vision of angels when the child was born. The Magi glimpsed something so unusual in the heavens that they left their homes and wandered in search of it, certain they would find something. There was not a spark out of our millennial sky. The stars were lovely as ever, beautiful in their multitudes. I watched for a further half-hour after midnight. There was no unusual movement, no slippage, no lightning. I listened intently, hoping to hear even the slightest grinding sound, as of one vast plate of creation touching against another. Anything that might offer the simple consolation of certainty to those who suffer pain and doubt. There was only the faintest rustle of breezes in the branches and far away the usual craven barking of Gunning's old dog.

When he was going to be twenty-one, poor Noel, I remember it well, that Christmas Eve, we had been sitting in the kitchen, after a slice of Christmas cake and a cup of tea, all cosy and content and quiet. At eleven thirty we were to make our way to the end of the lane where we'd get a lift with the Gunnings into Midnight Mass. I remember we had been listening to the radio. I enjoyed the Christmas carols. Even Gráinne seemed to be at peace. I had promised Noel that tomorrow we would celebrate Christmas and his special birthday together. I saved up for the occasion. I had a special set of keys cut for him. I had a fine new bicycle hidden away in the sheds, one with five gears on it, though what anyone would want five gears for I'll never know. Noel was very quiet all day. Then, at eleven o'clock he got up suddenly. He put on his coat.

'I'd like to walk into town by myself,' he announced, and he was out the door before I could remonstrate.

Gráinne touched me on the arm. 'Let him away,' she said.

'He's not been himself lately. A good walk'll set him up. An' he'll come back with us an' the Gunnings.'

One thing about time is that no matter how much alike every stitch along the way may appear to be, you can never tell what the next stitch will be like. If you could, you'd be in control of things. But we are not in control. Time is and time goes its own way. I know now that time is a thing to be endured, that we live always in the naked present, the past is lost to us because it's gone, the future lost to us because we have no hold on it. There is no break in the continuity. There is no flaw in time. No slip. It goes on and we are reduced by it to slavery.

We did not see Noel at Mass. We waited about afterwards and the Gunnings were most patient. It was a cold night, very cold. You could imagine the frost going noisily about its business, binding everything in its chains. We were home by two o'clock. There was no sign of Noel. This was not unusual, as he often took a tice and went off somewhere mooching about by himself. I called out over the black slopes of our holding, the hedges, the gate, the fences. I took a lantern and went among the sheds. Nothing.

I was standing outside the door of the cart-house, shivering with the cold of that awful night, the light of the lantern throwing shadows about the yard, when I thought I heard Noel's voice calling to me. I was certain I heard him. I have been half-certain of it for many years since that night. After the emptiness of the millennium darkness I have thrown even that half-certainty away from me. The fact is, Noel couldn't have called at that moment. He was already dead. But my belief was that his call had been sent out hours before that and only now, through some gracious kindness of the Creator, had reached me where I stood bemused, proving that there was a warp in the power of time that might yet redeem us all.

I found him lying in the lake, close to the shore, his face and shoulders and chest under the water, his hands clutching the weeds at the bottom of the lake. And all about him the water was frozen solid. His body was stiff with the frost and with death. But it was his hands – I found that difficult, as if his hands were trying to find something on the bottom of the lake. I broke the ice and hoisted his body onto the shore. His eyes, too, were frozen open, where they had been watching into the blackness of the water. Perhaps he had seen the great galaxies of stars reflected on that icy surface and had drawn down closer to find some light of hope shimmering there. I do not know. I know nothing.

After that millennial silence, more terrifying than any silence has ever been, I went back inside my empty house and poured myself a large glass of whiskey. I left the old calendar, 1999, hanging on the wall. Why should I take it down and put the new one in its place? What would be the point?